The Risk in
Crossing
Borders

A Novel

William McClain

The Risk in Crossing Borders

green planet books | Published by
Green Planet Books
williammcclainwriter.com

Book Design:
morninglitebookdesign.com
Cover skyline illustrations:
Michael Tompsett — www.michael-tompsett.pixels.com

Printed in the United States of America
Publisher's Cataloging-in-Publication data:
McClain, William
The Risk in Crossing Borders
ISBN: 978-1-7351598-0-5

Your children are not your children.
They are the sons and daughters
of life's longing for itself.
You may give them your love but not your thoughts,
For they have their own thoughts.
You may house their bodies but not their souls,
For their souls dwell in the house of tomorrow, which
you cannot visit, not even in your dreams.

—

And think not that you can direct the course of love,
for love, if it finds you worthy, directs your course.

—

Kahlil Gibran, The Prophet

Seattle

This was not the usual Seattle drizzle. Throughout the city, blasts of rain drenched anyone unfortunate enough to be caught outdoors, spawning small streams that raced down the steep streets. Traffic lights swayed in the wind, while tall evergreens bent and waved.

The pounding rain and wind didn't trouble Yana Pickering. She curled up on her living room couch with the newest book by one of her favorite mystery writers, a mug of green tea, and a Vivaldi concerto playing in the background. As the storm intensified around Yana's 1920s-era craftsman home, she simply increased the volume on her sound system.

The Pacific Northwest is out of reach of hurricanes, and tornadoes are practically unheard of. But the area makes up for it with winter storms that have been known to blow down entire forests out on the Olympic Peninsula.

This was one of those horrific storms. The gusts crescendoed into other-worldly howls, its giant waves attacking windows, lawn furniture, and anything not cemented to the ground. Yana heard a burst of sharp, loud cracks—a tree snapping in two. It sounded close enough to belong to one of her neighbors.

The wind was creating such a racket that Yana couldn't be sure if she heard someone knocking at her front door. Setting down her mug, she listened more intently. Unexpected night visitors were rare in her life, so Yana dismissed the sound as wind rattling her upstairs dormer windows. But there it was again—someone was definitely at her front door. She glanced at the microwave as she passed the kitchen. Nine thirty-eight was late for a caller, even for a Friday night.

Ducking into the bathroom, Yana ran a brush through her hair before deciding that someone calling this late would have to deal with seeing her as is. She peeked out the window beside her front door but could see no one. She opened the door a crack, then a bit more, until finally, she leaned out over her porch, peering into the darkness. There was no one. The wind bursting through the open door was stripping her of warmth, so she swiftly closed and relocked it.

She was sure she heard knocking. Hadn't she? Was this a sign she'd been living alone for too long? Or had she been so wrapped up in her book that her mind was inventing things?

Yana decided it was time for bed. She double-checked the dead-bolts on her front and back doors, as well as the locks on all her windows before turning in. She was annoyed that the mysterious knocking had brought her pulse up a notch. Yana savored her independence, but on certain nights, when her house creaked and groaned, it became difficult to dismiss thoughts of an intruder working his way up her wooden staircase.

Burrowing down into her bed in search of her lost warmth, Yana found herself jumping awake with each crash of the wind. Finally, giving up on sleep, she grabbed her thickest blanket and settled back down on the living room couch, returning to her book.

Someone was knocking at Yana's door again, both the front and back doors, but she couldn't locate either doorway. Had her house been remodeled during the night? Yana had been expecting someone, someone threatening disruption, but couldn't remember who it was. She hated the disconcerting sense of not remembering, that she was missing something that should be obvious.

Then Yana realized she had been dreaming. She became aware that the uneven surface she was lying on was not her bed. Opening her eyes, she remembered her move to the living room couch the previous night. The storm had passed, but there really was someone knocking at her front door. Her unsettledness from the previous night was out of place in the soft, gray morning light, as if last night's chaotic weather and mysterious noises were part of her dream. The calm was broken again by the insistent knocking. Wrapped in her blanket and feeling stiff from a night on the couch, she reluctantly made her way to her door.

The squat, balding man on her front porch raised his eyebrows in slight alarm at Yana's state. "Sorry—I've called 911—but there's someone in your front yard, and I think she's dead!" he told her, waving his phone as if he thought Yana needed the visual cue.

Yana struggled to wake up. It was too early in the morning to be told there was a body among her rhododendrons. Was this just a crazy person at her door? Her house was close enough to the University District that she did get some unusual characters from time to time. This man, however, dressed in neat blue jeans, button-down shirt, and newer walking shoes, looked quite normal. Yana wished he would stop talking at her as he walked around the side of her porch, evidently expecting her to follow.

"I just wanted to check whether you knew who she was," he called back to her. In slippers and blanket, Yana ventured a few steps off her porch to find there was a lady's body tucked between her evergreen huckleberry and the front siding.

Yana went over for a closer look. Beneath the spattering of mud and the dark hair pasted across the woman's cheek, Yana could make out a youthful complexion marred by a blood-encrusted gash running from near her ear lobe to the point of her cheek bone. Her jeans and heavy winter jacket with a lined hood did not show the wear of someone living on the streets. Yana reached down to touch the young women's head. In the delicate morning light, she could make out long dark lashes, full lips—slightly parted—and several bruises. Although the woman's cheek felt cold, Yana sensed the slightest touch of warm air. "She's still breathing!" Yana called back, while trying to decide if she'd seen the battered young woman before. Her face looked familiar.

Yana noticed the paramedics pulling up to her front sidewalk, having not even registered the approaching sirens in her concentration on the stranger lying in her front yard. Two paramedics, a man and a woman, ran up, quickly checked the young woman for a pulse, and then attempted to rouse her. A third worker brought out a stretcher. She was wrapped in blankets and bundled away, while a police patrol car pulled up to the curb. The police officer spoke to the paramedic and then walked over to Yana and the man who had knocked on Yana's door. They were standing together next to Yana's front porch. "Are you the owners of this property?" he addressed them both, mistaking them for a married couple.

"I just happened to be passing by and made the 911 call," the man immediately responded with a shrug. "I don't know anything about the young lady, or how she ended up here."

"Okay. I'll need to see your I.D. and take down your name and contact information." Turning to Yana, the officer impatiently demanded, "And you are?"

"I own the property, but I don't know the lady either." Yana paused for a moment before continuing. "However, last night during the windstorm, I was quite sure I heard someone knocking at my door. When I went to answer—" Yana cut her story short because the officer was inspecting around the side of the house. She wasn't sure if she was supposed to follow him. He clearly wasn't interested in the ramblings of an old lady living on her own. The officer came back around front, asked if she had noticed any unusual visitors to the neighborhood or seen any suspicious activity. Yana decided against a second attempt to describe the knocking at her door the previous night, and the officer returned to his patrol car.

She was left standing near her front porch, wondering if the officer was done questioning her. Looking outward, she finally noticed the crowds of people clumped in groups on the edge of her property, some engaged in conversations, and others simply watching. Nothing works to gather neighbors together quite like the blaring siren of an emergency vehicle arriving on an early Saturday morning before anyone has embarked on their weekend errands. Of course, her neighbors all wanted to know what had happened, but Yana had no explanation to offer. After the lack of interest from the police officer, she decided not to bring up the previous night's knock on her door. She could read disappointment in her neighbors' faces, as if she were holding back information.

Yana was not in the mood for small talk but knew her neighbors would consider her antisocial if she immediately disappeared into her house. After a sufficient period of circulating and offering comments such as "So Justin's started college already," and "I didn't realize Monica had a new job!" Yana escaped, at last, to the safety of her home. Only then did it dawn on her that she had reconnected with all her neighbors clothed in a tired old blanket and battered slippers—not to mention the horror she experienced when she confronted the state of her hair staring back at her from her bathroom mirror.

Running a brush through her hair, Yana felt reflective. Halfway through her sixth decade, she accepted the changes in her appearance that came with aging. Her blondish-brown hair, which she was keeping shorter these days, showed bits of gray—manageable with some highlighting. Her face had several new creases—that was to be expected. Although not an athlete, Yana stayed active, mentally and physically. And while no one would call her skinny, she managed her weight well enough. Looking at her tired reflection on this particular morning, however, Yana felt old.

Her reflective mood persisted as she brewed her morning cup of coffee. It was strange to think that most of her life was behind her—both kids raised, career winding down, marriage over. Her marriage had ended without fireworks. Kyle, their youngest, left for college, and minus the distraction and activity he generated, it was impossible to ignore the empty space that had become Yana's relationship with Reggie. Yana recalled sitting at dinner, a mere spider's web of conversation connecting them, when she informed Reggie that she wanted to part ways. He had turned his face up from his dinner plate to stare at her in surprise. She realized how seldom he did that anymore—actually look at her. He set down his knife and fork and was, for many long moments, speechless. His soft brown eyes that once, long ago, had stolen her heart, widened with hurt, confusion, and fear, but tellingly, no trace of anger or fight. That, more than anything, confirmed her decision.

Being divorced brought unwanted sympathy from friends. Yana could handle taking out the garbage and dealing with spiders. She missed having someone to share her small joys and pains. But she had lost that aspect of her marriage years ago.

Yana relished her uncomplicated, comfy lifestyle in her Wallingford-neighborhood home where they raised their two kids. Although she had recently posted a "Black Lives Matter" sign in her front yard, she was not the confrontational type and would never go looking for trouble.

Yana's phone buzzed, bringing her back to the present. It was a text from Ellen. Yana was supposed to meet her former colleague for coffee that morning, but she decided to reschedule. She was still trying to sort through the events from her disrupted morning. She couldn't stop wondering whether someone had, in fact, knocked on her door the previous night. If so, was it the same lady who ended up in her front garden? She must have been severely hypothermic after being out most of the night. Did she survive? And why did her face look familiar?

Yana knew that trauma victims usually went to Harborview Medical Center, so she tried calling there. Of course, they couldn't release information to someone who was not a family member. Yana didn't even have a way to identify who she was inquiring about, just a description and approximate time when the woman would have arrived. She asked to be transferred to their social services unit, and after several transfers and dead ends, she finally reached someone who she felt might be able to help her. Yana briefly described what happened and asked if she could leave her name and phone number. "If you have any way to let me know whether she's okay—I know you can't share personal information—but anything you can pass along, I'd really appreciate it!"

Next Yana tried the Seattle Police Blotter web site. Apparently, the incident in her front yard wasn't deemed important enough to post.

She was heading out to pick up groceries for the week when her cell phone rang. Seeing that it was her daughter, Kayla, she picked up. "Hey, what's up?"

"Mom, mind if we stop by? Zaid and I are having some friends over, and I need to borrow your large skillet."

"What time are you coming by?"

"About an hour. Zaid isn't back from his run, and he'll need a shower."

"Okay—see you then."

Yana sighed as she returned her purse and coat to her closet. How can it be that, living on her own, she still had no control over her weekend? Still, with their crazy schedules, she always welcomed a visit from either of her kids. After earning a nursing degree three years ago, Kayla was delighted when her cardiology-unit internship turned into a full-time position. Of course, the glamour wore off quickly working night shifts and weekends. Then, earlier this year, she switched to daytime shifts—three twelve-hour days—and suddenly Kayla was a little easier to be around.

Kayla had met her boyfriend, Zaid, when he was a structural engineering student at Seattle University. Now Zaid worked for a high-end construction company. The two met, where else, via a dating app. In retrospect, Yana considered it a wonder that anyone in her generation was able to find partners.

Kayla sat in her usual spot at the kitchen table. Zaid sat next to her, reaching up with one arm to massage her shoulder. As Yana started heating water for tea, she shared her morning's excitement. Kayla and Zaid couldn't offer any theories about how the young lady ended up in Yana's yard, nor any ideas about how to obtain information from the hospital. "You have no connection to her, so you're just going to frustrate yourself worrying about it," Kayla advised. Zaid nodded his head in agreement.

Yana felt fortunate to have Zaid as, not a son-in-law, since they weren't married, but they had been together long enough that he felt like family. Kayla had been through some "interesting" relationships prior to Zaid. But Kayla and Zaid were a good fit even though they looked so different. Kayla's blond hair, blue eyes and light complexion stood out next to Zaid's dark skin, jet black hair, and studious dark-rimmed glasses.

After finishing medical school in Damascus, Zaid's father, Sami, came to Seattle to complete his residency. Sami had married Amena right before they left Syria, and Zaid was born soon after their arrival. Over the years the family developed many connections to their Seattle community while maintaining ties to friends and family in Syria. Now a number of their Syrian contacts were either dead or displaced due to the conflict there.

Kayla got up to rummage through Yana's refrigerator, as was her pattern. "Mind if I have some of this stir fry?" she asked as she dished some on to a plate. Zaid was more polite and feigned disinterest.

"No, go ahead. Zaid, help yourself." Yana was happy that she could still nourish her "kids."

After Kayla and Zaid left, Yana resigned herself to probably never learning the identity of the young lady from that morning, or her outcome. However, she did tell Ellen all about it when they met for their rescheduled coffee the next day. Ellen had retired recently from the King County Crime Lab where they had worked together for thirty years, and Yana missed her dearly. It had been two years now since Ellen lost her husband to cancer, and of her three children, only one remained in Seattle. So, Ellen and Yana would frequently meet over lunch or share a walk while they discussed and dissected whatever was happening in their lives. Ellen was suitably astonished with Yana's story, curious about the identity of her mystery woman, and not so quick as Kayla and Zaid to dismiss speculation.

Although it wasn't the same without Ellen, Yana still enjoyed working at the crime lab. Over the years, she had grown weary of trying to explain to people that it did not resemble anything like detective dramas or crime shows. If TV did mimic reality, who would watch? There was a lot of repetitive work, and she was rarely involved in the cases themselves, just supervising the lab work behind the scenes.

Yana could not have predicted that her indecision as an undergraduate, which led to a double major in chemistry and human biology, would be the perfect background for a forensic scientist. But, as her entry to the job market coincided with the end of the "double dip" recession of the early eighties, she was appreciative of any employment opportunity she could find. At that time there were no formal programs in forensic science. Law enforcement agencies looked for general science or crime-solving backgrounds and then provided on-the-job training.

Forensics had changed radically during Yana's tenure, the greatest impact coming from the introduction of DNA evidence. This was soon followed by a proliferation of television shows glamourizing the CSI lab, which, in turn, helped launch degree and certificate programs in forensic science. Now Yana had to deal with a steady flow of millennials with technical expertise but little appreciation for the cross-disciplinary, larger-picture perspective that was needed in complex or unusual cases. Yana reminded herself that she only needed to stick with it for another eleven years before she was Medicare eligible, and, by her calculations, could afford to leave it all to the next generation of whiz kids.

Four weeks following the incident of the lady-in-the-night, Yana was enjoying another Friday night at home with a new mystery novel when there was again a knock at the door. This time, she didn't check her hair in the bathroom but went straight to answer the door, pulling it open a bit too abruptly, as if trying to catch a prankster. Yana gasped.

It was the same young woman who, four weeks ago, had been lying in her garden looking close to death. The bruises were gone, but there was still evidence of the gash to her cheek. She was wearing the same winter coat. It had been cleaned. Again, Yana had the distinct impression she knew this woman from somewhere in her past.

"Ms. Pickering? I'm the woman who was in your yard last month when the paramedics came. Sorry to bother you again, but someone from the hospital gave me your contact information and said you wanted to know what happened to me."

Her voice was lower than Yana would expect from someone that young—perhaps an early smoker? "Yes, my goodness! Are you alright? You look much better!"

"I am better, thanks. And thanks for calling the paramedics. They said that if I had been hypothermic for much longer it could have done lasting damage, or I might have died."

"Actually, I didn't call the paramedics. A passerby did and then came to the door to alert me. But how did you end up in my yard?"

The young woman hesitated. "It's a long story actually, and I'd like to fill you in. Do you think I could come inside for a few minutes so we can talk?"

"Of course." Yana opened the door wider to let her in. She wondered if this was a good idea, but she was curious about her story and why she looked familiar. "Would you like some tea?"

"Thanks, yes, if it's not too much bother."

Once they were settled in Yana's small living room with a tea tray resting on the coffee table between them, Yana looked up expectantly at the young woman. "I don't believe I know your name."

"Yes, I'm sorry." The mystery woman glanced out the front window before answering. "My name is Emma Thomas. But we've met before under a different name. I used to be Eddie Rossi."

The silence stretched out while Yana struggled to take in what she had just heard and to craft a response. Of course, now that she heard the name, she knew why this woman looked familiar. Eddie used to date her daughter, Kayla. "But you're going by Emma now?" She was repeating what Emma just told her, but it was all she could think of to say while she bought herself time to process this.

Did this explain why the relationship with Kayla hadn't worked out? Did Kayla know about the change? And how did she end up in my front yard? Was she stalking the family?

Emma, watching Yana closely, seemed to read her thoughts. "Ms. Pickering, I'm sorry to spring this on you. But I heard that you wanted to know how I ended up in your front yard, and I want you to understand that it wasn't coincidence, but it wasn't intentional either."

Yana leaned back in her chair. "Okay, I'm listening."

"Earlier that night I met a friend for dinner at Julia's Restaurant a few blocks from here. I noticed a couple of guys glaring at us during dinner—my friend is also trans. It was late by the time we left, and we had parked in different directions. The two guys followed us out, and after my friend and I parted, they kept following me down a side street as I headed back to my car. Then they started to harass me about being transgender—basically calling me every insulting name their pea-brains could come up with. I finally turned to tell them to fuck off. My big mistake. That's when they chased me down and attacked me."

Yana set down her teacup. "That's awful! I can't believe that happened in liberal Wallingford of all places."

Emma seemed resigned. "Yeah, well you never know. Anyway, I managed to get away from them. Outran them. But I wasn't sure if they were still following me. That's when I realized that I'd stumbled onto the block where Kayla used to live. So, I knocked on your door. When you didn't answer right away, I was afraid they might come by and see me on the porch, so I hid behind some bushes. I must have been hit harder than I'd realized—a slight concussion the doctor said—because that's the last thing I remember from that night."

Hearing this tale, Yana temporarily forgot the shock of learning that Kayla's old flame Eddie was now Emma. "My god, you could have died out there in that weather! Did the police catch them?"

Emma's eyes narrowed. "No, my description wasn't much to go on. The police checked with the restaurant, and apparently they paid cash."

Once Emma finished her story, Yana's thoughts returned to

the change that had come to the person she had known as Eddie. Yana considered herself a liberal and had both gay and lesbian friends. In fact, her son was gay. But she realized she didn't have any first-hand experience with transgender people. Yana leaned forward in her chair. "Do you mind my asking? Were you aware that you were transgender when you were dating Kayla?"

For the first time, Emma's face relaxed into a bit of a smile as she recalled how she used to appreciate Kayla's mom's straight-forward approach to everything. "No, it's okay to ask. A part of me knew, but I didn't really understand it back then."

Emma smiled again, this time apologetically, and started to get up from the couch. "Well, I just wanted to give you the background on what happened that night. I'm sorry for causing such a commotion, and I don't want to take up your whole evening."

Still processing what she'd just heard, Yana thought about the courage it must have taken to come out as transgender when that meant confrontations and scorn from a large segment of the population, even in liberal Seattle. "Eddie—I mean Emma, I just want you to know that I'm proud of you for taking this step, and that you have my support."

Emma took a moment to compose herself before responding. "That means a lot to me. I know my parents will get there too, eventually."

Yana, who had also gotten up from her seat, sat down again. "What do your parents have to say about this?" Yana had met Emma's parents once when Kayla and Emma were an item.

Emma sat back down as well. "Mom's taken it the hardest. She completely fell apart when I told her. Now, she hardly talks to me and refuses to acknowledge the change. She still calls me Eddie."

"Oh, Emma, I'm so sorry! What did she say to you?"

"She said that I was born a boy and will always be a boy, and that nothing I can do will change that. I think it was a real shock for both of them. And they think that I'm just following a trend or trying to focus attention on myself. As if anyone would want this kind of attention. I think it scares them. They're worried about me, and frankly, they're worried about what to tell their friends."

"How did it go when you came out at work? Where do you work?"

Emma relaxed a bit, taking a sip of her tea before responding. "Last year I graduated from law school at the University of Puget Sound and started work at the law firm Swanson & Yates. I'd been there just a few months when I came out. Most of my peers were supportive, but not some of the old guard. They'd say the politically correct things, but there was a definite drop in the level of opportunities coming my direction."

"That's disappointing. You would think, as attorneys, they'd at least be aware of their potential liability in discriminating against you."

Emma gave a short, cynical laugh. "Sorry, Ms. Pickering, but the fact is, there isn't much liability. There's just not much in the way of laws that address discrimination against trans people. Plus, it's not something you can easily document or prove."

Yana had transitioned from her state of shock into her mother role. "For heaven's sake, call me Yana," she said, and then continued, "So what will you do? You can't let this strangle your career just as you're getting started."

"You're right. That's why I moved on to another firm, Mather Anesson. They have a more inclusive culture. Plus, it was easier to be the new trans employee, than to be viewed as the man who's now dressing as a woman."

There was an awkward pause, before Emma continued. "Now I really have taken up too much of your evening. But thanks for your support." She got up from her chair.

Yana stood up as well. "Of course, Emma. If there is anything

I can do to help with this transition—anytime you're being chased by thugs, feel free to drop in!"

They both laughed and then parted with hugs. Despite Yana's desire to be as accepting as possible, it felt strange to hug this woman who had once dated her daughter.

As soon as Emma left, Yana called Kayla. "Did you know that Eddie is now transgender?"

"Oh, yeah, I saw that on Facebook. That was a while ago. It's great to see her embracing who she is."

Yana felt deflated. What she considered bombshell news, was so unremarkable to her daughter that Kayla hadn't even bothered mentioning it to Yana. Clearly this was a generational thing. Recovering herself, Yana went on, "Well, Eddie—now Emma—was the woman that the paramedics picked up from our front yard last month."

"Oh, you're kidding! Is she okay? How did you find out?"

Yana filled Kayla in on Emma's visit and the conversation that had ensued.

"That's awful about Emma's folks. I never did care for her mom. Good thing you could be supportive for her." Kayla's comments made Yana feel like the underachieving child receiving praise for taking basic steps.

After hanging up, Yana decided she needed to get together with her friend Ellen for another coffee—or perhaps drinks.

They met up the next day at Pam's Kitchen, where Yana updated Ellen over paratha roti and cocktails. As expected, Ellen was suitably impressed with the turn of events and fully appreciated Yana's open-mindedness regarding her daughter's former boyfriend. "That's too bad the police couldn't find the jerks who attacked Emma," she remarked.

"Yeah, you're right." Yana had been mainly focused on the personal connection and hadn't given the police angle much thought. "I wonder how much effort they put into solving it."

"Seems like this would qualify as a hate crime."

"You would think so."

"Well, can you sneak a peek at whether this case went to the crime lab?"

"I just might do that. Considering how beat up she was, there should have been some DNA evidence."

The following Monday Yana did some snooping around the King County Crime Lab web site. As deputy director of the lab, she had access to every case file. Yana wasn't sure if Emma had officially changed her name, so she checked under both her old and new names. She found a match under Edward Rossi, but the date was wrong. It was from last March, well before the incident in Yana's front yard.

The lack of any lab reports on the current incident made it clear they hadn't deemed Emma's recent attack worthy of lab evaluation. That could have been because spending a night outside followed by a rush to the emergency department degraded any available forensic evidence. Alternatively, it could be that, because Emma was transgender, the detective in charge didn't take the crime seriously. Yana knew several detectives who would fit that profile. But she couldn't come up with a way to shed more light on what really happened with the investigation. It could be that, because Emma wasn't permanently injured, the case didn't receive as much attention as it might have otherwise.

With a quick glance around the office to make sure no one was looking in her direction, Yana opened the lab report from last March. It was a violation of policy to open a file for any purpose other than completing a work assignment. She hastily browsed the file, her pulse quickening with the fear that someone might walk by and start asking questions about what she was working on, even though that was unlikely. Yana scribbled a few cryptic notes on the details of the case and then quickly closed the file. Afterwards, she sat for a while thinking about what she just read.

The case involved an accusation of embezzlement while working at Swanson & Yates. Apparently, the case was closed due to insufficient evidence. So, was this the real reason Emma had changed employers so soon after being hired? Embezzlement didn't fit the person Yana knew prior to her transition to Emma. Had there been other changes besides her gender? Could she trust the things Emma had told her—that she had been chased by a couple of thugs the night she ended up in Yana's front yard, and that her parents had rejected her?

Yana decided that she, like the police, should assume that Emma was innocent of wrongdoing until proven otherwise. But she needed someone who could help provide perspective and perhaps see something she was overlooking. She couldn't confide in Kayla and Zaid. They might let slip to someone that Yana had been examining case notes for reasons unrelated to her job, which, together with the breach of confidentiality, could land her in serious trouble. But Yana could trust Ellen with this, and she would understand the importance of keeping it confidential. Yana would need to arrange to meet up with Ellen yet again. That wasn't an unhappy prospect.

That evening Yana had her son Kyle, Kyle's partner Thomas, Kayla, and Zaid over for dinner. This was Yana's family. She looked forward to their informal gatherings even more than the traditional holiday affairs. Yana was an only child, and her parents had both perished in a plane crash back when she was in college, so her kids and their partners were truly the extent of her family.

Kyle and Thomas ate and ran. "Sorry we have to jet," Kyle apologized. "I've got a neuroscience exam tomorrow. The professor is a bloody pain in the ass the way she expects us to memorize virtually everything. Does she even realize that a good portion of her class are not med students?"

Working towards a doctorate in physical therapy at the University of Washington, Kyle was, as usual, obsessed about his studies.

Thomas good-naturedly rolled his eyes, as Kyle bewailed the un-reasonable expectations of his professor. Thomas, who could have passed as Kyle's brother, had the same sandy hair, blue eyes, and tall, lanky frame as Kyle. After they made their exit, Yana pulled some of her chocolate hazelnut cookies from the freezer and made a fresh pot of tea.

"Oh, I forgot to mention that my folks would love to accept your invitation for Christmas Eve dinner," Zaid said through a mouth-ful of cookie.

"Terrific!" replied Yana. "And on that topic, I couldn't help won-dering whether Emma had a place to go for the holidays, with the way things are between her and her parents. Kayla, would it feel awkward if I invited her to join us?"

"No, of course not," Kayla replied in a tone implying surprise that Yana even needed to ask. Yana felt she always guessed wrong, either overlooking something that offended Kayla, or at the other end of the spectrum, bringing up something that Kayla clearly considered a non-issue.

"Okay, great—I'll check with her."

Yana poured herself some more tea, before turning to Zaid. "Kayla mentioned that your dad heard from his friend in Aleppo." Kayla had already shared with Yana that Sami's closest friend, Elias, had lost his wife, Aliya, in the bombing of their city. Now, a year following that bombing, Sami and Amena had lost all contact with Elias and had been extremely worried.

"Yes—good news and bad news," Zaid responded. "The good news is, of course, that Elias is alive and well. Turns out dad hadn't been able to make contact with him because he was abducted by one of the rebel militias."

"Oh my god! How did that happen?" Yana replied, setting down her tea.

"On his way to work at the hospital. They took him to a village outside Aleppo where they needed his surgery skills for one of their leaders who was badly injured in a mortar attack. They kept him at their camp for over a month. When they were forced to retreat from the village, they finally let him return to Aleppo."

"Thanks goodness Elias is okay," Yana responded.

"Yes, but there is more to the story," Zaid replied. Kayla, watching Zaid intently, raised a reassuring hand to his shoulder. Zaid seemed not to notice as he continued with his story. "He said they treated him well but took away his cell phone and wouldn't let him communicate with the outside world during his captivity. When he returned to Aleppo, he found out that his two kids, Victor and Kamar, had fled the city."

Yana gasped. Zaid ignored that as well and plowed ahead. "Elias and his kids had moved in with his brother, Qasim, because Elias's apartment was destroyed in the bombing that had taken Aliya's life. When Elias disappeared, Qasim had no idea what had happened to him. The situation in Aleppo was deteriorating, so he took the kids and headed south towards Hama. He left word for Elias at the hospital saying that if they couldn't find a safe refuge in Hama, they would continue across the border into Lebanon. Elias wasn't able to establish contact with Qasim, but based on the situation in Hama, he thinks they probably continued into Lebanon. He's planning to relocate to Lebanon to search for them."

Kayla picked up on the narrative. "Amena and Sami are planning a trip to Lebanon in January so they can help the family resettle."

Yana reached for a cookie as she responded, "Elias is fortunate to have Amena and Sami for support. It's hard to imagine what this must be like for that family, and after having lost their mother."

Kayla got up to clear the empty plates from the table. At the sink, she called over her shoulder, "Zaid is planning to go with them to help in any way he can," Kayla paused before continuing, "and I may go with him."

"Is that safe? You would stand out more as not being from the Middle East."

"Yes, of course! Thousands of Americans travel to Lebanon these days," Kayla replied, returning to the table.

Kayla and Zaid said their goodbyes a short time later. Yana wasn't really listening at that point. Her mind was distracted with thoughts of two children, a father, and an uncle, scattered somewhere between Syria and Lebanon, and her own daughter heading out to help them.

Lebanon

Victor was having the same dream again. He and Kamar were searching for their mother and father. Everywhere they looked they found only collapsed apartment buildings, empty storefronts, and the remains of burned-up cars. The dust of pulverized buildings mixed with the soot from extinguished fires and seeped into every part of their bodies and clothing, permeating the air with its suffocating smell. They stopped to ask a grandmother sitting on the edge of the street. Her clothes had accumulated so much dust that you couldn't tell what colors they had been before the bombing reached their neighborhood. They knew her by sight, having seen her walking her grandkids to their local school. Now she was the only person in view. They pleaded with her for information about where their parents had gone, but she continued to rock slightly forward and back, and to stare at the collapsed building across the street from her. They heard gunfire down the street to their left. Victor grabbed Kamar's arm, and they retreated in the opposite direction.

The gunfire faded as Victor woke to someone rattling the entrance to their makeshift shelter. Victor had no idea what time it was. He could see through the cracks in their shelter that it was still dark outside. Kamar had backed into the furthest corner, her blanket wrapped tightly about her, with only the top of her head and her wide, terrified eyes visible.

"Who is there?" Victor demanded, trying to sound like the protector of their domain, but not able to hide the fear in his voice. Two young men ducked into the small space. "Who are you, and what do you want?" Victor demanded.

"Please sit," they said to Victor, but there was no "please" in the way they said it.

Victor remained standing. Victor had grown up quickly over the past year, and one of the important lessons he had learned was that passivity is dangerous.

"Sit!" they insisted. "We want to talk."

Reluctantly Victor sat, positioning himself between the two men and Kamar. Without invitation, the two men sat opposite Victor, ignoring the muddy floor. "Victor—" they knew his name— "you two are alone, and you have no way to provide for your sister. It is time you started looking to your future."

Victor's face hardened. "My business is my own. What has that to do with you?"

"You have a duty to your mother killed by the bombs dropped by the infidel Alawite tyrant. You have a duty to your tribe, to your family, and to Allah. We have come to provide you the means to fulfill your duty. Our brotherhood will ensure your sister remains safe while you join your brothers in liberating Syria from the Alawite savages. Allah has protected you thus far not so that you could waste your life hiding in this place."

Victor sat up straight and tried to make his voice a man's voice, tried to project a confidence that wasn't there. "Thank you, brothers. I will consider your offer."

The spokesman for the two visitors attempted a smile, but

there was menace in his voice. "You should consider your decision carefully. The brotherhood looks out for the families of those who stand with us but have not the resources to protect everyone in our tribe." They rose from their seats. "Omar, who works in the car repair shop in town, is able to contact us." Silently, the two men slipped back into the night.

Victor waited for several minutes before stepping outside to see if they had truly left. Then he ducked back into the shelter and sat next to Kamar, the two leaning into each other. "Why do those men want you to fight? You are only fifteen!" Kamar asked.

"I've heard what happens with that militia," Victor answered to the darkness in front of them. "They are not like the militia our brother joined. They use new recruits for anything that is too dangerous for their more valuable, experienced soldiers. If I go with them, it's unlikely I will ever return."

"Then you should refuse to join."

"Did you not understand the threat they made against you? They want me to come willingly, but if I don't, they will come for me. And then they will take you as well. I don't want to talk about what they might do to you!"

Kamar fell silent, as Victor placed his arm across her shoulder. "I will come up with something," he assured her. Victor had always been a quiet, serious child. Now, he accepted his role as his sister's protector with determination. Kamar found it natural to turn to her brother, who had always shown her kindness.

They continued to sit in the darkness. Eventually, Kamar lay back down on her blanket and slept. Victor, however, could not sleep, with his adrenaline flowing and his mind churning through the same dead ends.

It had been more than a year since Victor and Kamar's secure world imploded. Victor's life revolved around school, hanging out with friends, listening to his music, and playing on his neighborhood soccer team, where he was a tenacious defender. Kamar was the better student and more popular at school than her quiet brother. But Victor was never jealous of his younger sister's success. On the contrary, he felt it was his responsibility to watch out for her. Part of her confidence at school stemmed from having an older brother she could depend on.

The war had been going on for years. Even so, Victor thought they were safe in Aleppo. Then the tension between his parents, Aliya and Elias, began to escalate as they witnessed the worrying reports streaming in from radio and TV. There were arguments that ended abruptly when Victor or Kamar entered a room. Small things—a forgotten chore or dirty dishes left out—would bring a sharp outburst from his mother. Later, she would smile, as if the anger had not happened. Victor spent more time outside or at his friend's house to escape the tension at home.

When their school was bombed, Victor's parents argued openly about whether to evacuate south. Victor's mother wanted them to join her family, who had fled to Damascus. She came from old money, people who did not want Syria to change and were sympathetic towards the Syrian government. Victor's dad supported the aims of the rebels but had not openly joined them. As head of surgery at the nearby hospital, his focus was on maintaining medical care at a time when their city was in crisis.

Victor agreed with his father, but politics was not his focus. His entire school had disappeared in a single day—the center of his emerging social world, now a pile of rubble. Kamar, the one who never stopped talking, often trying to boss her older brother, fell strangely silent. Victor had never seen his sister act this way, and it worried him.

The next week Victor and Kamar's mother insisted that they remain holed up in their apartment while their father worked his long shifts at the hospital. Victor wanted to visit his friend's apartment. If they did evacuate the city, who knows when Victor would see him again? It didn't make sense—Victor wasn't any more likely to be hit by a bomb at his friend's apartment than he was at home.

Victor came up with a plan. His mother was in the bathtub with the ventilation fan running, so he yelled to her through the door. "Mom, Aimar needs me to return some stuff of his. I'll only be gone a short time."

His mother yelled back over the whirr of the fan, "No, you are to stay here."

"It will just take a few minutes—" Victor started to say more, but at that moment his heart froze. The roar of planes, many planes, filled the air above them. Where were the air-raid sirens? There had been no warning.

"Mom, we need to go now! To the basement!"

"What dear?"

Victor pounded on the door. "Mom, open up. The bombers are back!"

"Just a minute." Victor heard the tub draining.

"Mom, now!" Victor tried to force the door. It was locked. "Mom, there isn't time for you to dry off. We need to go!" Kamar had also heard the planes overhead and came out of her bedroom, yelling at Victor.

The world exploded. A roar of sound and dust engulfed them, and they were thrown to the floor.

From playing soccer, Victor knew what it was like to be flattened when a larger player runs over you at full speed from behind. That was nothing compared to this. On his way to the floor, Victor crashed into the wall opposite the bathroom door, and he felt the wetness of blood on the back of his head. His ears rang painfully. He wondered if he would lose his hearing. Kamar, who had been thrown into Victor, had been cushioned by his body. Looking over Kamar, Victor saw that their bathroom door had been blown open. Half of their bathroom was missing—it was the half that included their mother. Their sink was hanging out in space, suspended by its plumbing. Their bathtub had vanished. Sunshine, filtered by clouds of dust, illuminated remaining bits of floor. The smell was a mixture of a muddy construction site, staleness, and smoke, not campfire smoke, but dirty industrial-smelling smoke.

Shouts and screams could be heard over the sound of more planes. Victor stared at the empty space beyond their bathroom. He could not take in the fact that his mother had just disappeared. Kamar continued to scream. Victor had one thought—get Kamar out of here. He tried to get to his feet and slipped. He thought he must be dizzy. Then he realized their apartment floor was no longer level. Victor pulled Kamar to her feet. She was screaming for her mother. Another explosion went off close by, and Kamar grabbed Victor in terror. There was no time to comfort her. Victor pried himself from Kamar and took her arm.

Their living room was still there, but the floor was covered in glass, the contents of a collapsed bookshelf, and other debris. Sirens, shouting, and other street sounds entered unchecked through their shattered front windows. Victor didn't allow time to take in this scene, firmly guiding Kamar through their front door. No longer the bossy, confident younger sister, Kamar followed Victor's lead.

They had been instructed that, in a bombing raid, they should take the stairway to the basement, which their parents thought would be safer than the street. Having seen the total destruction beyond their bathroom, Victor was determined to get out of the building—they would take their chances on the street. The stairwell was intact, but as they stepped on to it, it swayed slightly. Stairwells were supposed to be solid. Victor paused momentarily, wondering if it was safe. They heard voices below them, and he hurried Kamar down the stairs.

Reaching the ground floor, Victor and Kamar rushed out into

the street, turning to stare up at their slanting building. The wailing of victims mixed with the sounds of airplanes and sirens. People and cars went racing past, while smoke drifted in from other parts of the city.

Victor wanted to go back and find his mother, but he couldn't see a way past the rubble to get to where their bathroom had disappeared—it didn't look safe. Seeing the complete destruction where their mother was buried, Kamar again became hysterical. Victor restrained her from going closer and gathered her into his arms. At first, she struggled against him, then she fell on to Victor's shoulder, sobbing. Looking over his sister at the pile of rubble, Victor had little hope that his mother had survived.

Victor still felt his throat constrict whenever he thought of his mother's death. He shifted his position on the hard dirt floor, as his thoughts turned to the events following that bombing. Victor, Kamar, and their father moved in with their uncle, Qasim. Their old apartment remained unsafe to enter, so they had been unable to retrieve their belongings. Just as well, since there was no room in Qasim's small apartment. Qasim's wife had died of cancer several years ago, and he had no family left other than his brother, Elias.

Their lives settled into a new routine. Their father found another school for Victor and Kamar to attend. Qasim, who had lost his employment to the war, helped run the household. Their father continued to work long hours at the hospital, trying to keep up with the never-ending stream of casualties.

Then a second calamity hit their family. Qasim received a call from the hospital—Elias had not shown up for work. Over the next week, Qasim repeatedly tried Elias's phone, with no response. He checked the hospitals, prisons, and morgues. Meanwhile the bombings accelerated. Aleppo had reached a breaking point.

Qasim explained to Victor and Kamar that they had no choice—they needed to leave Aleppo. They packed their few belongings and joined others from their neighborhood fleeing the violence. Hitching a ride on the back of a truck, they traveled south 140 perilous kilometers to Hama. There the group encountered more fighting, and no place where they could settle. So, they continued over the border into Lebanon. Qasim tried calling Elias's phone one more time, but there was still no answer. The battery on Qasim's phone was almost dead, and he had no means to recharge it.

The Lebanese border town where they landed was outside the control of the Lebanese government and therefore subject to whichever militia group happened to be controlling the area. The current ruling militia herded the new arrivals out to a barren, rocky landscape a mile outside of town to join the many refugees who had preceded them. When Victor first laid eyes on the settlement, he was reminded of a picture he'd seen on the news of the remains of an airline crash, with debris strung across a wide area. As he got closer, the smell became overpowering, and he thought he might be sick.

Each family was left to scrounge for materials to make a shelter. Some of the refugees banded together to construct sanitation ditches and provide some rudimentary structure to the settlement. Despite their efforts, lacking access to resources or support, the settlement remained a dusty, chaotic collection of shanties.

Victor and Kamar shared a shelter with their uncle. One night, their uncle become violently ill. Victor asked around the settlement but was unable to find anyone with medical training who was willing to help them. One of their neighbors, who had befriended Qasim, offered his help. Despite their efforts to care for Qasim, on the third night of sickness, he died. Their friendly neighbor helped Kamar and Victor bury their uncle a short distance from the settlement.

With Qasim gone, Victor and Kamar were on their own, although Qasim's friend checked in on them from time to time. As winter weather descended upon them, they were in a constant battle to protect themselves and their few possessions from rain and mud.

Now it looked as if even this pitiful home was under threat. Victor continued staring into the night, trying to remember his life before the war. The wind picked up, rattling the sticks and sections of plastic that made up their shelter, and sending shivers down his arms as it swept over his shoulders. Victor's thoughts returned to their current predicament. He knew they were not safe here. But where could they go?

Victor and Kamar's knowledge of Lebanon extended only as far as the small pocket of farms and grazing lands in the immediate vicinity of their settlement. They knew additional refugee settlements lay to the west and south, some of which might offer better living conditions than this settlement so close to the border. They also knew that further west was Beirut, a modern, prosperous city with many religions and cultures. What they didn't know about Lebanon could fill whole libraries. They didn't know how to get to any of these places, how far they would need to travel, what kind of terrain to expect, how populated the areas were, what types of people they might encounter, and whether those people would assist or assault them.

Two children traveling alone through unknown, ungoverned territory would be suicidal. Victor didn't want to risk making inquiries within the settlement because anyone could be a militia informer and pass along the information that the kids were planning to leave the settlement. Victor thought of asking Qasim's friend, but he didn't think he had knowledge of the area either. Besides, Victor didn't want to put him in danger by involving him with this. He had already done so much for them.

It began to rain—heavy, loud drops on the plastic ceiling close to Victor's head. The water dripped down onto the dirt floor of their shelter, the damp adding to the chill of the wind. Automatically, Victor gathered his blanket onto the slightly higher section of their floor in an attempt to avoid the puddles. Struggling to overcome despair, he turned his thoughts back to the problem of staying alive and keeping Kamar safe. He ached for his father to be there, remembering his calm, gentle authority. He tried to think of what his father would do in this situation. Finally, sleep and Victor connected in the wee hours of the morning.

Victor woke after less than two hours of sleep. He felt exhausted, but also settled on a plan. He peeked outside to see the faintest glimmer of dawn, then reached down to gently wake Kamar. "Quickly!" he whispered, "Get dressed for the day and roll all your other clothes into your blanket."

Kamar's eyes went wide at Victor's urgency, but she remained in her blanket staring at Victor. "What's happened? Are those men coming back?"

"No, we're okay. But I need you to act quickly, and I will explain later." Victor tried to sound firm yet reassuring to his sister, as he turned to gather his own few possessions and roll them into his blanket. He took both rolls and said, "Wait here. I will be back in a few minutes."

Victor peered through the gap in their shelter's doorway. He waited for his neighbor who had stepped outside for his morning pee at the sanitation ditch. As soon as the area was clear, Victor headed towards the gulley that ran away from town. He walked as quickly as he dared, knowing that if he ran, he might draw attention. For once, being on the edge of the settlement was an advantage. He found a cavity on the side of the gully beneath some brambles that would have to do for hiding their only possessions. Then, just as quickly, he made his way back to their tent.

Once inside, he sat Kamar down and sat himself opposite her. He looked directly into her large brown eyes. Why did his sister have to be so beautiful? It created such great risk that he dared not leave her alone. Victor, on the other hand, was below medium height for his age and below medium build, with straight dark hair, smaller eyes than his sister, and no distinguishing features. In fact, he looked so ordinary that people tended to overlook him. That suited Victor, as it allowed him to be the quiet observer.

But now Victor needed to act. "Listen carefully. Today we will walk to school and then go to work at the farm as usual. After we've completed our work, we will retrieve our blankets and continue on the road out of town. We can't stay here. If we can make it towards Beirut, we have a chance of finding a better settlement away from the militia groups. It may be that, if we find an aid group, they can help us search for our father.

"But it's important that no one knows about our plan. We must do everything the same as usual. We have two large plastic bottles. I want you to hide one under your coat, and I will do the same. We can fill them with water before we head out."

"Do you understand?"

Kamar's slender shoulders trembled slightly, but her face showed determination. "Okay," was all she said.

They fell into their usual routine—a small breakfast from last night's leftovers and then a few hours at the makeshift school run by the refugees each morning. Although Kamar and Victor were two years apart, they were grouped together with the other older kids and studied independently, as the mothers who had organized the school focused their attention on the younger students. There was little in the way of books or supplies. Victor was determined to work on math and reading, but that was difficult without a proper textbook or a proper teacher.

After school, they trudged off to the farm whose owner had hired them for manual labor. In exchange for the two of them working six hours, they received food worth about ten U.S. dollars.

Finishing their farm work and collecting their food allotment, they broke from their routine on their way back to the refugee settlement. Veering off the road and down into the gulley, they retrieved their blanket rolls and doubled back past the farm just as it was starting to get dark, continuing on into unknown territory. Victor had observed that most traffic in and out of town came over this road, so this is the road they would take, hoping to gain some distance in the cover of night before anyone realized they were gone.

Seattle

Yana peered out her window at the frosty ground and rob-
in's-egg blue sky. It was cold according to Seattle's weak
standard of cold, which meant temperatures in the thirties.
Figuring that the Olympic Mountains would be out from their
usual winter cloud bank, Yana suggested to Ellen a hike at Dis-
covery Park instead of their usual Saturday morning coffee.

They were not disappointed by the clear, winter-morning view
across Puget Sound to the rugged and freshly snowed range. The
exertion of hiking and the crisp air helped Yana sort through her
many thoughts springing from recent revelations. Yana started
with telling Ellen about the police report on Emma. Ellen couldn't
provide any additional insight but agreed that Yana should not
behave differently towards Emma because of the report. "Try
to look at it this way," Ellen reasoned, "If you worked at any job
other than at the crime lab, you wouldn't know anything about
this. The police had insufficient evidence to proceed with the
case, so maybe it's best to leave it at that."

"You're probably right," Yana agreed. Even so, there was no

way she could just dismiss this from her mind. She decided she needed to be a bit cautious around Emma.

Having talked out the situation with Emma, Yana switched the conversation to Zaid and Kayla's plans to travel to Lebanon with Sami and Amena. "I'm thinking I may go with them."

Ellen stopped walking to face Yana directly. "Really? Is it safe to travel to Lebanon now?"

"That was my initial thought as well. I think we hear so much in the news about the conflicts in the Middle East, it gives us a distorted view. But, to be honest, part of the reason I'm wanting to go is to make sure Kayla stays safe. Also, I think Amena and Sami might appreciate the additional support."

They continued their walk. "Have you ever been to the Middle East?"

"The only other continent I've been to is Europe. It's about time I widened my horizons. I've done some online research, and there's actually a lot to see in Lebanon."

"I hadn't thought of Lebanon as a tourist destination, but obviously it has loads of history."

"Yeah, I'm starting to get excited about the trip. Now I just need to get it past Kayla. I have a feeling she'll think I'm being overprotective."

"Well, aren't you?"

"Yes, of course! But I can't admit that to her."

They had come to an overlook point and stopped to gaze. Immediately below them, Puget Sound expanded 180 degrees, reined in by an array of islands and the Kitsap Peninsula, with the Olympic Mountains forming the backdrop. To the south, Mt. Rainier held court, while a state ferry made its way from the Seattle waterfront, destined for either Bainbridge Island or Bremerton.

As they continued their hike, Yana sighed. "I need to get on the stick and make arrangements, request time off and everything.

They plan to leave in three weeks. Of course, I have so much banked vacation, I don't see a problem getting it approved." For a time, they walked on in silence as Yana tried to picture her trip to the Middle East to help a family blown apart by war.

Lebanon

Kamar and Victor walked all through the night, following the road as it climbed, slowly at first, then more steadily. They kept their hoods over their heads and their eyes downcast to avoid inquiries from the few passing vehicles. Victor insisted that they needed distance between themselves and their former settlement before trying to secure help from anyone.

As they ventured further into uninhabited territory, Victor's thoughts spiraled downward. They had no idea where they were headed, how long their food supply might last, or who they would encounter. What had he been thinking, bringing his sister out into the wilderness in the middle of winter?

They relied on the moon to light their way, watching nervously as the ghostly landscape transitioned from dry plain to rocky hills and steep ravines. At one point, they both froze, seeing what at first appeared to be a lion crossing a rise in the road ahead of them. Noticing Victor and Kamar, it stopped to stare, its body tensing. As it bounded away and escaped behind some rocks, Victor realized it was too small to be a lion. "Only a caracal," he reassured Kamar. As dawn snuck up from behind them, they found a level patch next to a stream, offering shelter for the day under a rocky outcropping.

Their food supply consisted of their daily ration earned from their farm labor, supplemented by food they nicked from the farm on their last day of work—anything they could sneak out under their clothes. Victor decided that, given how much work they'd done and how little they were paid, they had earned the additional food.

Qasim had been a smoker, although cigarettes had been scarce at their settlement. Now, the small collection of matches he left behind proved extremely valuable as they kindled a small fire before starting their meal. The fire provided comfort, and they sat for some time as the morning light slowly revealed their surroundings.

Suddenly Kamar looked up from staring into the fire. "Do we have pictures of mom?" she asked.

"What?" Victor had been lost in his own thoughts.

"Our mother. Do we have any pictures that we brought with us?"

"No, of course not. We lost all that when our apartment was bombed."

"I can picture dad's face, but I can't remember exactly what mom looked like. How will we remember her without pictures?"

"After we find dad, he can find someone who has a picture of her."

Kamar was playing with a stick, holding it in the fire until the end caught. She stared into its flame for a while before asking, "What do you think happened to dad?"

"He disappeared on the way to work, so he must have been abducted."

Kamar poked the end of her stick into the dirt, grinding out the flame. "That's what Qasim said. Does that mean he's in prison?" She left unsaid the possibility that they both were thinking—that he had been killed.

"I don't think so. He's a doctor. If either side abducted him, they would put him to work with their wounded. I've heard about that happening to other doctors."

Kamar and Victor fell silent, each trying to imagine their future among the uncertainties about where they were headed and what had become of their father. Finally, despite the increasing daylight, sleep overtook the two. Exhausted from their journey, they slept soundly as the sun progressed across the sky and began to set.

The narrow valley where they slept pointed straight towards the setting sun, prolonging the waning daylight. Across the canyon, a golden jackal began his nightly rounds before the darkness was complete, knowing that his territory was little frequented by humans. He made his way to the small stream, remaining unobtrusive by keeping close to the juniper and wild almond that peppered the canyon slopes. Having drunk his fill, he raised his head to test the smells of the gathering night. His body tensed at the scent drifting from the opposite bank. Turning his head to catch the sounds, he heard only the soft murmur of the stream and the faint tap of a woodpecker in the distance. He stretched out his neck to gather in and taste the scent—it was coming from slightly upstream. He stared through the dim light, identifying two humps on an otherwise level patch of stream bank.

As the jackal stared, one of the two humps started to move. The jackal retreated noiselessly downstream, heading for the opposite corner of his pack's hunting territory, as far as possible from the humans.

Upstream, Kamar awoke stiff, tired, cold, and hungry. She sat up, pulled her knees close to her chest for warmth, and tried to take in her surroundings in the dim light.

Victor, hearing his sister stir, also sat up from his bed roll. The two hastily ate a meager meal of leftovers before breaking camp and covering the remains of their fire to hide the evidence of their stay. After refilling their water bottles, they hiked the short distance back to the road and resumed their journey.

Traveling by night had its advantages. The exertion of the upward climb kept them from feeling the worst of the cold highland winter nights. The moon, just past full, provided light sufficient to follow the empty road.

They maintained this pattern for several days, slowly progressing over a low pass and starting their descent into the Beqaa Valley, both secretly worrying about their disappearing food supply. Each evening the waning moon rose a bit later. In its absence, they started each night's journey by the light of billions of stars crowded between the jagged horizons etched by the mountains on either side.

Seattle

The clear, cold weather was ushered out with a few inches of snow, which always creates a bit of hysteria in Seattle. The snow was soon swept away by winter rain, and just in time for Christmas, Seattle returned to its usual chilly, dark, and very wet December weather.

Gloomy weather outside made homes decked out for Christmas all the cheerier in contrast. Yana's rustic stone fireplace and dark woodwork formed a perfect backdrop for holiday decorations, her backyard pine tree and holly bush providing material. Living on her own, she had made the switch to an artificial tree, but thought nostalgically of family trips into the foothills each year to cut their tree.

Yana selected a mix of music for their Christmas Eve dinner, including George Winston's album, *December.* Kayla and Zaid arrived early to help with dinner preparations. Yana had opted for baked salmon as the main course, which seemed to involve less fuss than turkey or roast. This also allowed more time to chat as they waited for the other guests to arrive.

"So, you're sure you want to go to Lebanon?" Kayla asked. "There's not going to be much time for touristy stuff, you realize?"

"No, I understand. I still think it'll be fascinating to visit a Middle Eastern country. I know I would never try to visit that part of the world on my own. Besides, I have non-refundable tickets, so I'm pretty much committed to going."

While Kayla worked on a salad, Zaid was busy peeling carrots for hors d'oeuvres. "We've been having some long talks with mom and dad about the trip," he said over his shoulder. "It's a challenging situation. Lebanon has taken on so many refugees—first the Palestinians, who've been there for decades, and now the Syrian mass migration. I heard that Lebanon now has one refugee for every four citizens."

"Wow! That's hard to imagine." Yana had just pulled the roasted vegetables from the oven. "That must be a huge strain on the country's resources."

"Not to mention the toll it's taken on the patience and sympathy of the Lebanese," Zaid continued as he began cutting up the peeled carrots. Yana paused from her prepping of the salmon to look over to Zaid and Kayla. She thought of the danger faced by Elias's family amidst the complexity of politics and war.

Yana's thoughts were interrupted by the arrival of Kyle and Thomas, closely followed by Amena and Sami. As her house filled up with activity, Yana took a few moments' pause to savor the conversations and laughter.

A short time later, the doorbell rang, and Emma arrived. Since Emma had never met Thomas, Zaid, Amena, or Sami, Yana did introductions. "Emma is an old friend of Kayla's and is not able to be with her family this Christmas, so we're delighted she can join us!"

"Did you know Kayla from high school or college?" Amena asked.

"We were friends in college," Emma replied, looking a bit uncertain as to how much these people knew.

"Oh, were you roommates or in the same study program?" Amena continued.

Emma quickly decided she might as well come clean and avoid an uncomfortable game of twenty questions. "No, Kayla and I were dating for a while. I've since transitioned to being female."

Amena's mug of hot, spiced cider made a terrific crash as it hit the hardwood floor. It was as if someone had pushed the pause button, and everyone froze for a full second, not knowing what to do. Then, just as suddenly, action resumed. Amena was apologizing for her clumsiness and saying that her arthritis was getting worse. Yana was providing many "No worries!" as she went for broom, dustpan, and kitchen towel. "Kayla, could you get Amena a fresh cup?"

Sami came over to Amena to make sure she was okay, while Kyle and Thomas made use of the distraction to check out the hors d'oeuvres counter. The only person standing still was Emma, who looked around awkwardly, unsure of what to do, or who to talk to. As Kayla came into the kitchen Yana asked her under her breath "Didn't you tell Zaid's parents about Emma?"

"No, I didn't see any reason to," Kayla hissed back.

"Well, I don't think they have much experience dealing with transgender people, so some warning might have helped."

Kayla took offense at this. "Amena simply dropped her mug. Don't overanalyze this!"

At this point they were interrupted by Amena joining them in the kitchen, so Kayla offered her the fresh mug of cider she was holding. "Anything I can do to help with dinner?" Amena asked.

"Kayla and Zaid have been so much help already—I think we're in good shape. The salmon just went into the oven, so we're just waiting until that is close to done before we start dishing up," Yana replied, trying to sound as if all was peachy.

As Kayla and Amena wandered back into the living room,

Yana followed, feeling frustrated that what had promised to be a cozy dinner with her family was now tainted by tension. She noticed Emma standing by herself, and neither Kayla nor Kyle—who were the only other people Emma knew—were trying to include her in conversation. Yana's ability to intervene was limited—she had to focus attention on getting the meal on the table. She wanted to check in with Emma without making her feel even more uncomfortable. "Emma, can I get your advice on something in the kitchen?"

"Sure," she responded.

"So, you're not interested in our expert opinions," Kyle interjected. He said it in joking fashion, but there was an undercurrent of accusation.

Typical passive-aggressive Kyle, Yana thought, exasperated. "The more the merrier!" she responded, not being quick enough to think of a way to keep this to just herself and Emma. With Emma, Kyle, and Thomas all trooping expectantly into her kitchen, Yana needed to come up with something for which she was in need of advice. "I can't decide which wines to open to go with the salmon. Also, should we set out some hard cider?"

This immediately occupied Kyle and Thomas as they pulled open Yana's pantry and started investigating her meagre wine collection, debating each bottle as if world diplomacy hung on their decisions. Thus, Yana gained a few moments to ask Emma how she was doing. "Fine," she responded in that closed mouth way that told Yana her questioning was just making Emma feel more uncomfortable.

Things seemed less awkward once they sat down, and Emma could more comfortably be a spectator to the communal table conversation. Much of the discussion centered around the pending trip to Lebanon and what to expect once they arrived. After dessert, Emma took her leave as soon as she politely could, saying that she had agreed to meet a friend for drinks.

Eventually, it was just Kyle and Thomas who remained. Being on winter break, they weren't the first to leave, as was usually the case. "What was Emma doing over here anyway?" Kyle asked.

"She was here because I invited her!" Yana said, her hands on her hips. Kyle and Thomas already knew about Emma landing on Yana's doorstep in the middle of the night, but Yana hadn't filled them in on the fact that Emma's family had disowned her.

"That's vile!" Kyle responded, when Yana described how Emma's family had responded to her transition. "But, you know, there are a lot of nutters in the trans crowd."

"What's that supposed to mean?"

"Just that a lot of them are messed up—bi-polar, that sort of thing. Not all of them, of course, but I know a lot of trans that really don't have their shit together."

"Kyle Pickering, are you prejudiced against transgender people? If they have more than their fair share of mental illness, might that be related to the rejection and mistreatment they're subjected to?"

"No, I'm not prejudiced! Just saying what we've observed," Kyle replied, glancing at Thomas in an attempt to pull him to his defense. "I don't have a problem with people being trans. And, no doubt they get a lot of crap thrown their direction. I'm just saying that there are some that are their own worst enemy with how they respond to those outside their group. Trust me on this. I've seen it in action."

Yana didn't know how to respond to that. She was relieved when she finally had her home to herself again and could collapse onto her couch, disappointed that her family holiday left her feeling sour instead of content.

Beqaa Valley

Unaware that Christmas was being celebrated elsewhere around the world, Kamar and Victor descended into the Beqaa Valley. As they lost elevation, the weather turned slightly warmer, but also wetter. Twice they endured heavy rain as they huddled under scrubby trees, arms around each other for warmth. They were also encountering farms and houses along the road and more traffic, so they decided it was no longer necessary to travel by night.

Their priority each day was finding food and temporary shelter. They also needed information about refugee settlements in the area, hopefully something close to an aid group. They approached farm settlement after farm settlement in their attempt to exchange work for food. Three times they were chased off at gun point. Only one farmer had been polite in his firm refusal to offer any help. Kamar and Victor were simply asking to stay one night in the shelter of a barn and were offering to trade any sort of work for a bit of food.

After many failed attempts to exchange work for food, Kamar

and Victor reached a point of desperation. They waited for the cover of darkness before raiding a farm for any food they could find. They took shelter under an old vegetable stand alongside the road. It was too wet and too risky to build a fire.

Secretly, Victor raged at their predicament and the hostility they faced. It was not their fault they were refugees. What had they done to deserve this treatment?

Victor looked over at his sister. She was shivering in the wind-blown rain that reached them despite their cover. Victor placed his arm over her shoulder and drew her in, trying to stretch his blanket to cover both of them. What had he been thinking taking his sister on such a doomed expedition? If he was more resourceful, if he knew how to survive in the wilderness, they wouldn't be in such dire straits. Long after Kamar had fallen asleep, her head resting on his shoulder, Victor continued churning his dark thoughts.

Beirut

Yana woke to the pilot announcing their descent. They had been in transit for nineteen hours, including a hectic change of planes at Heathrow. Despite finally finding sleep in the latter half of the London-to-Beirut flight, Yana felt exhausted and impatient to get off the plane so she could move about.

For this leg of their flight, Yana had a window seat, with Kayla and Zaid next to her, and Amena and Sami one row ahead. Kayla appeared to have just woken up as well and was asking Zaid to look for something from deep within their carry-on. Yana pulled up her window shade and peered down at the coastline. In the twilight, the occasional freighters created pools of light that stood out against the gathering black of the sea.

Slowly Beirut came into view, its hillsides awash with lights, its border marked abruptly by the Mediterranean. Yana was not prepared for the beauty of the city from the air. She remembered hearing how it was once considered the Paris of the Middle East. The plane passed over a point of land, the far side of which was bound by cliffs. Here the high-rises were jammed together, restrained from their march towards the jagged edge, as if in danger of coming too close and falling into the sea. They continued past the city, descending towards the Beirut-Rafic Hariri airport.

Their plane landed, and the spell of seeing Beirut from the air at twilight was broken. Despite being travel-weary, Yana felt excitement at being in a completely foreign city she thought she would never visit. Fortunately, Amena and Sami were familiar with travel in the Middle East and, more importantly, were fluent in Arabic. Yana appreciated the luxury of visiting a foreign city while others in her party dealt with logistics. They retrieved baggage, worked their way through customs, and then headed off to a pre-arranged taxi. It was inadvisable, Amena explained, to pick up an airport curbside taxi in Beirut.

Yana couldn't help noticing that Kayla was focusing her attentions on her in-laws rather than her mother. Kayla had come around slowly to the idea of Yana joining the trip. Yana suspected that having her mother tag along remained a source of some embarrassment for her daughter.

While Kayla conversed with Amena and Sami, Yana fell in with Zaid, who, despite several trips to Syria with his parents, was visiting Lebanon for the first time. Yana glanced over at Zaid. "If I'm remembering correctly, you're fluent in Arabic, is that right?"

"Yes, although I never learned to read in Arabic. That would be useful here."

Yana noticed that most of the airport signage was in Arabic, French, and English. It occurred to her that her college French studies might be of use as well, assuming she could remember any of it.

They reached the exit and were at last out in fresh air. The temperature was cool, but comfortable—a contrast to the cold they left behind in Seattle.

"Still no sign of the two kids and their uncle?" Yana inquired as they reached the pick-up location for their taxi.

"As of the last time we talked with Elias, they were still missing."

They were distracted for a moment by an approaching taxi, but it wasn't theirs. "What do you remember about Elias's kids?" Yana asked.

"Our last trip to Syria was eight years ago, so they were just seven and five at the time. Victor was the quiet one and Kamar fearless. Since war broke out, it's not been safe to visit, and communication has been difficult."

"I'm sure they will be excited to see you."

"I really don't know what to expect. We can only guess at the horrible experiences they've been through. I hate to think of what growing up under so much loss and violence does to children, or to their father. We've had some frank family discussions about being prepared for serious social, mental, and psychological issues."

Yana had no response to that. Their taxi had arrived, so their conversation broke off. She was glad she had come. If there was any way she could help this family trying to pick up the broken pieces left by war, it was well worth it. She just hoped she would not be a hinderance.

As their taxi approached the city center, the group's conversation trailed off. Yana noticed Kayla's head resting against Zaid's shoulder in the seat in front of her. Yana felt sleepy too but wanted to take in as many sights as possible from the highway. They followed a freeway north, and in the darkness, things did not look much different than many cities in the U.S., except, of course, the Arabic script on all the signs. It was late Friday night, but traffic was still heavy. They passed through a tunnel, caught a glimpse of a large sports stadium and then another short tunnel. A spire-like structure, probably a mosque, was lit up ghostly white against the night sky. Upon reaching their hotel, the exhausted party dropped off their luggage, convened for a quick supper in the hotel, and then headed straight to bed.

The family set aside the following day to leisurely explore central Beirut, adjust to the time change, and confirm arrangements. For breakfast, they decided on an assortment of sharable hot and cold meze plates. Amena ordered ful medames, consisting of fava beans stewed with chickpeas, olive oil, and lemon juice, and served with tomatoes, onions, and cucumbers. Sami added eggs with awarma, which turned out to be a lamb confit. Zaid insisted on man'oushe, a domed, airy flat bread spiced with thyme, sumac, and sesame seeds.

Sami, being the only member of their party who had previously visited Beirut, explained how the city's cuisine combined Ottoman, Persian, Arab, and French influences, while benefiting from its proximity to the sea. He reminisced about his visit at age fourteen, when Beirut was enjoying a golden age—one of many it has enjoyed during its 5,000-year history. "Not too long after my visit, the Lebanese Civil War broke out," he continued. "What's amazing is that the different tribal and religious groups held things together for as long as they did, especially considering that they had no pre-existing concept of Lebanon as a nation."

Yana felt she was beginning to understand some of the tangled politics that formed the backdrop to the refugee crisis. She pondered this, as they started their exploration of Beirut.

They headed towards the waterfront. There they were disappointed with block after block of high-end condos and hotels, all with secure parking, interspersed by a few sterile courtyards and little green. This section of the city had been rebuilt following the end of the civil war, but without consideration for preserving the culture of the city. Missing were the corner markets and cafes that Sami recalled as giving the city character, and in their place were representatives of every high-end merchandizer. Yana noticed a lack of foot traffic. Those they passed wore western-style clothes, including exposed legs and necklines.

Turning inland, they found the Beirut Sami remembered from his visit many years ago. The streets became crowded with grandmothers in head scarfs, teenagers sporting the latest western trends, and businessmen in a hurry. Small shops sold huge cases of everything from artichokes to flower petals directly on the sidewalk. The smells of garlic, cheeses, olives, and cardamom would overwhelm and then blend as they walked past. They exchanged hellos with an elderly man selling bananas piled onto a large wooden cart. As they waited at a crosswalk, Yana closed her eyes for a moment to take in the sounds—shouts from pedestrians and shop owners, music streaming from street musicians and open-air restaurants, and overriding everything, the incessant cacophony of car horns.

After wandering through a boisterous weekend market under a highway bridge, they eventually found themselves in an Armenian neighborhood. By then it was three o'clock, and the older ones in their group had walked themselves out. Yana, Amena, and Sami caught a taxi back to their hotel, while Kayla and Zaid continued exploring the city. Back at the hotel, Yana and Amena took naps while Sami called Elias to confirm plans to meet at the hotel the following day.

Elias flicked off his phone and started home from the refugee medical clinic where he had been helping out on a temporary basis. He thought back to the time eight years ago when he had last seen Sami and Amena, a time when he felt secure, both with family and career. Now his wife was dead, and he had just found out that his brother had also died, leaving his two kids on their own. Elias had informed the clinic that he was no longer able to help them, that this was his last day, as he needed to devote himself full-time to locating his kids. He barely made it through his final work shift. His mind was not on his work. It was playing out scenarios, edging close to panic.

Aliya had wanted them to move in with her family in Damascus. Had they done so, she would probably still be alive, and their kids would be safe. But Elias couldn't bring himself to desert his city in its time of great need. And after all that he'd seen, he could never aid or support the Assad regime—that would have been expected of him had they moved to Damascus. Was he guilty of putting his own feelings above the safety of his family?

Aliya could have taken the kids to Damascus without him. Their marriage had been drifting apart, their lives moving in different directions—they both had known that. Elias suspected that Aliya had not wanted the embarrassment of a failed marriage. She wanted Elias with her when she returned to her family and its prominent social circle.

What a lifeline it was to have Sami and Amena here to help. Anxiety and guilt over his missing kids were threatening to take him down. He needed to hold himself together so that he could work on finding them. He tried to turn his mind to other things.

Elias had many other worries to choose from. Would these refugees ever be able to safely return to Syria? Millions of refugees packed together without adequate support or infrastructure were extremely susceptible to sweeping epidemics and other medical disasters.

Elias thought morosely that they should put up a big sign at their clinic with its limited resources, "If you need help with something minor, you are dying, or are pregnant, please sign in. Otherwise, you need to try your luck at a private hospital." The Lebanese healthcare system had proven remarkably resilient, given the number of refugees needing support—but the stress was becoming too great, especially with both the Lebanese economy and international aid levels on downward trajectories. Elias allowed worries such as these to fill his thoughts, as this left no room for even gloomier thoughts about his lost family.

Upon reaching the modest studio he was renting, Elias

switched on his TV and started preparing his dinner. A Lebanese Premier League match had just kicked off—a good distraction. After dinner, he reviewed the information he had collected regarding Victor and Kamar. Although he had discovered where they had crossed the border into Lebanon, he had no idea where they were now.

The next morning Elias got up early to go for a run before driving into Beirut. Exercise provided stress management for Elias. He knew he needed, now more than ever, to maintain that practice. Despite the wear that years of war had inflicted on his body, he managed to maintain a fit, lean frame. His dark hair was now peppered with gray, but that did not diminish the intensity of the deep brown eyes he had inherited from his mother.

Elias arrived at the hotel freshly showered and feeling marginally better than he had the previous evening. As he rode up the hotel elevator, he couldn't help comparing his life's trajectory with his friend's, who had been sheltered from war and its calamities. He thought back to their many long days and late nights studying together as they worked their way through medical school. They shared a common background, both coming from upper-middle-class families and having attended the same schools in Aleppo. More than that, they shared a youthful idealism and passion for medicine.

After finishing their residencies, Sami's in Seattle and Elias's in New York, Sami remained in the U.S. He and Amena had married just prior to Sami starting his residency, and they were both settled in Seattle when he finished. As for Elias, Aliya was waiting for him in Aleppo when he completed his residency. She was from a wealthy family who had dictated that Elias finish his medical training before the marriage could take place. Elias decided it didn't help to dwell on what might have been, had he remained in the U.S. as his friend Sami had done.

Elias reached the hotel room, and Sami was at the door in two bounds. Sami bear-hugged Elias and then steered him into the room. Elias knew in that moment that their friendship was one of the few precious things that had survived the war. He was also relieved to see Sami sporting some gray hair, although not as much as Elias. Sami had always carried a larger frame than Elias. Now Elias could not help noticing that Sami had gained more than a few pounds around his midsection.

Amena had also aged in the past eight years. Her complexion was tighter, and thin lines radiated from the corners of her eyes. But she had aged more subtly and gracefully than either Elias or Sami. The shock, however, was how grown up Zaid had become.

Elias had little time to register all this as introductions were made to the two new people in the room. He had been anticipating the chance to meet Zaid's partner, Kayla, but was surprised to find that Kayla's mother had also made the trip. Why was she here? Was their misfortune now a tourist attraction? Americans looking to assuage their guilt by showing up and experiencing the culture? His stress and worry threatened to spill over into anger. Elias worked to contain them. Impeccable manners had been instilled in him by his father, who always held his own emotions under tight control. As he and Yana exchanged acknowledgements, however, he sensed in her eyes a perceptiveness that saw through his cover.

Sami efficiently marshalled the group to the restaurant where he had made reservations the night before. Elias suspected that Sami wanted lunch done so they could begin work on locating Victor and Kamar. He was reminded again of their time in medical school, where Sami was the driven, business side of their friendship, keeping them both focused on practical necessities. Elias brought balance, providing calm for Sami when his relentless self-drive threatened to consume him. Elias felt he was now the one in need.

At the restaurant, Elias and Yana ended up seated next to each other, as the group formed three neat pairs. In fact, Elias sensed that the waiter assumed that the two of them were a couple, just as the other two pairs obviously were. If this felt awkward to Yana, she didn't show it, and they exchanged bits of their background.

Sami helped Kayla and Yana with menu explanations and suggestions. Once the waiter had taken their orders, Sami turned his attention to Elias. "So, any updates on Victor and Kamar?"

"I was able to track down where Qasim, Victor, and Kamar went after they left Hama. They were living in a settlement in Lebanon near the Syrian border. I found someone who had befriended Qasim while they were staying at the settlement. My brother became sick and they were unable to obtain any medical care. He passed away while at the settlement."

There was a moment of shocked silence, before Sami rose up from his seat and walked around the table to give Elias a hug. "I'm so sorry, my friend." Elias said nothing. He didn't want to break down in front of this group.

Finally, they broke away. "I can't tell you what it means to have you here with me," Elias eventually managed.

Elias was dreading the sharing of this news, feeling that his telling of it and seeing the reactions of his friends made the passing of his brother a reality that he had not yet fully accepted. He was relieved to have that done. Now, he wished he could return to his studio and collapse onto his bed. But they had work to do.

The two sat down, and Elias continued. "My contact at the settlement said Victor and Kamar were living on their own for a while and then disappeared."

Amena gasped, but Elias plowed ahead. "He told me that they took their belongings with them, so it looks like they left of their own accord. It's helpful to have the information on where they'd been staying, as there are only two main routes out of that area. I'm pretty sure they didn't try to return to Syria, so that means they probably headed southwest towards the Beqaa Valley. The challenge is that there are a number of directions they could have gone once they reached the valley.

"I brought maps with me, so we can review the situation after lunch. Also, I tried to leave word with the main refugee settlements in that vicinity, in case Victor and Kamar show up. There's no real structure or administration over these settlements, so that makes things difficult. Then, there are the many smaller settlements we'll need to canvass before widening the net by contacting settlements further out."

Eventually, the lunch conversation turned to less weighty topics, as Zaid, Kayla, and Yana filled Elias in on their respective careers, and Elias talked about his experiences at the refugee medical clinic.

When they returned to Sami's and Amena's hotel room, Sami, Elias, and Amena poured over the maps of the Beqaa Valley and lists of refugee settlements in the area, while Zaid started calling refugee relief offices to register the two children as missing. Kayla was not feeling well and had retreated to her room for a nap.

Yana tried to follow the map discussion over the others' shoulders, but they had reverted to Arabic, and Yana felt it would be a further intrusion to ask them to converse in English. She wanted to stay informed but was uncomfortably aware of her role as an outsider and didn't want to get in anyone's way. She didn't feel she was contributing anything, but at the same time, felt that going off on her own to read a book or explore the city would be inappropriate, given the gravity of the task they faced. For the first time on the trip she had serious second thoughts about the wisdom of her joining the expedition.

Yana had been intrigued to meet this old friend of Sami's. The manner in which his name was passed between Sami and Amena told Yana that the friendship had played a significant role in Sami's life. That morning, Sami hadn't been able to focus, picking up his book, only to put it back down again two minutes later to circle around the small hotel room. Yana attributed his behavior to his anticipation of the reunion after such a long period apart and to anxiety about Elias's family.

Yana's anticipation at meeting Elias evaporated when they actually met. She noticed Elias's eyes widen and anger flash across his face when he found out that Zaid's almost mother-in-law had attached herself to the expedition. Just as quickly the anger disappeared, as he shook hands and graciously welcomed her to Lebanon. However, she saw through his politeness to the judgmental eyes. Who was he to decide whether she should or should not be here?

Yana was disappointed to be seated next to Elias at lunch, feeling that he did not welcome her presence on this trip. However, after hearing the news about Elias's brother, she felt ashamed at how quickly she had become judgmental towards someone facing so much loss. His story put her minor worries in perspective.

Trying to make up for her early dismissal of Elias, Yana inquired about his experiences working in the refugee clinic, the type of cases he dealt with, and the state of their equipment and supplies. Elias reciprocated, asking about Yana's career. Yana was used to people being intrigued by the concept of working in a crime lab, but quickly losing interest in the actual details of her job. Elias, however, continued asking questions and delving into her craft, his eyes on her, more than on his plate of food. Yana noticed how quickly he picked up on her strong technical background and that he did not talk down to her. They discovered a shared respect for, and dependence on, science.

As the lunch drew to a close, Yana realized she had become so drawn into the comparisons between their careers that she had momentarily forgotten the rest of the party at the table. Feeling a bit self-conscious, she turned pointedly to Amena and asked her how she had enjoyed her lamb dish.

Once they returned from lunch to the hotel room, Elias, Sami, and Amena were lost in their maps and notes. Yana thought how strange it was that the two children were likely within a few hours driving distance, and yet they had no way to locate or contact them.

Beqaa Valley

While a group of people in a Beirut hotel room talked strategy, the focus of their search, Victor and Kamar, were only two hours away by car, steadily progressing south and west. They had been offered rides on occasion, but Victor would not risk riding with strangers. This afternoon brought steady rain, and the skies offered no hope for a respite. Unable to find shelter, the two were soaked through all their layers of clothing, and the chill was robbing Victor of the ability to think. He was particularly worried about Kamar, who had picked up a steady cough. When two men offered a ride in the back seat of their battered sedan, Victor weighed the risks and then acquiesced. They were both older men—perhaps in their fifties. Victor thought he saw kindness in their faces. The driver was slender and wiry, and the other in the passenger seat was a large man with an even larger belly.

The men engaged them in conversation, showing interest in Victor and Kamar's story. Victor spoke for the two of them and tried to share a minimum of information while not appearing unfriendly. They were originally from Aleppo and were heading west in search of a refugee settlement and aid.

Victor's radar went off when the car suddenly turned off the main road, taking a dirt track pointing off towards some low hills. "Where are we going?" Victor tried to make his voice sound neutral but was unable to quell panic's higher pitch and slight quaver.

"Just a short detour—we need to pick up something from a friend. Will take just a few minutes," the driver responded offhandedly.

They drove about a mile before the road started to climb through empty, rocky terrain. The men in front became silent. Finally, the road ended at a small, square house with a sagging roof and broken out windows. The area around the house was littered with random objects, soda cans, a metal rod, the decaying remains of an old cabinet. The house clearly had not been lived in for some time. Victor looked over to Kamar's wide frightened eyes. She silently mouthed a message to Victor, but he couldn't understand what she was trying to say. He scanned their surroundings for escape routes. He might be able to outrun these men. Kamar probably could not. He looked around the yard for possible weapons.

When Victor looked back, the man in the passenger seat had a gun pointed at Victor's head. He ordered him out of the car and onto the ground a short distance away. The driver also pulled out a gun and pointed it at Kamar. She was shaking so hard, she had difficulty opening the car door. The man in the passenger seat, the overweight one, grabbed Kamar's arm, dragging her into the house. Kamar looked back at Victor. He had never seen such an expression of silent pleading. The image remained, even after Kamar disappeared into the house.

A few moments later, Victor heard Kamar scream. Instinctively, Victor started to get to his feet. The driver fired a shot, close enough for Victor to feel the drag of the bullet in his hair. A branch splintered behind Victor, and the sound echoed from the nearby hills. Victor fell back on the ground and started to shake. He was no longer Kamar's protector. From the house, Kamar's screams turned to sobs. Victor wanted to block the sounds. He wanted to do something, somehow stop this thing that he could not believe was happening to his sister. He wanted to attack these evil men. He did nothing—there was a gun pointed at his head.

Eventually the first man returned, and the driver took his place. Kamar's sobs continued unabated. Once more Victor waited, powerless. A bird sang from a nearby judas tree, unconcerned about the attack on Kamar. A wasp buzzed through the grass near to where Victor was seated. Finally, the driver returned. The two men got into their car, throwing Victor and Kamar's belongings onto the ground. From the window the overweight man smiled and called out to Victor, "Your slut of a sister will soon be laying down for all her fellow Sunnis. It is why your kind are overrunning the valley and taking away our Maronite lands. We just gave her some early lessons. Go back to your Syrian hole where you belong!"

The car spun off down the dirt track, while Victor ran into the house. Kamar was on a sagging bed, lying on her side, her knees pulled up to her chest. Victor fell down beside her, feeling utterly impotent, unable to protect his sister, unable to comfort her, unable to find a way out of their personal hell.

The smell from the bed was a horrible stew of mildew, sweat, urine, and alcohol. There was an old couch in the second room that smelled not as bad. Victor slowly led Kamar there, placing the cleanest cushion he could find under her head, and she resumed her position, curled up against the world. Victor sat at the end of the couch near Kamar's head, staring into the coming night while Kamar's sobs slowly ebbed.

At the first hint of dawn, Victor gently gathered Kamar from the couch. Neither of them spoke as they picked up all the belongings they had in the world and followed the dirt track back to the main road.

Beirut

The group established a daily pattern. Each morning Elias and Sami took off to scour the countryside and visit refugee settlements, often joined by Zaid and Amena when the area they were visiting was considered safe. They had decided that Sami and Elias, traveling together as two doctors, would arouse the least amount of suspicion when passing through checkpoints. At each refugee settlement they posted signs and left contact information with whomever seemed to be in charge. As they traveled, they slowed down to check out any pedestrians they passed.

Those remaining in Beirut fell into a routine of spending the morning on their phones following up with aid groups and UN refugee officials. Here, at least, Yana could help, as many of the aid group contacts spoke English. At lunchtime, they would find a new restaurant to try and then spend some time exploring the city, making sure to be back to the hotel in time to greet the returning travelers. Zaid, Kayla, and Yana used some of their free time to visit the American University of Beirut, learning about the history of one of Beirut's premier institutions and taking in the spectacular views of city and coastline.

Thursday morning of the second week, Sami and Elias set off for a two-day trip reaching further north and east. Although the rest of the group remaining back in Beirut knew that the men would call with any news, it was particularly discouraging when the exhausted pair arrived home late Friday evening with nothing to show for their efforts.

Being on the ground in Beirut made the enormity of the task sink in. Even though Lebanon was a small country, their individual case was one among millions. Yana knew it was unlikely that a breakthrough would occur in the two weeks they had left before returning to Seattle. She worried about Elias being left to continue the search on his own. Something could have happened to his two kids, and he might not ever find out about it.

Saturday, the group again poured over maps. When Sami and Elias took a break from their planning, Yana asked whether it would be an inconvenience if she visited Elias's former refugee medical clinic and the nearby settlement the next week. She suggested that Elias and Sami could drop her off on their way out to explore the settlements. Kayla jumped at the idea, and Zaid expressed an interest as well. It would be a chance to see the countryside outside Beirut and to learn first-hand what it was like for the refugees. Perhaps they could make themselves useful in some way.

Elias and Sami were skeptical at first, but upon consideration, agreed that the route between Beirut and Elias's clinic was a safe one. Sami and Elias could drive them out and then continue on with their canvasing of refugee centers. After two weeks of feeling marginally useful, Yana felt excited at the prospect of a more concrete way to help.

Beqaa Valley

Victor was worried about Kamar. Her cough kept getting worse, but he was more worried about her mental state. Her shoulders and head drooped. She hardly ever spoke. She did everything slowly, reminding Victor of his grandfather. Whereas before, she might complain about the cold or lack of food, now she expressed no emotion. She did whatever Victor told her to do. He did not like this new, compliant Kamar.

Victor felt his worry deep within, and it filled him with dread and panic. He was responsible for the unthinkable things that had happened to his sister. He should never have taken the ride from those two men. How could he have been so stupid? Never trust a stranger. Never again! He and Kamar were on their own.

By late afternoon, Victor and Kamar were approaching another small town. Desperately hungry, they needed to steal some food before finding a place to spend the night. They were no longer trying to exchange work for food, having no success with that approach and needing to conserve their energy.

At the edge of town, they came upon a small farm. Victor surveyed the area and didn't see anyone about. An empty field was bordered by low bushes and scrub, which allowed Victor and Kamar to approach the farm's out-buildings unseen. They could hear chickens. Victor knew better than to check for eggs, as the chickens would create too much noise. A bag of feed grain hung from a post. Victor and Kamar scooped the grain into any of their pockets that didn't have holes, while three goats stood in a nearby paddock, staring at the two intruders. They could chew on the grain, and that would provide something for their empty stomachs.

Then they heard the sound of a door opening behind them. They turned to see an old woman standing in the doorway to her farmhouse, her white hair escaping from its ties in loose strands. Despite the curvature in her diminutive frame, she was aiming a shotgun straight at Victor who slowly backed away. When the woman's gaze turned to Kamar who was staring despondently at her shoes, her expression softened as she slowly lowered her weapon. "Okay," she finally said, "I can feed you one meal. Then you must be on your way."

But Victor did not respond to her offer of help. He continued backing away until he reached Kamar, and grabbing a fistful of her jacket, pulled her away as well. They continued past the town and found a campsite for the night under the shelter of a small grove of scrub trees. The land immediately around them was flat and featureless. They chewed on the coarse grain they had stolen and tried to find sleep as the skies began to rain. Victor had heard someone talking about an aid group operating near a refugee settlement just outside the next town, so he took solace in the thought that they might be close to their goal.

The next morning, it was once again raining, and Kamar would not get up. Victor explained to her that the aid group was only as far as the next town. He would carry her bed roll for her. He tried to pull her to her feet, but she was a dead weight. When he let go, she sank back down, coughing. Numb with cold, Victor sat down next to her, thinking desperately of what to do. He didn't dare ask anyone passing along the nearby road for help. He would not risk that again. If only Kamar could keep going for one more day—they were so close.

As Victor sat in the rain, he thought about his home and his school, both destroyed, their uncle who had been so kind to them, dead. He thought of his mother killed in the bombing raid, his father missing and probably dead—if only his parents could be with them now. Victor tried to hold it back. He had to remain strong or they would have no hope whatsoever. He looked over to his sister, shivering in the rain, staring down at the ground in front of her. Victor had failed to protect his sister. She would probably die too, out in this cold, desolate place. Victor could not hold it back. Ashamed that he was letting his sister down in yet another way, he could not stop the heaving sobs.

Victor felt an arm across his shoulder. It was his sister. He leaned into her and cried until there was no more left. Then, without saying a word, Kamar stood up and pulled Victor to his feet. They both picked up their bedrolls and started the long trek to the next village.

Victor and Kamar walked all day, their pace drooping as the day wore on. Finally, near dusk, they approached the aid facility. There was a line stretching outside the office. After twenty minutes, they were allowed into the small, cramped office.

The office was heated. It had been so long since they had felt the sensation of warmth. As it slowly penetrated their bodies, it kindled within them the depth and misery of the cold they had endured, making unbearable the thought of eventually having to leave this office and return to their cold existence.

A lady who looked to be in her forties asked them to sit on the two old wooden chairs that stood in front of her simple metal desk.

The woman looked European, but she spoke fluent Arabic. Victor explained that they were brother and sister, that their mother was killed in the bombing in Syria, and their father had gone missing. They were looking for shelter and a place to attend school. They were willing to work for food. The woman began asking them a series of questions and typed the information onto a form on the small laptop at her desk.

Victor had already coached Kamar on the false names they were going to use. He still worried that the militia recruiters would be furious that he had given them the slip and would track him down.

After months of being either in a refugee shelter or on the road, Victor and Kamar were thin, ragged and, above all, dirty. With their hair and nails uncut and the accumulation of dirt, they appeared more like feral cats or stray dogs than human children. The aid worker seemed not to take notice. She had seen so many similar cases, that these two did not stand out. She calmly and efficiently provided Victor and Kamar with information about the nearby refugee settlement and told them that the closest school was a three-mile walk from the nearby settlement. She strongly suggested to Victor that he take his sister to their medical clinic to have someone evaluate her cough. Then she directed them to the back room, where a young man led them to a large storeroom. They were each given a clean blanket and allowed to select from an odd assortment of used clothing. They both found shoes close to their sizes with some wear still left in them and some clothing to replace the battered and smelly articles they had been wearing.

Victor and Kamar were paired with a newly arriving family of three—mother and father with a child of about two years. They were to share a large one-room tent with this family, who did not appear happy with the arrangement. Despite the animosity, the prospect of being off the road and having shelter felt like a luxury.

An aid worker led the group to their newly assigned shelter.

Due to the flat terrain, Victor and Kamar's initial view of the settlement was a long row of tents bisected by a narrow road. As they proceeded down the central roadway, they passed branch roads, stretching off into the distance on either side. Each branch road was lined with tents, side-by-side. Victor lost count of the number of branch roads they passed, and they began to comprehend the immensity of their new settlement.

The air was filled with a noxious mixture of mud, human bodies, and limited sanitation. Children were running in and out amongst the mud puddles and tents. Their shouts to each other punctuated the background noise of crying babies and the hum of adult conversation. Finally, they turned down a side road to their left and were shown their shelter.

The following morning, the group from Seattle ate a hasty breakfast before heading out. Sami had rented a compact to save on gas and draw less attention as they traveled the countryside. With Sami and Amena occupying the front seats and Zaid and Kayla in back, Elias had offered that Yana might be more comfortable riding with him. Yana saw this as an opportunity to talk with Elias about his work and about the conditions in the nearby settlement.

Yana was looking forward to seeing the Lebanese countryside, but due to their early start, it was mostly dark when they set out. Elias began by explaining how the 29-year Syrian occupation of parts of Lebanon during the Lebanese Civil War, including the Syrian detention and torture of Lebanese civilians, had fostered a deep animosity towards the Syrians. In addition, certain ethnic groups feared that the huge influx of Syrians, together with the additional Palestinian refugees displaced from Syria, would, over time, upset the precarious power balance in Lebanese elections. Their worry was that the refugees' descendants might eventually become citizens, even though there was no path for them to do so. "Wow, I had no idea," Yana responded. "This explains the hostility."

"Exactly," Elias confirmed. "It also helps explain why the Lebanese government stopped allowing the UN or aid groups to set up official refugee settlements for Syrians. Many of the new refugees are forced into makeshift settlements or whatever shelter they can find. I think the government is hoping they will find the situation so intolerable that they will either return to Syria or move on to another country. The government also stopped the UN from registering Syrian refugees, which prevents them from establishing legal residence or obtaining work permits. In some places they have been forcibly deporting refugees back to Syria."

"How is it that you're able to work?" Yana asked.

"Because I'm a physician, the Lebanese are willing to overlook my nationality. The need for skilled labor outweighs their aversion to Syrians." With Elias watching the road, Yana had the opportunity to study him as he responded. His face was creased and worn, yet remained open. It was a face Yana felt she could trust.

"What will you do once you find Victor and Kamar? Will you resume working at the refugee clinic?"

"Perhaps for a while. I haven't thought that far ahead. I know I need to move on or the enormity of this mess is going to take me down. But I find it hard to turn my back on these people in such desperate need."

"Where would you go if you did move on?"

"We were well along in the process of applying for visas to France before my wife was killed. My father was from France, and he registered me with the French government when I was a child, so I have dual French-Syrian citizenship. My parents raised me to be bi-lingual—French and Arabic."

"You certainly could pick worse places to live. I consider Paris my favorite city, after Seattle, of course!"

There was an accident ahead. The cars involved were on the

shoulder. Even so, traffic had slowed. Elias looked over and smiled at Yana. "Home of Starbucks, Microsoft, and Amazon. Doesn't it rain constantly there?"

"That's what everyone thinks. Actually, it's more that it's constantly cloudy, or at least ten months of the year. July and August are dry and not terribly hot, so our summers are pleasant. The rest of the year we do get a lot of drizzle, so you just get used to it and go about your business in the rain. In fact, most Seattleites don't use umbrellas. It typically doesn't rain hard enough to be bothered with them."

"When I did my residency in New York, I visited many of the cities along the east coast of the U.S., but I've never been to Seattle. I'd like to see the city some time."

"You should definitely come visit us. It might be the break you need from working with so many people whose lives have been torn apart."

Yana went on to describe a bit more about her work and told Elias about her son. "Do you have other family in the area, or elsewhere?"

Elias was silent for a few moments. "Neither of my parents are still living. My father was quite old when he started his family, so I had only one sibling—my older brother. My wife and I had four children. My oldest joined one of the rebel militias and was killed two years ago. Our second child died as an infant. So now it's just Victor and Kamar."

Yana noticed Elias's grip tighten on the steering wheel. He was staring ahead, determinedly. Yana wanted to do something for this unfortunate man, pat him on the shoulder or take his hand. But she didn't know him well, and he was busy driving the car. "I'm so sorry for what you've gone through."

"I'm actually fortunate to have escaped from Aleppo. Many of my colleagues were killed. The Assad regime specifically targets hospitals in their bombing of the city."

"It's hard to fathom a policy like that. You do need a break from all this, or you will find one day that you no longer have anything left to give."

Neither knew what to say after this. Yana felt she had intruded as far as she dared. They drove on in silence for a short while, both staring straight ahead, absorbed in their private thoughts. Finally, Yana asked Elias about his daily routine at the clinic and how he had decided on medicine as a career. "My father was a physician. I think it was always assumed that I would follow in his footsteps," Elias explained.

"How did he end up in Syria?"

"He came to Syria as a medic during World War II. They let him graduate early because of the war. He never returned to France. He'd been living in Syria for some time when he fell in love with my mother, who was quite a bit younger. He never talked about his war experience or his relations in France."

"Did he keep in touch with his family back in France?"

"Not as far as I'm aware. I don't even know if I have relatives in France. Somehow, growing up I knew not to ask. He was a good father to me, but not someone you felt like you really knew." Elias suddenly seemed to catch himself. "Not sure how we returned to my sorry personal life. Tell me more about your family."

By the time they reached their destination the conversation had returned to safer territory. Yana realized she had failed to take in any of the scenery along the way.

Elias showed the group around the clinic, which included a tiny space that served as both physician office and exam room, an equally tiny front office, a small lab, and a two-bed infirmary. Their supply room was in reality a large walk-in closet. He pointed the group towards the refugee settlement and gave them a lunchtime recommendation for a restaurant in the nearby town.

Elias and Sami took off to track down more settlements, and Zaid decided at the last minute to join them. Kayla, Amena, and

Yana headed down to the aid group office to pay a visit and discuss their search for Kamar and Victor. After that, they walked over to the refugee settlement. There wasn't much to see at the settlement except tents, makeshift shelters, and lots of mud. Sanitation appeared to be barely functional and laundry facilities non-existent, so the smell was overpowering. They came upon some aid workers who explained to them what their top needs were at the settlement and described their efforts to establish some schooling for the youngest group of school-age children—those too young to walk to the nearest Lebanese school. Amena described Victor and Kamar to the aid workers in case they had encountered them.

At lunchtime, they drove Elias's car to the local restaurant he had recommended. It was a bare-bones establishment. The food was simple but surprisingly good. Amena had fattoush, a salad consisting of fried vegetables with bits of flat bread, topped with more chopped vegetables and feta, while Kayla had kibbeh, a spicy concoction of lamb and sautéed pine nuts, and Yana had kafta, consisting of lamb meatballs barbequed on skewers. Each of the dishes, including their sides of hummus, were seasoned with a complex of spices that brought to mind their earlier exploration of the Beirut street markets.

After lunch, Amena and Kayla decided to go back to the refugee settlement to see if they could be of help to the aid workers, while Yana went back to the medical clinic to see if there was something useful she could do there. The filing system, being in Arabic, was beyond her, but she could match up names in the supply room to help with a much overdue inventory. She was also not useless in the lab, as some of her forensic skills and her experience working in cramped lab spaces transferred over.

Being busy helped the day pass quickly. On the way home, the group agreed that they would like to continue helping out at the settlement and at the clinic. That meant returning to Beirut, grabbing a quick supper, and calling it an early night in anticipation of another early start the next day.

Yesterday had been a disappointment for Victor and Kamar. They had walked the three miles into town, and, after several mis-directions, finally found the school, only to be told that their classrooms were full and that it was impossible for them to enroll. The administrator, a short bald man with a neatly trimmed mustache, told them he was sorry, but the look he gave Kamar and Victor did not seem at all sorry. It was the look of someone who wanted to have nothing to do with them and who wanted them not just out of their school, but also out of their town and out of their country. Victor did not believe for a minute that their school was full. He could try to complain, but there was no one to complain to. He had heard that those who caused trouble were being rounded up and sent back to Syria, with no regard as to whether Syria was safe for them.

Today, since attending school was not an option, they would go to the medical clinic to see about Kamar's cough. When they arrived at the clinic, the line curved outside the small building and around the side. Many of those in line were mothers with small children, some of whom were fussing loudly, while a few remained listless. Victor and Kamar noticed some who were clearly mothers-to-be. There were those who looked almost too sick to be waiting in line. Kamar and Victor took up their place in line, and after two hours it was their turn to talk to the lady in the front office.

Again, there were many questions that were written down on a paper form. Victor and Kamar used the same fake names they had used at the aid facility. Better to be consistent, and besides, Victor didn't know who might have access to the records at the clinic. He needed to be sure the militia recruiters wouldn't trace them to their new settlement.

The doctor who examined Kamar seemed kind but tired. He gave Kamar a shot in her arm and impressed upon her and Victor how important it was that she return in two days so that he could examine her arm. He told them that she didn't need to wait in line again for the follow-up visit but could go directly to the front office. After so much waiting, it seemed a disappointment to have no resolution. There was nothing for them to do but head back to the settlement.

As they passed through the front office, there was another lady with lighter hair conversing with the nurse in English. She looked directly at Kamar and Victor as they headed out the door. In fact, she stared at them, making Victor uncomfortable. Kamar didn't notice the lady's stares, as she had now taken to always looking down.

Victor wanted to get Kamar out of the office and away from the stares. He took her by the arm and, in his haste, accidentally called her by her real name. They were out the door heading back to the settlement when Victor heard someone call his name—not the false name he had given—his real name. He turned to see the lady had followed them out of the office. He urgently hurried Kamar away. The lady continued to follow them. She called out Kamar's name, and Kamar stopped to turn around. Victor grabbed his sister and urged her forward, but she resisted him.

The lady was talking in English so Victor and Kamar couldn't understand her. Then he heard other names—Elias, Sami, and Amena. The militia they were running from would know their father's name, but they wouldn't know the names of their father's friends in America. The woman smiled at them. Victor did not trust smiles. Then she said another word that Victor and Kamar understood. She pointed at herself and said, "American."

Victor paused. She looked American, and she was speaking English. Then she might know Sami and Amena. "Where are

Elias, Sami, and Amena?" Victor demanded in Arabic. The lady smiled again and beaconed them to return with her to the clinic.

Victor hesitated but Kamar did not. She started following the lady back to the clinic. Victor, not willing to leave Kamar alone, had no choice but to follow. As they entered the office, the lady gently but firmly took Kamar's arm and lead her right past the startled nurse into the office, even though the doctor was with another patient. The doctor looked up in surprise, and anger flashed across his face. "I'm with a patient!" he said to the lady in English.

But she replied simply "Victor and Kamar! Elias's kids."

The doctor's face switched from anger to shock. He dropped to one knee in front of them. "Victor? Kamar?"

Victor hesitated to answer. This man looked kind, but so did the drivers who attacked Kamar. Before he could stop her, Kamar looked up at the doctor and replied, "Yes, we are Victor and Kamar."

"But why did you give us false names? Your father is here looking for you."

Victor finally spoke up, his hand across Kamar's shoulder, pulling her back. "No, our father was abducted in Syria."

"He was, but now he is here looking for you. If you wait here, we can call him now, and you can talk to him."

The doctor was looking up Elias's phone number, but the American lady already had her phone out. She talked briefly on her phone before handing it to Victor.

"Hello," Victor spoke tentatively into the phone.

"Victor? Oh my god, Victor!" It was his father. "I've been so worried. Are you okay? Is Kamar okay?"

"Yes, dad. We're okay." Victor didn't want to cry in front of these people. "What happened to you?"

"I was taken by a militia. They wouldn't let me have any outside contact—they took my phone. I've been trying to find you two ever since I was set free. I can explain everything when we get back. We're about thirty minutes away. Is Kamar there?"

"Yes, she's right here. She's okay, but she has a cough."

Sami, Elias, and Zaid were already on their way back to the clinic when Yana's call came through. As Elias talked with his son and then his daughter, Sami didn't give a second thought to the ramifications of possibly getting a speeding ticket in a foreign country. He was intent on getting back to the clinic as soon as possible. At one point they lost the phone connection but were able to reconnect a few minutes later.

At last the entire group was reunited, all standing outside the clinic. It had been many years since Victor had seen Amena and Sami, but he thought they looked familiar. Everyone wanted to embrace Kamar and Victor. Amena was crying profusely. In fact, there were tears all around, except Victor.

Elias was overwhelmed with the relief of having his two kids in front of him, where he could see they were in one piece. With the emotional surge he also felt exhaustion. He wished there was somewhere quiet where he could sit with Victor and Kamar and simply be with them.

Sami was having trouble standing still and was pacing about the group. The anticipation of Elias's reunion with his kids, postponed by the drive back to the clinic, had created a backup of adrenaline. Now this energy was directed towards Kamar and Victor. "How did they find you? Where have you been staying? Is your health okay?"

Yana, still the outsider, was observing Victor and Kamar. Finally, she broke in. "Sami, these two look incredibly tired. I'm guessing they're also quite hungry. Perhaps some food and a bath, and maybe some rest as well, and then they can share their story?"

For a moment Sami looked ready to blow up at Yana. She was not part of this circle. She had not endured the anxious waiting, the worry that had fallen as a suffocating blanket upon Sami, Amena, and Elias. Who was she to interfere at such a time as this? Then Elias, who had been thinking the same as Yana, intervened with a smile to Sami. "I think the order of business is food, bath, sleep, and then a chance to tell their story."

Sami exhaled a long calming breath. "Sorry, Elias. Of course," he finally agreed.

Elias realized his studio apartment was not suited for the three of them, and that it would be good to be in the city where they would have access to the goods and services Victor and Kamar needed to recover from their ordeal. Sami called the hotel and booked a two-bedroom suite. This would allow Victor and Kamar to each have their own room. Elias would not mind sleeping on the couch.

Elias turned to Victor and Kamar. "We should gather your things from the settlement, and then we'll drive to Beirut. Are you hungry? We can stop for something to eat before we head out."

This last suggestion received an enthusiastic response, so they quickly gathered Victor and Kamar's few possessions and headed to the same nearby restaurant. Victor and Kamar sat down to their first proper meal in many months. Their appetite was ravenous. Elias, however, intervened with the ordering to avoid rich foods, realizing that their digestive system would not handle them well after such a long period on a spartan diet. Over dinner, Elias explained who Kayla and Yana were and gave Kamar and Victor some background on their efforts to try to locate them. The group refrained from grilling the two on what they had been through.

It was decided that Victor and Kamar would ride with Elias and Yana, while the rest rode in Sami's rental. On the drive to Beirut, Kamar was soon asleep. Elias tried to engage Victor in conversation, but Victor responded to each overture with single-word responses. Finally, Elias gave up on his efforts. Victor sat silent, staring out the car window as the scenery transitioned from dry hills and small towns to chaotic metropolis. He thought he would feel ecstatic at finally finding his father. Instead he felt empty. The knot deep inside continued to fill him with pain, banishing any sense of hope.

Beirut

When they reached the hotel, Kamar and Victor marveled at things that, in another life, they had once considered so commonplace as to be beneath their notice—warmth, soft carpet, light switches, running water, warm baths, flush toilets, and most astounding of all, beds—beds with sheets and blankets, dry, warm, and sheltered from rain and wind.

The part of their rescue that would not assimilate was that they were at last safe. It was quiet now, but in the dead of night the sirens would sound, and the bombs would rain destruction and chaos all around them. The streets looked safe, but there were surely snipers on the next block. The car cruising past them had darkened windows to conceal the armed militiamen who were on patrol, ready to snatch anyone they could recruit or exploit. These fears were now embedded deep within their innermost survival instincts. They were untouchable by the logic or reassurances of others.

The next morning, at Yana's suggestion, Victor and Kamar shared breakfast in their hotel room with just their father. Victor, especially, was grateful for the chance to share his story away from the larger group.

Over toast and poached eggs, they talked about the trip to Hama and their unsuccessful search for somewhere they could settle. They described the ordeal of crossing the border and setting up a makeshift shelter, how their uncle had died, leaving Kamar and Victor on their own. They talked about the night they were visited by the militia recruiters and their realization that the settlement was no longer safe. In describing their journey across Lebanon in search of help, each of the two siblings were secretly relieved that the other declined to say anything about the attack on Kamar. Each, secretly and illogically, harbored guilt and shame for what had happened. It was as if they had made an unspoken agreement to bury the incident, just as they buried the true horrors of their refugee experience, which their telling of their story could not adequately convey.

Elias's elation at having found Victor and Kamar was tempered by the state they were in. Unlike the traumatized children he had treated in the hospital in Aleppo, and later at the refugee clinic, these were his own children. They had always been nourished, loved, and vibrant. Were the two individuals in front of him the same children? It was more than their physical state. Kamar felt hollow, her face empty of expression, with eyes that would not look directly at anyone. Victor was wary to the point of seeming hostile. His eyes were watching, measuring, giving nothing. Always, he kept Kamar close to him.

Elias also felt overwhelmed by all that needed to be done. He decided that the first order of business was clothes. Elias and Amena took the pair of them shopping, while the rest of the group stayed in the hotel to rest and catch up on e-mails. The group reconvened for lunch, after which Sami and Amena took Victor and Kamar for haircuts, while Elias scheduled dental appointments and physicals. He also picked up cell phones for the kids in case either of them accidently became separated.

The group from Seattle had one week left before they needed to return home. Saturday morning, Elias examined Kamar's injection site from two days ago, confirming what they had suspected—Kamar had been exposed to tuberculosis during her time in the settlements. That afternoon, while Kayla and Zaid took Kamar and Victor to check out a local market, Elias took advantage of a chance to talk with Sami and Amena without the kids. "We need to set up a treatment regime for Kamar right away and also get Victor tested. I've been hearing of drug-resistant strains among the refugees, so I hope that's not the case here."

Sami was nodding in agreement. "This is going to make it all that much harder for you to get the kids to France."

"How long do you think the treatment will take?" Amena asked.

"First thing is to get Kamar in for a sputum sample and chest x-ray to confirm whether she has active TB, which I suspect she does. Treatment can last six to nine months, but that's if it's not drug-resistant," Elias responded.

"It's good you have Kamar sleeping in her own room," Sami added.

Listening to this conversation, again as the outsider, Yana was struck by the imperative to get these kids into a safe, normal environment where they could start to heal. Looking across the room, her eyes met Elias's, and she felt he was thinking the same thing.

By Wednesday, medical tests revealed that Kamar did indeed have active TB with mild lung involvement. Victor had been exposed to the disease but did not have an active infection. Their doctor decided to quarantine Kamar at the hospital for the first few days of her antibiotic regime as a precaution. Victor was also started on an antibiotic regime to destroy his latent TB infection.

By Friday, they had a clear picture of the medical situation, with Kamar due to be discharged from the hospital Saturday morning. Friday evening Zaid and Kayla took Victor to a movie. Yana declined the offer to join the younger group at the movies, and once more, found herself in the role of outside observer as Sami, Amena, and Elias discussed the situation. Fortunately for her, they were talking in English.

Elias had started the search for an apartment in Beirut and for permanent employment in the city. Next week he would resume work on the application to emigrate to France that he had started at the beginning of the Syrian conflict.

As Yana surveyed the group, she wished she could do something to speed the recovery process. Her time here was drawing to a close. In less than twenty-four hours she would be on her way home. She knew she would never view the world, and its far-flung problems, with the same secure detachment.

Seattle

On the long plane ride home, Yana had many hours to reflect upon the trip. She had no regrets about tagging along. In the excitement of locating the missing children, no one had acknowledged her as the one who had recognized them. But that was how it should be. The focus should be on getting Kamar and Victor on the path to putting their lives back together.

Yana's return to home and work felt surreal, as if the world consisted of harsh realities where life was a day-to-day struggle, and her Seattle existence was a sheltered fantasy. Of course, that wasn't true, she told herself. Her work in the lab was a critical link in the chain of justice that protected the citizens who carried out their lives here.

Her first weekend back in Seattle, Yana drafted an email to Elias:

Elias, I want to thank you for your hospitality and guidance during our recent visit. I hope my presence was not an intrusion on the long-standing bond you share with Sami and Amena.

Experiencing first-hand the desperate plight faced by millions of people from your unfortunate homeland has changed my perspective on the world. I was also touched by your sharing with me some of the horrible personal losses you have carried, while continuing to care for those around you. It was a privilege to visit your clinic and see the resourcefulness of the staff in leveraging their limited resources.

I hope, once circumstances allow it, you can take up my invitation to visit Seattle, and that such a trip could provide a much-needed break from your corner of the earth, involved as it is in so much strife. In the meantime, if there is anything I can do to help with your situation or with Victor and Kamar, please let me know.

Yana.

Having completed that, Yana felt she could put the whole Lebanon experience away for now. Being back in Seattle, her thoughts returned to Emma and the situation around Emma's work. The embezzlement charge still bothered her. It felt unsettled. Yana had a friend who worked at Swanson & Yates. She reached out to him to see if he could shed some light on the situation. After speaking with him, she decided to text Emma to see if they could get together.

Hi Emma. We're back from Lebanon, and I'm happy to report that we recovered the two missing children. Wondering if you have some time to catch up—we haven't talked since Christmas. How about a walk around Green Lake next weekend? I can tell you about our trip.

Next, Yana texted Ellen to see if she was free. They had a lot to talk about.

It was one of those bleak, cold-and-rainy February days that remind you of how far off spring really is, so Ellen and Yana decided to forego a walk and meet for lunch at the Frye Art Museum. Yana told Ellen all about her trip, including her impressions of Beirut, what is was like being the outside observer to the search for Victor and Kamar, how she had been the one to actually recognize them, how she tried to prevent Sami from grilling the exhausted kids with questions when they were so obviously in need of rest and food, and that, fortunately, Elias was also perceptive to that and backed her up.

"Speaking of being perceptive," Ellen interrupted Yana's monologue with a sly smile, "I'm noticing that Elias comes into this narrative a fair amount. Mysterious physician from the Middle East who has lost his wife and now cares for refugees. Is this the beginning of some cheap romance novel?"

"Oh, of course not! But, yes, now that you bring it up, he's not bad looking for someone in his 50s." Yana couldn't help a small smile.

Ellen barked a laugh at her friend. "Yes, I've known you too long not to notice something in the way you mention him."

Yana tried to straighten her face and busied herself with her salad. "Yeah, well, I certainly don't need another man in my life. Plus, he has dual French-Syrian citizenship, so if he leaves Lebanon, it would be to go to France, not the U.S."

"Ooooh, mysterious French physician from the Middle East. It gets even better."

"Stop it, will you! Anyway, he needs to remain in Lebanon until Kamar finishes her TB treatment and they are able to arrange emigration to France."

"So, you really have thought this through, haven't you?"

"For that, you can pay for lunch!"

Wanting to change topics, Yana asked Ellen's advice on how to bring up with Emma the incident that had occurred at Emma's former employer, Swanson & Yates. "I've decided that 'Hey,

Emma, you haven't been involved in any embezzlement lately?' is a bit too direct."

"Do you really think you should bring it up at all? I can think of any number of ways in which the discussion does not end well."

"Yes, so can I—that's the problem. But there's more to the story that I found out since we last talked. I spoke to a friend, Malick, who works at Swanson & Yates. I didn't tell him about Emma's police case. I just said I knew Emma and asked him if he knew anything about Maria Burns. She's the attorney who made the accusations against Emma. Malick told me that Burns is nasty piece of work. Also, Malick remembers Emma. He said that, while Burns didn't make any overt remarks, you could tell that she had nothing but contempt for Emma after she came out as transgender. He also mentioned that Burns is the type who gravitates towards people in power, and being transgender makes you quite vulnerable."

Yana and Ellen finished up lunch and headed back outside to their cars. The sun had finally broken through and reflected brightly from the wet roads and sidewalks. "So, you think Emma was set up because she was transgender?" Ellen asked.

"That's exactly what I think. Also, who knows what else is behind this. Maybe this was a way to create confusion and cover the tracks of whoever really did the embezzlement."

"First, it was the cheap romance novel, now it's the dime-store detective. Maybe it's time for you to give up reading for a while." Ellen replied with a grin.

"Yes, very funny. You're not much help! It's just that I'm beginning to realize how vulnerable someone is when they make public something as personal as being transgender. I feel protective of Emma, and I want to get to the bottom of this. I need a diplomatic way to raise the topic with her."

It turned out that Emma was busy the following weekend, so they arranged their walk for the next Saturday. The weather cooperated beautifully—sunny and warm for late February. The big swaths of daffodils around Green Lake were just beginning to bloom, always a welcome promise that winter would eventually relinquish its hold. It seemed to Yana that their blooms arrived a bit earlier each year.

The scar on Emma's cheek had faded to where it was hardly noticeable. She seemed more confident to Yana. Yana described her trip to Lebanon, having become well-practiced at its retelling. They paused to watch a great blue heron explore the shallow lake shore as Yana turned to Emma. "So, what's new in your world? Any improvement with your family?"

"No, although my dad has been texting me now and then. Not sure if my mom knows he's doing that."

"Well, I think your mom is being short-sighted. From my vantage, she has a wonderful, successful daughter, if she could just get past her prejudice."

"I think she'll get there eventually. Though I don't think our relationship will ever be quite the same."

"I think I understand. Sometimes things are said and done that can't be undone."

They continued on their walk. "By the way, I hope that Christmas Eve was not too uncomfortable for you. I thought Kayla would have told her in-laws a bit about you ahead of time. I'm sorry for the awkwardness."

"Thanks, but it's okay. It was kind of you to include me."

They walked in silence for a minute before Yana changed subjects. "So, how are things at Mather Anesson? Are you dealing with any discrimination there?"

"No, they've been great. The organization has worked hard to foster an inclusive culture, and it shows compared with Swanson & Yates."

"Speaking of Swanson & Yates, a friend of mine works there— Malick Diallo. Did you work with him much?"

"Yeah, I worked on a couple of projects with Malick. He was

someone who didn't have issues with my being transgender. Seemed like a nice guy."

"Yes, well, he was telling me about another attorney, Maria Burns. Said she was quite the piece of work!"

Yana studied Emma's reaction. For a fraction of a second, she looked up at Yana, startled. Then she quickly diverted her gaze out across the Lake. "Yes, Burns was the main reason I left."

Yana decided to dig a bit deeper. "Malick mentioned something about a disagreement between you and Burns. He said that you were not the first person for her to go after."

"I really haven't talked to anyone about this. She tried to frame me."

Yana feigned surprise. "No! Did she really? What happened?"

"Bogus expense reimbursement checks were issued in my name. They weren't for huge sums—a few thousand dollars each. I have no idea how it happened, but I'm quite sure she set me up. We were working together for a client in Portland, and we had to take several short trips down there."

"Did you guys drive, fly, or take the train?"

"Are you kidding? An attorney as self-important as Burns? Of course, we flew. Then, she asked me to do her expense submission along with my own."

"Doesn't she have an administrative assistant to do that?"

"Yes, she certainly does. But she said that it would be easier for me to do it, since I was also on the trip, knew what all the expenses related to, and could make sure nothing was left out. She was heading out of town again and claimed she didn't have time to work with her AA on it. I figured it was best to swallow my pride and do what she said. I knew her reputation.

"Anyway, she gave me her password for her account within the reimbursement software they use so that I could create expense reports under her name. Also, she sent me her password via e-mail. That left a record for the police showing that she had shared it with me. She claimed that I created bogus expense reports for myself and then signed onto the system as her to approve them. She's high enough in the organization that she has authority to sign off on expense reports. Of course, no one can sign off on their own expense reports."

"Were the checks cashed?" Yana and Emma had to dodge as a boy on rollerblades sped past them.

"Yes, they were. But I had nothing to do with it. I saw photos of the endorsed checks. They were close to my signature, but enough off that I could tell they weren't mine. The police had a handwriting expert examine them, and they concluded the signatures could be forgeries. That's why the case was dropped."

Yana only had Emma's version of the events, but she believed Emma was telling the truth. "What doesn't make sense to me is why this Burns lady would go to so much trouble to frame you. Does she really hate transgender people that much?"

"She certainly seemed to hate me. I think she saw me as weird and not fitting in. Also, being transgender made me weak and vulnerable in her eyes. She's had to be tough to rise through the ranks as a female in the firm. Somehow, she viewed me as a threat, and despised me as a weakling."

Yana considered this as they stopped to watch another heron as it waded further offshore, and with a sudden swoop, snatched a fish from the water. The heron took a moment to secure the fish in its beak before taking flight powered by its over-long, angular wings. Yana turned back to Emma. "But this seems like a lot of effort to go through and not without risk. Have the police tried to track down the person who committed the forgeries?"

"No. I think from the police point of view, I'm still the guilty party. They just concluded the evidence wasn't solid enough to press charges since their expert allowed that someone might have forged the signatures. But there is a bit more to the story in terms of Burns' motivation."

Yana raised her eyebrows. "What? Did the two of you have a disagreement?"

Emma sighed and turned as they resumed their walk. "I don't know how I end up telling you all this stuff that I haven't shared with anyone else."

Yana half smiled. "I do seem to end up as surrogate mom a lot. Honestly, Emma, I'm happy to listen if I can be of help. On the other hand, if this is getting too personal, I completely understand."

"No, it helps to talk. It all started about a month after I joined the firm. Burns suggested we meet for drinks after work so that she could help me with some of the office politics and how things operated. She made it sound as if she were taking me under her wing. So, I met up with her, and she did share some helpful tips. But it soon became clear that she was coming on to me."

Yana was shocked. "You mean she was making sexual advances?"

"Yes. And she, not too subtly, made it clear that she was offering me an inside track to better work opportunities in exchange."

"Did she really!" Yana replied, although she knew this type of thing was more common than a lot of folks realized. "How did you respond?"

"First, just to be clear, I would never trade sexual favors for work advancement."

"No, of course you wouldn't."

"The thing was, this happened shortly after I had come to a resolution about being transgender, after many agonizing months of questioning. I was getting ready to come out at work and was apprehensive about the reception I would receive. As you can imagine, this was the last thing I needed at that point in my life." Emma was looking straight ahead, as if reliving the episode in her head.

"That must have been so upsetting."

"Yes, and I'm afraid I may have reacted a bit strongly."

"Emma, what happened?"

Emma looked over at Yana. "I told her she was pathetic. Then followed up with 'So this is the only way you can get someone to sleep with you?'"

"Ouch!"

"Yes, that was below the belt. I know I should have found a way to exit gracefully, with Burns' ego still intact. But, as I mentioned, I was in a difficult space. I had originally thought her attention had something to do with the potential she saw in me as an attorney, not as her sex toy."

Yana considered this for a few moments. "Well, it would explain her vehemence in trying to take you down, especially once you revealed that you were transgender. I can see where someone like Burns would not like the fact that she was attracted to someone who was on the verge of coming out as transgender. Even so, I wouldn't apologize for standing up to her. I'm not sure I could have. The world needs more people doing that, not less. In my book, you demonstrated integrity and guts."

Emma laughed. "I think you missed one—integrity, guts, and unemployment."

"But this doesn't impact your standing at your current position, does it?"

"I don't think so, but I really don't know. The attorneys in this town all seem to know each other. It wouldn't be out of character for her to plant stories about me with some of the leadership at Mather Anesson."

In light of the prejudice and hatred Emma faced, Yana was starting to feel protective of her in the same way she felt towards her own kids. If Burns was a threat to Emma, was there a way to neutralize that threat? Yana almost said something more to Emma but decided that first she needed to give this some thought.

Beirut

Elias knew that Beirut had many physician specialists and offered excellent medical care to those with the means to pay for it, drawing patients from the greater Middle East region. However, the city had a shortage of physicians providing basic care. This allowed Elias to find a new position in general surgery despite his Syrian nationality. His dual citizenship and his medical residency in New York City helped. His new position was a step down compared to the responsibilities he had shouldered in Aleppo, but the hours worked well with Victor and Kamar's school schedule. Thankfully, their TB was responding well to first-line antibiotics, and both kids were far enough along in their treatment to be able to attend school.

They had settled into the Armenian quarter of Beirut. Elias recognized the importance of everyone having their own room, so he spent his housing budget on space rather than quality. The apartment was clean and functional but far from glamorous, with their only view being that of other apartments of similar style.

Elias was returning home from a long workday. A packed

schedule left him physically and emotionally drained. Now, as he climbed the three flights of stairs to their apartment, he thought of how nice it would be if he could simply grab a beer from the refrigerator and relax—read or watch TV. That was not an option.

It was hard for Elias not to draw comparisons to the way things were before the war. Aliya managed the household, and they faced the normal challenges of raising a family, including some strains in their marriage. Now, Elias felt unequipped. Victor and Kamar's level of need was beyond anything he'd encountered previously, and he was on his own to meet that need.

Kamar was spread out on the gray carpet of their combined living room-dining area. Their small television was on, and she was working on her math. Elias didn't understand how someone could concentrate on math amidst the noise from the television, but he was happy to let that go.

Victor was, as usual, holed up in his tiny bedroom. Kamar seemed to be adjusting to their new school, but Elias worried about Victor. Both kids were enrolled in classes a year younger than their peers, due to the interruptions in their schooling. Kamar was keeping up with her classes. Victor was struggling. Earlier today, Elias had received a call from the school, informing him that Victor had been involved in a fight during lunch break.

Elias knocked on the door to Victor's room and found Victor sprawled on his bed, wearing his earbuds. He didn't appear to be working on anything in particular. Elias sat in the only chair in the room and Victor removed his earbuds. "What's new at school?" he asked.

"Nothing," Victor replied. Elias had gotten used to Victor's sullen and withdrawn behavior, so he plowed ahead.

"Are there any kids at school that you've made friends with?"

"No, not really."

"The school called today to say that you were involved in a fight with some other kids."

Victor didn't respond.

"What were you guys fighting about?"

Victor shrugged. More silence.

"Well, I can guess that some of the other kids are not welcoming to someone who is Syrian. Is that right?"

Victor nodded his head.

"Victor, I know this is difficult. And you've been through so much already. I want to help you, but I can't if you won't be open with me."

"It won't happen again," Victor replied, and he put his earbuds back in.

Victor was relieved when Elias left the room without trying to probe any deeper. Victor liked and respected his father. His father simply didn't understand the situation. Victor didn't belong in this place. There was no reason to talk to him about it, as there was nothing that could be done. Moving to a new school wouldn't help. He would still be the Syrian refugee that they wanted out of their country.

Everyone talked about going to France as if that would make it all okay. That was the country that outlawed the wearing of a face-covering hajib. He would be the unwelcome intruder there as well.

Victor accepted that it was his lot to be rejected by the community. He still could not be around Kamar without being reminded of how she had been violated as a result of his failure to protect her. There was no point in telling his father about that either. What was done could not be undone. Why bring further shame to Kamar? At school, Victor would see Kamar sitting alone during lunchtime, hunched over her books. He would walk past without acknowledging her. Kamar understood why. It was better not to draw attention to her, better if no one knew they were brother and sister.

Now that Kamar was in safe hands, perhaps the best thing

would be for Victor to go back to Syria. He could follow in the footsteps of his older brother, Saif, and fight against the Assad regime. If he died in the fighting, so be it.

Saif, being six years older than Victor, had been in some ways a second father. Tall and strong, he had appeared to Victor as invincible. Victor recalled the talks around the family table when the fighting first broke out. Saif was convinced that this was Syria's time to break free as a country. Elias had tried to temper Saif's zeal with caution, but Saif would hear none of it. Victor had initially been hopeful about the outcome of the fighting and envious of Saif. Now he felt skeptical that anything in his country would change, but he could at least honor the sacrifice made by his brother.

Elias walked back out to the living room and slumped down at the kitchen table, resting his elbows on the table and his forehead against his palms. He had been at a loss for anything further to say, and he couldn't just remain sitting in Victor's bedroom staring at him, so he left. Was he really up to being a parent to these kids? Perhaps he was too depleted from his own losses to have anything left to give them.

Elias tried to think of something he could do to help Victor. His brain was having trouble filtering out the chattering noise of Kamar's TV show. Last week, Elias had inquired about setting up an appointment with a child psychologist. He found that, in Beirut, demand for child counseling services far outstripped supply, and he couldn't find anyone who was scheduling less than nine months out. It occurred to him that he shouldn't be surprised by that, given the history of conflict in the region. Elias had gone ahead with scheduling an appointment anyway. He knew something needed to happen sooner but was at a loss as to what he could do.

Elias had been conversing with Sami and Amena about his concerns. He decided to write to Yana as well. Yana had sent him an e-mail shortly after returning to the U.S., and they had exchanged a few follow-up e-mails. From the time Elias spent with Yana while she was in Lebanon, he had seen that she was a keen observer of people. Perhaps she could provide some insight.

Seattle

Yana wrestled with how to respond to Elias's request. She was not surprised to hear that Victor was struggling. She had asked Zaid about his impressions of the younger Victor from his family's visits before the Syrian conflict. Zaid remembered Victor as a quiet but otherwise normal and happy kid. While in Lebanon, Yana had observed how closed Victor was. But she had also observed how protective he was around his sister. She suspected that, behind the silence and withdrawal, was a person who cared about the people around him.

Yana thought she knew what was needed, but what if she was totally off base? She had already intruded on this group and had sensed some resentment both from Sami and from Kayla. Even so, with Victor's welfare at stake, now was not the time to be timid. So, she began composing her response to Elias:

Hi Elias,

I'm sorry to hear that Victor is struggling, but I'm not too surprised, given all that he's been through. Thanks for asking my advice. As an outsider, I'm hesitant to respond, so please don't feel obligated to follow it. If it seems helpful, great. If not, then please disregard.

People who have been traumatized have a funny way of blaming themselves, especially young people. For Victor, the trauma comes at a critical time as he is entering adulthood and figuring out what it is to be a man. And if that were not enough, he has lost a parent, as well as the support of the community he grew up with.

I'm sure Victor shared much of his experience with you, but I wonder if there isn't more that he has held back. I think the key with Victor is getting him to talk about all that happened to him and how it is affecting him.

There are a couple of things working against Victor. First, he is, by nature, a quiet person—more an observer than a doer. This is not a bad thing, in itself, but is likely reinforcing his tendency to withdraw. Second, there's an aspect of this that is harder for boys than for girls in that being a victim goes against society's male stereotype. The successful male is seen as the winner or conqueror, not the loser or victim. So, simply the fact that Victor is a victim (or refugee) may be causing him shame. I don't think Victor is thinking this overtly, but it may be affecting his mental state, keeping him closed down.

I believe it's important to get Victor talking about his experiences and feelings with someone who feels safe to him, either with you or with a skilled counselor. If you decide to work with Victor yourself, you may want to consider going away for a few days, just the two of you. I hear there are some beautiful areas up in the mountains in Lebanon, or perhaps along the coast. Somewhere away from all the noise and distraction of Beirut.

One additional consideration is that, even though Victor is the one whose behavior is causing concerns, Kamar is also dealing with her own private trauma, as you well know. Victor seems to be the immediate need, but it's important for Kamar to process her experiences as well. I feel bad adding to your burden by bringing this up, but the two stories are linked, so their resolutions may be as well.

Elias, I hope this is helpful. As I said, if this doesn't fit, please toss it, and no need to explain or justify anything to me. If there is any way I can support you in helping these two kids, I hope you will ask.

Yana

Yana felt considerable apprehension about how her advice might be received. Would Elias understand what she was referring to with regard to the male shame associated with being a victim? Would he think she was acting as a know-it-all? Yana had prior experience with her attempts to help being considered interfering. But then, Elias had asked for her advice. In an impulse of bravery, she hit send.

Exactly one week after sending her response to Elias, Yana received a phone call from a distraught Kayla. Victor had gone missing.

Beirut

Shortly after arriving home from school Friday afternoon, Victor told Kamar that he was heading out to the store. He never returned. Two hours later, Elias came home to a very worried Kamar. He started calling the few contacts who might possibly know something about his whereabouts. When that yielded nothing, Elias went back out to his car and began driving around their neighborhood in expanding circles, scanning the sidewalks, and stopping in at cafés and other locations where he thought he might find Victor.

At nine-thirty that evening, Elias returned to a frantic Kamar. He did his best to calm her down and get her to bed. He then called the police station, but they didn't have any information or assistance they could offer. Next, Elias started calling the various hospitals in the city. All this time, he kept trying Victor's phone, with no response. Finally, having run out of options, he called Sami and Amena to fill them in on the situation.

The following week was hell for Elias and worse for Kamar. She was too upset to go to school. She hardly ate and spent most of the time in her bedroom. Elias tried numerous times to talk with her, but she would tense up each time, her arms and hands drawn inward, her eyes down. Elias was unable to elicit anything but the most basic responses from her.

After having weathered so many losses in the past five years, Victor's disappearance felt to Elias like a finishing blow. Perhaps it was the cumulative effect of so much stress and loss. Or perhaps it was the fact that Victor and Kamar had come to represent to him a victory amidst the endless valley of tragedy and destruction that had become his life.

Elias took as much time as he dared from work. He was still new to his position at the clinic, and being Syrian, he would not be given much slack for missing work. He devoted all the time he could to following up with the police, tracking down leads from the local Syrian community, and trying to pull Kamar out from her shell.

The police had little time for, or interest in, Victor's disappearance. Still, Elias checked in each day to see if any new information had surfaced. He didn't trust the police to reach out proactively to him in the unlikely event that something useful did turn up. His contacts within the Syrian community were more sympathetic but unable to provide much help. Victor's case was one among literally tens of thousands of missing Syrians. With their help, Elias found reliable contacts within the various political factions among the Syrian refugees, and this gave him some people to follow up with.

The Friday evening following Victor's disappearance, Elias was on his way home from work. Exhaustion engulfed him like a vast ocean of sand, sapping his energy as he tried to keep moving forward through the knee-high drifts that seemed to extend in all directions. Between his work and the issues he faced with Victor and Kamar, he had no time for himself. He couldn't remember the last time he'd gone for a run. That had always been his way to manage stress, but now he lacked the energy to do anything extra, and he didn't want to leave Kamar home alone any more than was necessary.

With effort, Elias drove home, pulled himself out of his car and climbed the many stairs to their apartment. He didn't want dinner. He wanted to go straight to his room and throw himself on his bed. But there was Kamar's bedroom, the door closed tight. Elias stared at the closed door. Somehow Elias knew she held the key to why Victor ran away.

Elias came to a decision. Without giving himself time to reconsider, he knocked and entered Kamar's room. Closing the door behind him, Elias sat down on the floor next to the bed where Kamar was reclined with her phone and ear buds. Kamar sat up with her back against the headboard, removed her ear buds and looked up briefly at Elias before averting her gaze once more.

Elias tried to be both gentle and firm. "Kamar, we need to talk. I understand how difficult this is for you, but you need to tell me everything you know about what was going on with Victor before he disappeared. The only way we can help Victor is if you can trust me and we can work together."

Kamar fidgeted with the cord to her earbuds, wrapping and unwrapping it around her fingers. "I think Victor may have joined one of the militias," she finally said, her voice barely audible.

"Did he say something to you about this?"

"No, he didn't tell me this, but I could tell he was thinking about leaving."

"Do you have any ideas as to why he would want to do that? What was bothering him so much?"

Kamar hesitated. "I think he felt responsible for all the stuff that happened to us. With mom gone and you missing, he felt he had to take your place."

"But you guys made it here. You were both safe again. Wasn't that your goal? How could he be responsible for the war that tore us apart?"

Kamar didn't respond. She pulled her legs up to her chest and wrapped her arms tightly around them, making herself as physically withdrawn as was humanly possible. Then she started to shake.

Elias sat beside her on the bed and placed an arm across her shoulder. "Kamar, what is it? What happened?"

But Kamar was unable to respond, as her breathing became short and ragged. Then her body began to wrench as her tears flowed. Elias continued to sit with her, trying to provide comfort. Eventually she became still, and the sobs subsided. Finally, she was able to speak. "It wasn't Victor's fault," she said.

Seattle

Yana could not concentrate on her book. Finally putting it down, she turned on her TV. Nothing could catch her interest. She had an hour to wait for Elias's call. What worried her was not knowing why he wanted to talk. His e-mail from that morning had been brief, "Can I call you Friday evening around seven Seattle time?" Yana responded by providing her phone number but resisted asking him what it was he wanted to discuss. She figured that if he wanted to tell her ahead of time, he would have. But she didn't like being left to wonder. Most likely it was about Victor. Had he followed her advice with the outcome being that Victor ran away? If that were true, what would there be for them to discuss? Elias did not strike her as the type to call her just so he could throw blame around.

With enough time for a short walk around her neighborhood, Yana decided the fresh air and physical movement would clear her brain and calm her nerves. She grabbed her coat and headed out her front door.

March had finally arrived, that contrary month, with the

promise of spring around the corner, but the reality of yet another stretch of cold and rain. Yana found March to be even more dreary than February—the wet and cold having long worn out their welcome. Once outside, despite the wind and slight drizzle, she felt her mood improve as she wound through her neighborhood to where she had a clear view of Lake Union, with the sparkling Seattle skyline on the opposite shore. Darkness was filling the spaces around her like water seeping into a sinking boat, pressed down by low, brooding clouds. Yana didn't mind. The gloom made the lights of downtown stand out warmly, while a faint twilight from the recently set sun illuminated the lake in a soft gray sheen. A handful of Canadian geese honked overhead as they headed down towards the lake for the night.

Yana decided that whatever the situation with Victor, her advice was not unsolicited, and was given in good faith. She, of course, would feel terrible if it somehow contributed to Victor's departure, but she realized that there was another, different sort of worry contributing to her anxiety. She didn't want Elias to think poorly of her.

Elias called promptly at seven, his voice a bit hushed, as if not wanting to be overheard. "Yana, thanks for being willing to talk at such short notice."

"Of course, Elias. Is everything okay?" Hearing those words coming out of her mouth, Yana realized what a ridiculous thing it was to say, given what was going on.

"Honestly, things are far from being okay. I'm sure you're wondering why I'm calling you, so I think first of all I owe you an explanation."

"Elias, if there's anything at all I can do to help, I'm here."

"There are some new developments, and I need a sounding board. Sami is my best friend, but I think you know he reacts strongly to things. I'm wondering if I can impose on you? I need your calm intuition and understanding."

Yana realized that at least this was not sounding like she was going to be blamed for Victor's running away. "Of course, you can. What's going on?"

"I need to share this with you in confidence. I haven't yet told Sami and Amena, and it's important that they hear this from me rather than indirectly."

"I understand." Yana thought to herself that this was sounding more and more ominous.

"Yana, you were spot on in your advice about Victor. The problem is, I wasn't able to put it into action soon enough. He ran away before I had a chance to arrange some time for us. Anyway, last night—it's Saturday morning here—but last night I decided I needed to get Kamar to talk, that she might be the key to Victor's disappearance. It was your e-mail that helped me see that. So, I went into her room and told her she needed to tell me everything she knew about what was going on with Victor. Ever since Victor left, Kamar has withdrawn completely. It took a lot of anguish on her part, but she finally confided that she had been raped."

"Oh my god! Those poor children. On top of everything else they've been through."

"Apparently, at a point of desperation, they accepted a ride from some people who appeared to be okay but were not. Because Victor made the decision to accept the ride, he felt responsible for the attack. Kamar thinks that Victor didn't want to tell anyone about the rape because he didn't want to bring additional shame to her. And Kamar didn't tell us sooner because she didn't want to make Victor feel worse for what had happened."

"This is starting to explain Victor's disappearance."

"Yes. Kamar also told me that she had seen Victor being singled out at school. It was made clear to him that Syrian refugees were not welcome."

"Wow, so much for a kid to handle!"

"I keep thinking about how I should have realized what was

going on when Victor got involved in a fight at school. I should have known that getting time with Victor, getting him talking, needed to happen right away. The truth is, if he's joined a militia, I'll probably never see him again."

Yana sensed that Elias was on the verge of losing it. This conversation was not at all what she had been expecting. "Elias, the first observation I'd like to make is that we've had a situation where Kamar and Victor were each blaming themselves for something that had in fact been caused by outsiders and for which they had no blame. We don't want to add you to this same list of casualties. Your life has also been torn apart by this conflict and yet you have done everything you possibly can to help Victor and Kamar. You are not to blame for any of this. In fact, in my book, you've been a terrific father to these kids. Unfortunately, no matter how hard we try, so much of life is outside our control. I think you've seen enough of life to know that dwelling on what might have been doesn't get you anywhere."

"This is why I wanted to talk with you—I knew you would help me see a different perspective. It's just that this is hitting me hard. I thought that at least in Victor and Kamar's case we could salvage something positive."

"Yes, we still can salvage quite a bit that's positive. Kamar needs you right now. There's not much you can do for Victor at this point in time. I know it's not a lot of consolation, but at least, if he did join a militia group, he did it on his own decision, not because he was forced. There is some value in that. It may be a way for him to feel that he is fighting back. Of course, there are much better ways he could fight back, but we're not in a position to do anything about that at the moment."

"Of course, you're right. I think that Kamar opening up about the rape is the breakthrough she's needed. Once she calmed down, we talked until late last night. She hasn't been that open the whole time we've been in Lebanon."

"In the clear light of morning, she may return to the conclusion that Victor's disappearance is her fault because of his feeling responsible for the assault and trying to protect her. Whatever you do, keep her talking. What's the plan for getting her out of Lebanon?"

"Next month, her TB should be to the point where she can travel. We were waiting for the emigration visa to come through. Now I need to rethink all this, with Victor missing."

"Elias, I think it's really important for you to stay close to Kamar right now. It would be easy for her to be overlooked with all the concern for Victor. It sounds like there's not much you can do for Victor at the moment, but there is a lot you can do to help Kamar. I think getting her to France would be a very positive move. Does she know any French?"

"Some. She's continuing her French studies at her new school, so that's helpful."

Having finished her call with Elias, Yana remained in her comfy chair for a long time, staring though her front window into the darkness that had become complete during the course of their conversation. There was much to think about. She had no experience with rape victims and couldn't imagine the terror of being raped. And then to think of that happening at age thirteen. How do you help someone recover from such an experience, especially someone who has lost a parent and now, perhaps, her only remaining sibling? She decided she needed to educate herself about rape recovery. She was determined not to volunteer information for Elias. But, if he came asking, she wanted to be ready to help him.

She also thought of Elias moving to France. She wondered what part of France he would choose to live in. Probably not Paris—too expensive. Probably wherever he could find employment. Yana had taken French in high school and continued for two more years in college but was not sure how much of the language she retained.

The next morning, Yana met Ellen for a walk around Green

Lake and told her about her conversation with Elias. Yana figured that this did not risk breaking Elias's request for confidentiality, since Ellen was good at keeping secrets. Yana found it helpful to talk things through with Ellen, even if Ellen couldn't provide any new insights.

They walked on for a while in silence, Yana thinking about all the trauma Kamar had endured, Ellen perceptively giving her space. Yana's thoughts then turned to Elias, thinking of the openness he continued to show with her. Finally, Yana broke the silence. "I hadn't anticipated that Elias would confide so much in me. We haven't known each other that long."

"Are you wondering if there's more to it than just seeking your advice? Do you want there to be more to this relationship?" Ellen responded. One area of common ground that tied together Yana and Ellen's friendship was their mutual tendency to be direct.

"Maybe. I appreciate that he is open and willing to seek advice from a woman. Most men prefer giving advice."

"Ha! True." Ellen interjected.

"It just seems pointless to pursue the relationship seriously as our paths are so divergent, his to France, while I'm firmly rooted in Seattle."

They had to divert around an exercise group of young mothers and one young father, all with strollers carrying children of approximately the same age. "So, perhaps it's destined to be a distance friendship," Ellen continued once they had passed the group.

"Yes, and that would not be a bad thing."

Having run out of things to say about the situation with Elias, Kamar, and Victor, they turned their attention to Emma. "I'm so incensed at that Burns lady—I want to do something about her. I hate what she did to make Emma's transition so much more difficult," Yana confessed.

"Looking for revenge?"

"No, I don't relish revenge. I'd just like to bring her down a notch so that she perhaps will think twice about attacking people who are vulnerable. Mostly, I'm worried that she might do something to sabotage Emma's new position. Anyway, I've set up a lunch with Malick, my friend from Anderson & Yates, and Emma."

"Yana, what are you cooking up?"

"I don't know. But I don't like seeing vulnerable people being stepped on, and I don't like just standing by and letting it go if Emma is at risk. My first step is to find out if Malick and Emma are both interested in doing something about it."

Beirut

Nearly two weeks following his call with Yana, Elias had finally finished another grueling work week and was glad to be heading home to Kamar. After opening up to Elias, Kamar's mood had gradually improved. She was spending less time in her bedroom and more time with Elias, helping him fix meals, watching television together, even sharing some of her music with him.

Sharing the news of Kamar's assault with Sami and Amena had been excruciating. They were both, as expected, extremely upset. Elias could picture Sami pacing the room. Sami asked if Elias was going to try to hunt down those responsible. Elias knew he would never be able to find the two men, and if he did, would not be able to prove culpability.

As was his habit each day after work, Elias checked their mailbox in their apartment building's drab, 1960s-era lobby before starting up the stairs to their unit. Glancing through the junk mail and bills as he walked across the lobby to the stairs, his eyes fell on an envelope addressed by hand to Kamar and Elias. He recognized Victor's precise, miniature handwriting.

Ripping open the letter on the spot, he stood in the bottom stairwell and read the letter twice.

Hi Dad and Kamar,

First, I am sorry for leaving without letting you know where I was heading and for any worry this caused. I left to join a militia and to fight for the liberation of Syria. I joined a unit from the same rebel group that Saif fought with, not the group that was recruiting me in the refugee settlement. I did this on my own decision and am happier here than I've been since we left Aleppo, knowing that I am contributing something.

Please do not try to track me down or contact me. I will try to send you updates from time to time. I've lost my phone, but I have both of your phone numbers and will make sure not to lose them.

My love to you,

Victor

Elias sank down onto the bottom step. Victor's birthday had passed, uncelebrated, during the three weeks he'd been gone. Barely sixteen now and fighting in a hopeless war because that was the only way he knew to drown out the burden he should never have carried. Elias had always been the calm, resilient one, but that was now spent. He had nothing left for this war that kept taking, even when he thought there was no more left for him to lose.

But the letter was not addressed to him alone. Kamar, who was just beginning to rebuild herself would need to receive this news as well. How was Elias to tell her? He longed to remain in the empty stairwell.

Slowly Elias got to his feet and climbed the stairs to his apartment. Kamar was fixing a snack in the kitchen. Elias said he had some news from Victor and asked her to come sit with him on the couch. She came immediately into the living room, her eyes wide, questioning Elias. When she sat down next to him, he simply handed the letter to her to read while he placed his comforting arm around her shoulder.

Kamar took the news better than Elias had expected. "Well, at least he's alive," she spoke thoughtfully, "and it was his decision to do this."

"Yes, I don't think there's anything more we can do for Victor at this point. If he doesn't want to be found, I don't think we stand a chance of finding him." Elias suspected that Kamar didn't fully appreciate the danger that Victor was in as part of a rebel militia but thought it best not to go down that path with her.

They both sat together in silence, each absorbing the news. Finally, Kamar broke the silence. "Do you still think we should move to France while Victor's in the militia?"

Elias considered for a moment before responding. "Yes, I think it's important that we move ahead on that. Neither of us feel at home in Beirut, and we don't know how long the war will continue. What do you think?"

"What about Victor? What if he comes looking for us?"

"I will try to get a message to him through my contacts within the Syrian refugee community in Beirut. But even if I can't reach him, he mentioned in his letter that he'll keep our phone numbers safe. I think that might be his way of telling us that we should move ahead with our lives. Of course, if Victor ever reaches out to us, I would be on the next plane back to Beirut."

Kamar sat silently for a while. "Where in France were you thinking we'd move?"

"I don't know. Probably a mid-sized city and hopefully somewhere in the south of France where the climate is closer to what we are used to. Of course, it would depend on where I could find employment."

Kamar picked nervously at a frayed bit of couch upholstery. "What about the kids at my new school in France? Will they resent us as refugees?"

Elias, as always, tried to be as honest as possible with Kamar. "Yes, I expect some of them may resent us. But many of them will not. One thing that will be key is for you to learn French as quickly as possible. I want to enroll you in some intensive French courses, both before and after emigrating."

Again Kamar was silent, and Elias allowed her space to think. Finally, she looked over at Elias. "I agree that we should move ahead on France. You're right. I've not made friends at school, and I don't feel that Beirut is home."

Seattle

Yana, Emma, and Malick met at Duke's restaurant across the street from Green Lake. The three of them seemed an unlikely trio. Yana had gotten to know Malick and his wife when Kyle and Malick's oldest son were in high-school drama together. Originally from Senegal, Malick immigrated with his parents to New York City when he was four. Their story was not an uncommon one for immigrant families. His parents took whatever work they could and saved as much as possible so that their three kids could attend college, and, eventually, graduate school. Malick was the youngest of the three and chose law instead of engineering as his older siblings had. He was tall, with a broad physique and easy laugh. It was his dark-rimmed glasses that gave him his serious look, hiding his mischievous nature.

Once they had placed their orders, and Emma and Malick had a chance to catch up with each other, Yana launched the conversation about Maria Burns. "I'm an outside party to this whole thing. I just don't like bullies and Burns sounds like she fits that profile. I'm wondering if there's a way to clip her wings so she's not as able to harm the people around her, Emma in particular."

"She definitely fits the profile," Malick responded, leaning back in his chair, "and I think she has some vulnerabilities."

"Is this something that you guys want to get involved in? Of course, we would want to make sure that anything we do can't be traced back to either of you." Yana wanted to make sure this was a joint initiative, not something they were going along with just because she had proposed it.

Malick didn't hesitate. "I would love to see her wings clipped. Emma is not her only casualty, by a long shot. Just the other day she got one of our AA's fired, and it wasn't even her own AA."

Emma perked up at this news. "Who got fired?"

"Michael. Burns had overlooked a report that had been promised by end of day. Her own AA was out sick. She dropped it on Michael's desk at four fifty-five and told him it needed to be mailed by five-thirty. Michael had his own work and deadlines to worry about, so he told Burns he couldn't promise anything but would do his best. When the report missed the delivery deadline, Burns lied to the office manager saying that she had told Michael about the deadline that morning and had been promised that it would go out. When it's an attorney's word against an AA's word, you can guess who they believe."

Malick continued, scowling, "Of course, she's in cozy with the office manager because they live in the same Newport Hills neighborhood, belong to the same golf club, kids go to the same schools, that sort of thing."

Emma's eyes widened. "Wait, you mean she's married with kids and she still hit on me?"

Malick looked over at Emma with a concerned look. "I hadn't heard about that. I'm assuming this was before you transitioned?"

"Yes," Emma responded, "and we're guessing that's why she reacted so negatively when I came out a few weeks later."

"Oh, she would have hated you just for being transgender all right, but she definitely wouldn't like feeling she'd been made a fool." Malick paused for a moment, frowning. "How did you respond to her?"

"Not as gracious as I might have been in turning her down. She caught me off guard at a point where I wasn't at my best."

Yana chimed in, "You are not in any way to blame for this. You should never have been put in that position by someone who has power over your career."

"Absolutely right," Malick affirmed. "Burns likes to use her influence to her advantage, and she doesn't care in the slightest about being ethical. I think that might be exactly where she is vulnerable."

"What do you mean?" Yana replied. At that moment their food arrived, so the conversation halted until they were settled with their lunches and no longer had waitstaff hovering within earshot.

"I don't know details, but there are plenty of rumors that bear investigation. Also, Burns considers AAs, receptionists, and file clerks to be beneath her notice. I, on the other hand, have no compunctions about hobnobbing with anyone. You'd be surprised how much they know about what's going on in the office. I think it's time to set that network into action. Also, the timing couldn't be better. As you know, Emma, Michael was popular among the other office staff, and Burns has a long history of treating office staff like dirt."

Yana finished her bite of food. "This sounds quite intriguing. But, Emma, I never heard from you in response to my original question. Is this something you want to be involved in?"

Emma looked out towards the lake before responding. "Part of me wants to forget this whole chapter and move on, especially with all that I have on my plate. But I think I owe it to those still working at Anderson & Yates, so, yeah, I'm in."

"Wonderful!" Yana beamed. "Malick, what can we do to help you?"

Malick seemed a bit lost in thought. "Nothing at this point. Let me think on this, and I'll get back to you both."

Emma remained serious as she looked over at Yana. "What about you? What's in this for you?"

Yana was caught off guard that Emma had turned her own question back on her but quickly realized that it was a fair thing to ask. "If there's a way to keep her from doing additional harm, that will be worth it for me."

Malick appeared to break away from his thoughts. "Burns is, without a doubt, skilled in how she manipulates people and situations. But she has a serious weakness. She gives no thought to the people who are below her level in the organization. Her consideration is strictly tied to the level of power she thinks you have."

The following week, Malick took Kara to lunch. Kara was the administrative assistant that Malick shared with several other attorneys and legal assistants. The two of them often swapped stories about their kids, whose ages overlapped. They considered each other friends, and he felt confident that he could rely on Kara to keep their conversation confidential.

They met at Tulio, which was a few blocks from their downtown office. After catching up on each other's families, their conversation turned to Michael's unfortunate departure. They started to trash Burns, as they had done numerous times in the past. For Kara, who was close friends with Michael, his sacking had crossed a line. "I don't know if I can keep working for this firm, Malick. Burns is in too tight with our office manager, and I don't see this behavior changing. I feel like my only option is to take care of myself in this situation. That probably means finding a different place to work, although I hate to do that after twenty-two years here."

Malick set down his fork. He had wondered how he was going to present his ideas to Kara. She had saved him the trouble by providing the perfect opening. "There might be another way, Kara. I confess to having ulterior motives in inviting you to lunch today." Malick proceeded to fill Kara in on what had happened to Emma, including how Burns had tried to come on to her and then, in retaliation, tried to frame her.

"Wow. I heard rumors about Emma being involved in embezzlement, but I thought that just couldn't be true. It didn't fit her at all."

"I'm pretty sure that Emma did no such thing. The alternative explanation fits too well. Anyway, Yana is a friend of ours that Shelly and I got to know through our kids' school. Yana is also friends with Emma, and she found out about the embezzlement charge and Burns' role. So, she, Emma, and I recently met and decided we needed to do something about Burns. My question is, are you willing to help?"

"I'd be delighted to! What did you have in mind?"

"I have several ideas in mind that I don't think run too much risk of repercussions. But this isn't risk-free, so I will completely understand if you don't want to get involved."

"What's life without some risk? Now you have me intrigued." Without thinking, Kara gave the other tables in the restaurant a glance to make sure there was no one from their office.

Malick followed her glance before continuing. "Part of this you're not going to like. With Michael gone, they are reassigning AA roles, and you're going to be picking up Burns."

"Oh, crap! I was afraid that might happen. Why does Burns need a new AA? Her old one is still here, isn't she?"

"Yes, but you know Burns. She's never content. The shake-up provided her an opportunity to snatch the best AA for herself. Also, you're not supposed to know about the reassignments until they're formally announced, so please keep that to yourself for now."

"No problem. I appreciate being forewarned. But we had better come up with a good plan, because with this news, it's definitely the only thing keeping me here."

"That's why I thought that if we put our heads together, we could come up with something. Also, as her new AA, you will be well placed." To that, Kara simply smiled.

Beirut

It had been four weeks since Elias and Kamar had received Victor's letter and subsequently had their talk about moving to France. Immediately after Kamar indicated she was on board with the move, Elias arranged additional French lessons for her. Between the lessons and her French class at school, she was progressing rapidly. They started speaking French at home whenever possible, which was helpful to Elias as well, since his French was rusty.

Elias felt the bond with his daughter strengthening as they became a close-knit family of two. He realized that, back in Aleppo, when they had been a complacent and distracted family of four, he had underappreciated the value of family.

Elias and Kamar worked together on researching various regions of France and were beginning to form ideas on which ones looked most promising. Besides being a great activity for the two of them to share, it helped them focus on their future rather than dwelling on past miseries. Privately, in the evenings when Kamar had gone to bed, Elias also researched which areas in France they might want to avoid due to strong anti-immigration sentiment. He was determined to give this endeavor the greatest possible chance for success.

Elias found that the northeastern regions of France were reported to have some of the strongest anti-immigration attitudes, despite having relatively low levels of actual immigration. In contrast, Montpellier seemed to have a lot going for it. In addition to offering a Mediterranean climate, the city housed numerous universities and educational institutions, giving it a large student population. Elias noted that the city had a history of welcoming immigrants. Being close to the Mediterranean coast, the Montpellier housing market looked a bit more expensive than many regions of France, but Elias still felt it was doable, assuming he could find decent employment.

In addition to researching France, Elias started tracking down his relatives on his father's side, whose family originated from the city of Lyon. Through public records, he found the names of his dad's siblings—a sister and two brothers. His research uncovered that his aunt and one of his uncles were deceased, but it appeared that his Uncle Marcelin was still living.

Elias found an address for Marcelin and had written to him several weeks ago. He finally received a reply, but it was from Marcelin's daughter, Yvonne. Elias knew none of his cousins on his father's side, so Yvonne was new to him. She informed Elias that Marcelin was not mentally capable of responding, but she offered to help him if she could. Yvonne said that she was aware that her uncle had been in the French medical corps and had remained in Syria when the French withdrew. After that, there had been no contact between the families. From the tone of the letter, Elias sensed there might be more to the story that Yvonne was not telling him.

Elias was composing a longer letter to Yvonne describing his family and what had happened to them as a result of the conflict in Syria. Elias explained that he and Kamar planned to emigrate to France, which had prompted his outreach.

With his reply to Yvonne ready for posting, Elias turned his attention to employment opportunities in the region around Montpellier. As one of the fastest-growing cities in France, it offered a number of possibilities worth exploring, and Elias felt heartened.

For the first time, Elias allowed his imagination free reign to picture their new life in France. A place where all residents received medical care, not just those with means. A place where a bombing made front page news and people were not wary of every parked car they passed. A country, in fact, a whole collection of countries where you could visit the furthest corners and feel relatively safe. He pictured weekend train excursions to Paris, where, with a luxurious, unhurried pace, he could introduce Kamar to the treasures of the Louvre, the Musée d'Orsay. They could visit Notre Dame, climb the hill to Montmartre, or simply soak in the ambiance of the place Elias considered the greatest city in the world. In fact, the possibilities seemed endless—a day trip to walk the promenade in Nice, a weekend to catch a Barcelona FC match, while marveling at the city's quirky architecture.

The funny thing was, in all of these imaginings, Yana was there, subconsciously. Elias didn't imagine her outright or purposely, and yet he felt her presence. With just Elias and Kamar by themselves, it felt incomplete. Elias knew this was crazy, as they didn't know each other that well, and she was on the other side of the world. Elias wasn't sure if she felt any of the same things about him. The thought of Yana uprooting herself to move to France was ridiculous, and it was impractical for Elias to emigrate to the U.S. with Kamar. Nevertheless, tonight he had let his imagination loose, and this is where it had taken him.

Seattle

Kara's pulse was racing. She knew Maria Burns was in San Francisco and would not be returning until tomorrow. But that didn't prevent someone else from walking in on her. As she searched Burns' office, she kept herself facing the doorway so that she would immediately spot anyone's approach. She had her story ready in case that happened. If questioned, she was looking for the draft report for McFarland, Inc. She had already planted the report under some other papers, allowing her to "find it," if necessary.

Two months ago, before Kara had become Burns' AA, she had been in Burns' office covering while Michael was out on leave. As Burns didn't place much value on an AA's time, she thought nothing of keeping an AA standing, waiting for extended periods while she searched for something, or made edits to a document. Although Burns thought she was being discreet, Kara's sharp eyes picked out a slip of paper at Burns' elbow that appeared to be a list of passcodes for various office systems. Kara remembered being told emphatically, during a required office training session, to avoid writing down passcodes and that if you did need to write them down, to keep them secure at all times. Of course, leave it to Burns to feel that the normal rules and admonitions didn't apply to her. Now, Kara was hoping that the list still existed and that it had been left unlocked somewhere in this office.

Burns' office was devoid of anything personal, other than two framed certificates—her law degree from Loyola and a certificate from the Washington State Bar Association. There were two large framed works of art, both in the same modern-industrial style involving bold blocks crafted in metallic blues and greys. Her desk and credenza were covered in piles of documents and files, but bare of anything that was not job-related. A low coffee table, small couch and matching side chair echoed the tones and style of the artwork. The surface of the coffee table carried only a thin layer of dust.

After searching through each stack of files on the desk and credenza, Kara cautiously began opening drawers. While it was not unusual for an AA to search an attorney's desk for a paper or file he or she needed, the opening of drawers was taboo.

Sensing motion just outside Burns' doorway, Kara closed the drawer she was searching as quickly as she could while trying to minimize the tell-tale scraping sound of the drawer against its slides. It was Margret, the file clerk. Margret was a frequent visitor to Burns' office, as Burns was not the most diligent about returning files she no longer needed.

Kara couldn't be sure whether Margret saw her closing the drawer. She tried to cover her nervousness by remarking that, "It's just like Burns to need a report delivered while she was out of the office but neglect to provide the marked-up copy!"

"Or, to ever return a file." Margret replied, but she gave Kara a shrewd look. Margret found the file she was looking for and left.

Margret was the last person Kara wanted to run into. She was a highly-skilled gossip and not to be trusted—ever. Nothing she could do about that now.

With one more drawer to search, Kara decided she might as well finish what she'd started. It was the bottom drawer closest to the door, which made it the hardest to discretely search. She was surprised to see a framed photo of Burns' two kids. It had been taken a while ago, because they looked quite young. Wondering why she kept the photo hidden in her desk, Kara lifted the frame. There was the document she sought. She slipped it into the McFarland Report she had planted as her excuse for searching the office and smuggled it out to be copied later in the day. She would eventually need to replace the paper, but that could wait until Margret had left for the day.

Kara waited until lunchtime, figuring that the copy room would be less busy. She had the list of passcodes embedded in a report to be copied, so it would not be directly visible to a casual observer, even if someone wandered in mid-job. She had just pushed the copy button when two things happened in close succession—Margret walked into the copy room, and the copy machine jammed.

Kara worked hard to keep her cool, so as to not act suspicious in front of Margret. Thankfully, Margret didn't offer to help unjam the copier and stood instead, watching Kara, with her hip resting against the opposite counter and her jaw working energetically against her chewing gum. Kara was forced to open the machine and pull out the jammed pages under Margret's watchful eyes as she waited to use the machine. There was the list of passcodes, incompletely printed due to the jamming of the paper. Kara had no choice but to include that page with the other jammed pages and slip them into the recycle box sitting next to the copier.

Having finished her print job, Kara headed back to her desk. She slipped the original list of passcodes along with its copy into

a blank folder and set it in the bottom of one of her desk drawers. Then, as soon as the copy room was empty again, she snuck
back in to retrieve the jammed copy from the recycle box. Not
able to immediately find it, she grabbed the top layer of recycled
papers and slunk back to her desk to look more closely. The other
jammed papers from her report were there, but the list of passcodes was definitely gone.

Kara panicked. Had Margret taken it? That seemed to be the
only explanation. If she'd seen it when Kara was making her copies, why didn't she say something? Would she link the copying
incident to Kara's search of Burns' office that morning? Otherwise, how would she know whose passcodes they were?

Kara tried to get on with her work, but she couldn't concentrate. Finally, when she saw that Malick had no visitors in his
office and was not on the phone, she slipped into his office and
closed the door. Malick looked up from his computer monitor.
"Kara, what's up?"

Sinking into a chair across from Malick's desk, Kara relayed
all that had happened. "Jesus!" Malick replied, "That was bad
luck." He paused for a moment while it sunk in. "We need to
think this through and not panic."

"Yeah, I've had a bit of time to think," Kara replied. "We need
to get the original list back into Burns' desk, and I need to hide
the copied version."

"Right. Well I got you into this, so I think it's my turn to step
in," Malick said with a smile.

"I was hoping you'd say that." Kara handed Malick her blank
folder. "This has both the original and the copy. I think it's better if you keep the copy, just in case someone decides to search
my desk. Also, can you find an excuse to be in Burns' office this
afternoon? It would be great if you could return the original."

"Yep, I can come up with some reason to snoop around. Where
exactly did you find it?"

Kara described the precise positioning of the original as she had found it. They agreed to talk that evening from home.

When Kara called Malick later that evening, she was relieved to hear that he had replaced the original without incident. "So, what do we do now?" Kara asked.

"I suggest we lay low for a few days. Let's wait to see if anything comes up related to the missing copy. If we haven't heard anything by next Monday, we can move forward with step two."

"Sounds good. I'm not even sure how much of the codes were successfully copied onto the jammed page. I didn't have a chance to examine it closely with Margret watching."

By the following Monday evening, nothing unusual had surfaced at the office. Margret was acting normally around Kara, and Burns had been back in the office for several days. Kara poked her head into Malick's office on her way out, giving him a thumbs-up.

That evening, Malick went to the public library and reserved a computer in a far corner. He pulled up the law firm's internal web site and tried out the stolen passcodes. They were still current. He was able to log into Burns' office account and then into her Outlook account. Her calendar was crowded. It was quite interesting to troll through it. But he was looking for something specific, and finally he found it. She was meeting Greg Soriano for dinner a week from Thursday at the Seastar Restaurant in Bellevue.

Malick made a note and then closed out the account. Once he returned home, he gave Yana a call. Yana would need to be the one to document their meeting, as she would not be recognizable to Burns.

Yana, in turn, called Ellen to see if she was free a week from Thursday. Yana thought it would look more natural if she was with someone, rather than dining solo. With that set, Yana decided on a dry-run dinner at Seastar the following evening, which would allow her to scope out the restaurant.

The following Thursday, Yana and Ellen parked their car a few blocks from the restaurant. Even though Ellen remained skeptical about the plan Yana, Malick, and Kara had cooked up, she was totally on board with helping Yana with her clandestine operation. She confessed to having always harbored a secret desire to be a spy and was approaching the evening as if it were an elaborate party game. Yana, on the other hand, was nervous. Being a spy was definitely not something to which she aspired.

Not wanting to draw attention to herself, Yana had chosen a gray and white checked blazer paired with a soft grey scoop-necked top and black pencil skirt. At the last minute, she decided to wear her pearl earrings.

They had worked through their plan in detail. By the end of the night, Yana needed to obtain photographic evidence that Maria Burns and Greg Soriano were dining together. Burns' Outlook calendar listed a seven o'clock reservation, so Yana had made a reservation for seven ten. Yana headed into the restaurant at exactly seven ten, while Ellen waited in the car for an additional five minutes. This would give Yana some time while waiting for "the other person in her party" to survey the restaurant in search of Burns. That way they could request a table with a view of Burns and Soriano. Malick had provided two different photos of Burns, which he had pulled off their firm's web site and which Yana had committed to memory.

Greg Soriano was the Chief of Operations for the construction conglomerate Stannis, Inc. Malick had heard rumors that Soriano and Burns were having a fling. This was problematic because Burns was the lead attorney on the team representing King County in a big-stakes lawsuit against Stannis for failure to meet design requirements and missed deadlines in construction of a new county detention facility. It was a messy case with accusations flying in both directions. Soriano was heavily involved in defending the work done by Stannis, and Burns being in a relationship with him was a clear conflict of interest, worthy of disbarment. The fact that her client was a governmental entity made the breach even more serious.

Having confirmed her reservation at the restaurant's reception desk, Yana declined to be seated right away. Instead she took a seat in the waiting area where she had a view into the restaurant. So far, so good.

The restaurant's large back-lit glass wine racks, shiny scalloped wall coverings and hanging glass decorative balls felt upscale. Yana could understand why Burns would choose to dine there. She didn't immediately spot Burns, but there were a couple of women with their backs to her that she couldn't rule out, plus some tables that were hidden from view around a corner.

Yana's next ploy was to use a trip to the ladies' room as an excuse to wander through the restaurant so she could check out the portions of the dining area that were hidden from immediate view. From her previous visit, she already knew where the restroom was located, but she planned to feign ignorance. Unfortunately, the receptionist, in an apparent effort to provide exceptional service, smiled knowingly when Yana rose from her seat and discreetly informed her where she could find the restrooms. Yana then had no choice but to proceed directly, still unable to locate her quarry.

While in the restroom, Yana cooked up another plan to wander the restaurant. On her way back to the waiting area, she would look around the restaurant pretending to search for Ellen in case she had already been seated. But as she exited the restroom, straight ahead of her was the ever-helpful receptionist, standing with Ellen, waiting for Yana to emerge. Thwarted again, they were forced to take a table, still having no idea of where Burns and Soriano were sitting or how they might maneuver into a position from which to take their photos.

They had just ordered drinks when Yana spotted Burns bursting through the front door. A man who had been among those waiting in reception rose to greet her. Yana assumed this must be Soriano. He was tall, with an athletic build and dark hair.

Of course! Leave it to Burns to show up late! From a distance, she appeared to be apologizing to Soriano, and he appeared to be responding with a bit of humor. Too late, Yana thought to whip out her phone. By the time she had the photo app opened, the party was moving away towards their table. With only a view of their backs, Yana and Ellen watched as they disappeared around the corner into a section of the dining area hidden from view.

While Ellen seemed to be enjoying herself, Yana couldn't remember a meal out that she enjoyed less. She couldn't taste her food, but spent the entire time cooking up ideas with Ellen about how they could catch their photo, none of which seemed sane. They could wait and try to snap a shot as Burns and Soriano left, but that seemed chancy. What if one of them decided to stop in the restroom on the way out? They needed a shot of them together.

Finally, Yana collected her courage and decided on a direct approach. She would simply walk over to their table and snap a picture. If she had her phone ready, she was sure she could capture a photo before they had time to react. And, so what if they saw her taking it? They didn't know her, and she didn't have any reason to see them again in the future. Ellen tried to dissuade Yana from her plan, but Yana decided that Ellen didn't like it because it was too straightforward—not the cloak-and-dagger stuff that she had been looking forward to this evening.

"I'm just going to do it!" Yana finally announced to Ellen. She immediately got up from her chair, afraid that, if she hesitated, she would lose her nerve. Once she started walking toward the other dining area, she felt there was no turning back, as if she had stepped on to a roller coaster, and it had started on its inevitable track. Feeling her heart thumping against her throat, she spotted the couple. Without breaking stride, she walked straight over to them, capturing their startled expressions on her phone.

What happened next, she hadn't counted on. With reflexes that seemed to anticipate just such an occurrence, Burns jumped from her seat, grabbed Yana's wrist with surprising strength, wrested the phone out of her hand, pulled up the photo and deleted it.

Burns was tall for a woman, at least six feet. She put her face right up to Yana's and said quietly and calmly, but with menace that would make a mafia enforcer envious, "I don't know who the fuck you are, but if you and your phone are not out of this restaurant this instant, you will be very sorry." Before Yana could react, Burns pulled Yana's top forward with her index finger and dropped the phone, which settled somewhere below her bra.

Yana was devastated, humiliated. She fled the restaurant, forgetting momentarily that Ellen was still back at their table. She thought of Ellen just as she reached the door but couldn't bring herself to go back inside. I'll text Ellen when I get to the car, she thought.

As Yana hurried past the front of the restaurant, she glanced inside. There was an unobstructed view of the two of them sitting at their table, heads close together, probably laughing at Yana's undignified exit. The restaurant lighting clearly illuminated the pair, while the darkness outside kept Yana hidden. She dug her phone from the depths where it had settled, zoomed in, and snapped four perfect shots in quick succession.

France

Elias and Kamar had just finished their third week in Montpellier, France. Their travel visas had arrived on the first of May, and they left Beirut as soon as Kamar's school year finished. One advantage of having so few possessions between the two of them was that they had little that needed to be shipped.

Elias felt an overwhelming sense of relief, tainted by guilt in leaving behind his fellow refugees and his country of Syria at a time when doctors were desperately needed. There were also times when he wondered whether he was abandoning Victor in his move to France. But he couldn't see how remaining in Lebanon would help Victor's situation.

Elias had little time to dwell on his conflicting feelings as there was so much to do. They took up temporary lodgings in the outskirts of the city, as they narrowed down their options for a more permanent situation. Elias kept busy with job interviews, most of which he had lined up while still in Lebanon. Then there were the countless tasks needed to establish residency and set up a household. Both Elias and Kamar continued work on improving their French, as that was of paramount importance in integrating into their new community. A final decision on schooling would need to wait until they determined which neighborhood they would call home, and Elias was hoping to confirm where he would be working before committing to a long-term lease.

One of the first things Elias did upon arriving in Montpellier was to find a counselor for Kamar. Kamar was reluctant at first. Elias tried to frame the concept of counseling in terms that would make sense to her and not seem threatening. "Counseling is not much different from the work I do. I help the body heal when there has been a physical injury. A counselor is trained to help people heal from emotional injuries. You've been through an emotional injury that is, I'd say, the equivalent of a major car crash. It would not be very smart to be involved in a car crash and then insist that you didn't need a doctor—that you just want to see if your body will heal all on its own. No matter that your broken arm might heal at a funny angle and prevent you from being able to use it normally." After a few sessions, Kamar seemed content to continue with counseling, although she never shared specifics about her sessions, and Elias didn't pry.

Kamar immersed herself in all things French, and Elias prioritized their time spent getting to know their newly adopted city. Most mornings, in the cooler part of the day, Elias and Kamar explored a new site or neighborhood and then, during the warm afternoons, retreated to their apartment to work on applications or to practice their French. One morning they visited Pavillon Populaire to catch a photography exhibit, followed the next morning with a trip to the beach. Another morning they drove north of the city past vineyards and sunflower fields to the trailhead for Pic Saint-Loup where they were rewarded for their climb with a stunning 360-degree view of the surrounding territory. Often, in the evenings, they wandered Écusson, the old quarter in the center of Montpellier, discovering a new restaurant to try with each excursion.

Today however, they were venturing for the first time outside the Languedoc-Roussillon Region—a train trip to Lyon to meet up with Yvonne, who had agreed to introduce Elias to some of his relations. As the train pulled into Lyon's Part Dieu station, Elias's excitement at reconnecting with his father's roots mixed with anxiety over how he and Kamar would be received and what he might discover about the past that his father had kept from him. Elias could feel Kamar's excitement at visiting a new city, but also sensed her apprehension at meeting so many new people.

Elias's father never spoke of his upbringing in France. He had been a good parent—Elias could depend on him to be fair and even-tempered. Even so, he felt he didn't know the person behind the impeccable manners. His dad's even temperament was an impenetrable barrier. How could you find fault with or react to someone who presented so benignly?

Elias thought back to his departure to the U.S. to start his residency. His parents accompanied him to the airport to see him off, as did his fiancée, Aliya. There were embraces all around, but it was his father who held on to him that extra moment, as if afraid to let go. He thought his father was about to say something to him when Aliya broke in, taking Elias's hand and saying how she wasn't sure she could stand the long wait for him to complete his residency. His father busied himself with checking Elias's luggage instead. Elias thought he saw tears in the corners of his father's eyes—the only time he had witnessed that.

Elias's father passed away while he was in New York, so that had been the last time he saw him, the man who had played such a role in his life, whom he had followed into the medical profession, yet who remained a mystery to him. Perhaps these people could shed some light.

The train had come to a stop. Kamar had to nudge Elias back

to the present. They grabbed their bags and joined the crowds navigating the station, which was undergoing a major renovation. Elias texted to let Yvonne know that they had arrived. She responded immediately with her location, adding that she was wearing a bright red dress, so they could easily spot her.

Yvonne appeared to be older than Elias but shared his compact build. Her earrings and shoes matched her dress with the smart sense of style that is stereotypically French. However, it was her sharp, brown eyes that caught Elias, communicating intelligence and awareness.

Although they were essentially strangers, Elias greeted Yvonne with a kiss to each cheek. Then Yvonne turned exclaiming, "So this must be Kamar. Welcome to Lyon!" Kamar responded somewhat shyly, but managed a smile, and her smiles suited her. Elias sensed Yvonne's motherly instinct kicking in and felt reassured that this would go well.

They made their way to Yvonne's car and started towards her home, where they would be connecting with more relations that evening. On the way, Yvonne stopped at the residential care facility where her father, Marcelin, lived. Yvonne prepared them for the fact that her father was typically not fully cognizant. "On good days, he seems to know who everyone is and can carry on a conversation," she explained.

They found Marcelin sitting in a common area. The TV was on, but it appeared that he had been sleeping. A large man, he looked like he could have been a farmer or construction worker during his active years. However, Marcelin was well-groomed and well-dressed, more so than some of the other residents sharing the room. Yvonne walked over to him, stooping to give him a kiss, and then said loudly "Daddy, I have some people here for you to meet."

Marcelin looked up at his daughter and then slowly looked over and locked eyes with Elias. His countenance transformed, and his face became flushed. He rose unsteadily from his armchair and came at Elias as fast as his shaky legs would take him. "You!" he yelled with a volume that did not seem possible from such an elderly man. "You dare show yourself here! Get out! Get out of my sight!"

Elias, in total shock, retreated. The other residents stared with open jaws. Two staff members dashed in, trying to lead Marcelin back to his chair, but he was resisting them. Elias grabbed Kamar's arm, and they quickly left the facility to wait outside, wondering what had just happened.

Some minutes later, Yvonne emerged, looking distressed. "This is my fault. I should have seen that this might happen. Please, can we sit for a minute?" She motioned the bewildered Elias and Kamar across the facility's front lawn to a bench facing a flower bed filled with summer roses in yellows and reds.

Yvonne seemed on the verge of tears. Taking a breath to compose herself, she turned to Elias. "What do you know about the time that your father left for Syria?"

"My father never talked about the war. That was a closed chapter in our household. Is that related to what just happened?"

"Yes, I'm sorry to say. I think you must look a lot like your father. I tried to explain to Marcelin who you were and that you would be visiting, but I don't think he understood me. You probably triggered memories of your father. That's who Marcelin thought you were just now."

"Wow. I've always wondered why my father had no contact with his family. Obviously, there was a falling out."

"Yes, to put it mildly."

"Can you fill me in on what happened?"

"If you're sure you want to hear this. I don't think this is what you had in mind when you decided to reconnect with his family."

"I really didn't know what to expect. But, yes, I think this is something I need to know, if you're okay with sharing."

"Of course. As you probably know, your father was the oldest of four children, three sons and one daughter."

"I know almost nothing about his family, so please start from the beginning."

Yvonne turned on the bench to face Elias more directly. "Well, there was your father, then his sister Eva, then Marcelin, and finally Leone. When the war broke out, your father was in medical school. I remember my Aunt Eva telling me that, being the oldest, your father was a serious child. While in Paris for medical training, the loose attitudes in the city shocked him. So, when the propaganda from the Vichy leader, Pétain, talked about making France neutral and reversing the country's 'slide into decadence,' it appealed to your father's Catholic background. I think he was also afraid of what might happen to him amidst all the chaos of war. Having worked so hard on his medical training, he had more to lose than his younger brothers."

Elias turned from staring at the bright roses to face Yvonne. At last, he was hearing the story of his father. Yvonne continued, "Marcelin was the firebrand in the family. He got involved in the Resistance about the time your father signed up as a medic with the Vichy Army. He tried to talk your father into joining the Resistance instead, and they had a huge row."

"Okay, I'm starting to understand why Marcelin reacted the way he did."

"That's only part of it," Yvonne replied. "Leone also became involved in the Resistance, under Marcelin's influence. Leone lied about his age and joined the Free French Army under de Gaulle. He was part of Operation Exporter, the British and Commonwealth invasion of Syria and Lebanon. Not too many people realize that the Free French were part of that operation, at de Gaulle's insistence. Leone lost his life in the battle that liberated Syria, and your father was supporting the Vichy Army in Syria that was fighting against him."

Elias struggled to picture his father's family ripped in pieces by this tragedy. It felt surreal. Here he was sitting outside a care facility in a city he'd never seen before, with Kamar and a cousin he had just met, and he was, at last, discovering the key to his father and, in some ways, to himself. War had blown apart his father's family, just as it had blown apart his own family. Yvonne was watching him with great concern. Kamar placed an arm across his shoulder.

Finally, Elias found his voice. "That explains a lot," was all he could manage.

"I imagine it does. I'm so sorry that you never knew this and that you had to find out in such a manner."

Elias looked back out at the roses, watching a wasp as it buzzed from flower to flower searching for its insect prey. "My middle name is Leone. Was that my father's way to memorialize his younger brother?" Yvonne didn't have an answer to that, and after a pause, Elias continued, "I don't fault your father at all for his reaction. Totally understandable."

"After you left, I tried to explain to him who you were. I don't know if any of it penetrated. And, to be honest, I'm not sure he would react much differently knowing that you were his nephew, not his brother."

"Sounds like a rift that was too big to heal."

"Yes, I'm afraid it was. I think Marcelin also blamed himself for recruiting his younger brother into the Resistance, and that's part of why he never could get over his death. Eva told me that, when they were growing up, Marcelin always watched out for Leone."

"Yvonne, I'm sorry to resurrect such painful history. I really had no idea. I'm wondering if it's a good idea to hold this get-together you've been so kind to organize."

"Nonsense. You have nothing to apologize for. This was our parents' battle. It is not a battle that our generation needs to have."

"Are you sure the others in your family will feel the same?"

"Yes. And I would try to get my father to see reason as well, but

I'm afraid that's beyond his capacity at this point. Come on. It's time we put an end to this family rift."

They returned to the car and headed to Yvonne's house. "So, who will be there tonight?" Elias asked.

"Eva passed away a number of years ago, so Marcelin is all that's left of our father's family. My brother and his wife, and also my sister and her husband, will be joining us. Oh, and my husband Denis, of course. Our Aunt Eva met her husband while studying at the University of Paris after the war, and he was from Lille, so that's where she and her extended family settled. None of them were able to make the trip. The younger generation is mostly dispersed and tied up with work and family, so, out of all your second cousins, just my daughter, is able to join us."

"That sounds perfect—not too overwhelming a group. I really appreciate your organizing this."

Seattle

Yana had thought, with Elias and Kamar safely resettled in France, that she would probably not hear from them again. She reflected on how, as she aged, she had accumulated an entire closet full of people she once knew but had lost touch with—friends from high school and college who had moved on with their lives and fortunes, people who came and went at work, parents of her kids' schoolmates she had gotten to know and that, despite good intentions, she no longer had contact with. She assumed that Elias, Kamar, and Victor would be three more to set into a dusty box among the shelves of her memories, likely never to be opened again.

Yet, here was another e-mail from Elias. The man certainly was open about himself. Yana had encountered few men with that quality.

Hi Yana,

I hope you are enjoying one of those splendid Seattle summers that you boasted of when we were in Beirut. The warm climate in Montpellier suits Kamar and me just fine, and we are both happy to now be calling France home. Unfortunately, we have no update from Victor, and can only hope that he is okay.

While we were in Lebanon, you inquired about my father's history and the events that led to his settling in Syria. I was sorry to have no information to share. But now, thanks to reconnecting with my father's family here in France, I have filled in most of that picture.

You may have heard about this from Sami and Amena. I wanted to share it with you all the same. When you leave the country you've called home since birth, and sever nearly all your connections, it makes the few remaining, such as Sami and Amena, as well as the new connections, such as yourself, and my new-found French relatives, all the more important. So, I hope you will not mind so much my ramblings to you, as I have few to share this with and none so perceptive as yourself.

It appears that I have an ignoble past. Fortunately, the current generation of my father's family are not inclined to hold the children responsible for the decisions of their parents.

My father, being the oldest of four siblings, and of a serious nature, was drawn to the doctrine espoused by Pétain calling for a reversal of France's "slide into decadence." They offered him the chance to graduate early if he enlisted with the Vichy Army. Also, work as a medic may have seemed to him a convenient way to hopefully survive the war. This decision resulted in his being stationed in Syria, supporting the Vichy Army as it tried in vain to prevent Syria and Lebanon from falling into Allied hands. Unknown to him until later, his youngest brother was fighting with the Free French Army supporting the British operation and died in that battle.

As you can well imagine, this ended any possibility that my father might be forgiven by his family for joining the Vichy Army. I don't know whether he was able to forgive himself. My guess is that this haunted him to his grave. So, now at last, I know the reason my father kept such a large part of himself cut off from everyone and why I never felt I knew him.

My cousin tells me that, as a young man, my father was a devout Catholic, and the Catholic Church's support of the Vichy Government influenced his decision to sign up. I think his faith was another war casualty. Growing up, our household was not very religious, although my mother was nominally Muslim.

This revelation explains so much of my family, but also opens up more questions. I find myself sitting for long periods staring into space, lost in my thoughts. I'm hoping that sharing this with an accomplished listener will help bring my focus back to the many details of setting up our new life.

Speaking of our new life, I start a new position next week with one of the major medical centers in town, so now I really do need to be more focused.

While in Lebanon, you invited me to Seattle. I don't think that will happen anytime soon, since Kamar and I are adjusting to our adopted city and not eager for more travel at this point. So, I will extend the invitation in the other direction. Montpellier is a lovely town and well situated to exploring southern France, Barcelona, or even northern Italy. I'm sorry to say that the town will not meet your standards for quality and quantity of rain. Perhaps you can be without for short periods?

Please let me know what's happening with you, and I trust that you are doing well.

Elias

Yana didn't respond to Elias's e-mail right away, as she needed time to think. Clearly, he was interested in continuing their relationship and in a personal, rather than distant fashion. Yana was interested in continuing as well, but she couldn't see a future in it. The prospect of something more serious seemed impossible. She was firmly rooted in Seattle. All her family and friends were here, and it was the place where she had grown up. On their end, Elias had finally found a safe place for Kamar. It wouldn't be good for her to move to the U.S. and have to learn yet another language and culture, not to mention how long it might take them to gain permission to immigrate.

Surely Elias understood all this. Was he naively optimistic that things would just work out? That didn't fit the Elias she had come to know while in Lebanon. If not that, then he must value the relationship as is, even if it was not "going anywhere." That was something Yana could also accept and feel comfortable with.

Yana decided that she would respond in kind. However, she didn't have time this afternoon, as she was meeting up with Malick, Emma, and Kara to talk about next steps. She had informed the others about the photos she had captured of Burns and Soriano.

They were meeting at Malick's home in Laurelhurst. Yana couldn't help feeling a bit jealous as she walked up the front steps and turned around to take in the view across Lake Washington to the Bellevue skyline, with the Cascade Mountains in the distance.

But Malick was so far from being pretentious that Yana couldn't begrudge him the wonderful location.

With the four of them gathered around Malick's dining room table, Yana passed around her phone so each could flip through the four shots of Burns and Soriano. There was general agreement that the photos provided sufficiently clear views of the two individuals, so there would be no question as to their identity. Kara handed the phone back to Yana. "So, what's our next step?" she said, looking over to Malick. "Do we file a grievance with the Washington Bar Association?"

"No." Malick leaned back in his chair. "We would need to complete an official form to do that, and it would involve disclosing our identity. Much better to leave that to the county, since they are the aggrieved party. All we need to do is set things in motion. While I had access to Burns' files, I copied down contact information for everyone in her contacts list working for the county."

"So, we just need to forward the pictures to them?" Kara continued.

"Yes, but it wouldn't hurt to send copies to the Bar Association, as well as our dear old office manager. That way it's all in the open, and folks would be forced to deal with it."

"What about sending a copy to the Seattle Times?" Kara wondered out loud.

"I don't think that will be necessary, as the county and the Bar Association should be compelled to take action. Also, keeping in mind that our goal is to take down Burns, we don't want the firm to be a casualty, which could happen with a lot of adverse publicity."

Yana was trying to take all this in. "What could the county point to in terms of damages?" she asked.

Malick leaned forward again. "From the state bar's point of view, the conflict of interest is sufficient. If the county wanted to sue for damages, they would need to demonstrate that they were harmed. Several ways that could happen—Burns could have fed useful information to Soriano, which allowed his company to craft a more effective defense. They could argue that Burns didn't represent them effectively because she had a personal attachment to the defendants, or Burns could have provided information about the level of settlement the county might be willing to accept, which would erode their negotiating power."

"And the fact that the plaintiff is a governmental agency, the aggrieved party is really the taxpayers," Emma contributed, speaking up for the first time.

Once they all agreed on the plan of action, Malick volunteered to do the actual mailings. Yana texted the pictures to Malick's phone, so he could download them to individual thumb drives. He printed out address labels and a short description of the significance of the photos. He then mailed them from a downtown post office box.

The wheels had been set in motion. Now all they needed to do was sit back and watch.

Montpellier

Elias felt a lightness in his mood, a sense of being that he thought would never be his to experience again. Kamar was enthusiastic about her school. She was making friends with both French students and with fellow immigrants. Most of the immigrants at her school were from Algeria, and they shared some common ground with Kamar.

In particular, Maisah and Kamar were quickly becoming inseparable. If Maisah was not hanging out at Kamar's apartment after school, then it was a sure bet that Kamar was over at Maisah's apartment. The two girls even looked alike, same large eyes, dark hair, and winning smiles. Most heartening, Kamar was becoming silly. That was the way a fourteen-year-old girl should be. Maisah's playful, accepting personality played a big role in bringing out Kamar's silliness.

Their apartment was small for a three-bedroom unit, and modest, but it was on a second floor and looked out over a central courtyard with a small fountain, garden, and play area for younger kids. They were some distance from the city center but close to a tram station and within walking distance of the medical center where Elias was now working. For the most part, Elias was happy with his new employment, although he was once again working at a level far below the roles he filled back in Aleppo. Importantly, he was finding a sense of purpose in the clinic's mission, which was to serve everyone in the community.

Over time, Kamar and Elias achieved greater distance between themselves and the violence they had experienced. They both knew their experiences from the Syrian conflict would always haunt them, but those memories gradually occupied a smaller part of their conscious existence.

While Elias was overjoyed with Kamar's progress and how well they were settling into Montpellier, the thing that really made him smile during his private, reflective moments was that Yana had taken up his offer to visit Montpellier. She was planning a trip in late October and indicated that a friend of hers, Ellen, would be accompanying her. At first, Elias was disappointed to hear that Yana was bringing her friend. Then he realized that it would be less awkward for Kamar that way, avoiding the possibility that she would feel herself to be a third wheel tagging along with just Elias and Yana.

Elias found himself imagining all the places they would take Yana and Ellen. There were a lot of details yet to be worked out. Did the two women want to spend most of their time in Montpellier, or did they intend to use it primarily as a base to explore more widely? Did they want or expect that Elias and Kamar would join them in their excursions, or was Montpellier just a stop in their itinerary where they would have a short visit and then move on with their trip? This nervous anticipation reminded Elias of high-school dating. He would need to sound them out without putting any expectations on them. Probably Yana was still working this out with her friend.

Elias had also spent a lot of time thinking about his father. He and Kamar had made another trip to Lyon in August while his cousin from Lille, Eva's daughter, and her husband were in Lyon visiting Yvonne's family. His cousins had gathered together old family photos and placed them in an album, which they presented to Elias. They showed his father and his father's family before the war. These were scenes that Elias had never seen before, and he had gone through the album numerous times trying to extract as much information as he could from the images.

Elias found out that his grandmother had died shortly after Leone's death. Whether the family blamed her death on the stress caused by her youngest son's death, the banishment of her oldest son, the deprivations of war or a combination of all of the above, no one ventured an opinion. Apparently, Elias's grandfather took his wife's death badly, and he survived only an additional five years.

At least none of the current family appeared to blame Elias in any way for the tragedies of World War II, and they welcomed him as family, apart from Marcelin, of course. Yvonne told Elias that she picked one of Marcelin's more lucid moments to try to explain to him who Elias was, but she wasn't sure how much penetrated. When Elias told her that he felt it would be best not to chance another visit, she didn't disagree.

Despite the tragic family history, Elias was glad that he had reconnected. His French relatives, Kamar, and Victor were now the only family he had.

Edmonds

Yana was starting to get excited about their upcoming trip to France. She and Ellen had driven out to Rick Steves' Travel Center in Edmonds, just north of Seattle, where they picked up the most recent editions of the relevant guidebooks, and talked to the experts about practicalities, such as train connections, local festivals that would take place during their visit, and tips on places to stay. Then they walked the few blocks down to the beach and found a bench in a small park next to the ferry dock where they sat to look through the books and discuss their trip.

A ferry from Kingston on the Kitsap Peninsula was approaching the dock as kids and dogs chased seagulls through the beach grass. Across the water, the Olympic Mountains had lost their winter snowpack from all but the higher elevations. Yana set her book on France aside and turned to Ellen. "We need to talk about how we want to approach our visit with Elias."

"Well, how do you want to approach it?"

"I'm not sure—that's the problem. I don't know how serious this is with Elias. Plus, it's your vacation too, so I don't want it to revolve around me."

"Yeah, I get it. Sounds like we may need to play this a bit by ear. I'm okay with that."

The approaching ferry sounded its deep, abrupt horn, making them both jump. Yana looked up for a moment to watch the churning water from the ferry's reverse engines, as it slowed down to dock. She turned back to Ellen. "Okay, let's start with our itinerary. What we have so far is flights in and out of Paris and three weeks to spend as we want. I think we'll need at least a week in and around Paris."

Ellen smiled at the prospect of a whole week in Paris. "That sounds good to me. Should we allot a week for Montpellier? That would allow an additional week for either Barcelona, northern Italy, or Switzerland, minus a day or two getting back to Paris for our flight home."

"Are you sure you're okay with a whole week at Montpellier?"

"Yeah, that will be fine. Plus, I don't want to deal with you pining away."

"I don't pine for anyone. I'm done with that sort of thing. I just don't like things being unsettled."

"Maybe a bit of unsettled is good for you. Your life was becoming pretty settled, almost, one might say, to the point of being boring?"

"And what's wrong with boring? I used to be boring and proud of it!" Behind them, the cars were starting to drive off the ferry. Those on foot were also disembarking and scattering in various directions.

"Well, I have a feeling that may be changing."

"Yes, and that's what's so unsettling." Yana paused for a second. "This conversation is starting to sound circular."

"Well why don't you float that itinerary with your mysterious Middle-East-French physician and see how he reacts. That may tell you something."

"Yes, it might," Yana said thoughtfully, looking out across the water.

"I'm changing the subject, but I haven't heard any update on your espionage project. Any developments?"

Yana had to pull in her thoughts, which were far away, drifting over southern France. Maria Burns was a much less pleasant topic to consider. "There's been nothing! It's very strange. It's been a month since the pictures were sent out, and both Malick and Kara say they haven't picked up any mention of it anywhere. Apparently, Burns is still assigned to the King County account. Malick was going to try the stolen pass codes to break into her account again to see if there are any e-mail exchanges that can shed some light. But the pass codes may no longer be valid, so that may not work."

Seattle

That evening, Malick returned to the public library to try to access Burns' accounts. He was surprised to find that the password for her e-mail account was still valid. Clearly, Burns was not diligent about changing her passwords. After about an hour of sifting through e-mails, he was losing hope of finding anything pertinent to the photos. If there were dealings related to a potential conflict of interest, it would make sense that she would avoid mediums that left a record and would be handling things via phone.

Malick was close to giving up when he opened one more e-mail from Burns' main contact at the county. At last, here was something on the photos:

Maria,

Thanks for your follow up and for providing additional information regarding the anonymous photos and the conflict-of-interest accusation related to your firm's work for King County (the "County"). In

accordance with the King County Ethics Policy, our legal depart-
ment has completed its review of the situation.

As you probably are aware, we conducted an interview with your
Office Manager, Mr. Weston, who corroborated your account that
you and he had met after work for drinks, and that Mr. Soriano's
presence at the same restaurant was coincidental. Mr. Weston pro-
vided us with a copy of his credit card receipt from the restaurant
dated that evening. We separately interviewed Mr. Soriano, who
also corroborated your account of the evening, and that the only
time the two of you were alone was a brief period when Mr. West-
on was at the restroom.

After conferring with our internal counsel, we are agreeable to
letting the matter stand. As a condition for continuing to engage
your firm in a legal capacity, we are requesting that you, and any
members of your team working with the County, or with access to
the County account, refrain from any contact whatsoever, wheth-
er planned or unplanned, with Mr. Soriano or any members of
his team involved in the litigation with the County, other than as
needed as a direct outcome of your work with the County, and al-
ways with County personnel present. This policy should avoid any
future incidents that might be construed as a breach of confiden-
tiality or ethics. Our legal department will be forwarding formal
documents stating the above conditions, which we are asking you
and every member of your team working on the County account
to sign.

We appreciate your assistance in resolving this matter. Please let
us know if you have any questions or concerns.

Malick read the e-mail through twice and then sat thinking.
Now he knew not only why there had been no repercussions, but

also how far Weston was willing to stick his neck out for Burns. Finally, he pulled out his phone, took a photo of the e-mail, closed down the account and made his way home.

Two weeks later the foursome met again at Malick's to discuss the e-mail message. Out of all of them, Kara seemed the most incensed. "How could she wiggle out of this? It should be no surprise that Weston covered for her. They're thick as thieves. But he had a receipt from the restaurant for that evening. How did he manage that?"

Yana was similarly incensed. "Burns was definitely there to meet Soriano. We saw her come in and greet him. There's no way that was a coincidental crossing of paths."

Malick seemed more resigned. "I suspect that your walking up to their table to snap a picture might have tipped them off," he said with a wry smile. "She could have phoned Weston and told him he needed to get down to the restaurant to create a paper trail that would substantiate the cover story that she and Soriano agreed to."

Yana was skeptical. "Do you really think he would cover for her to that degree? Doesn't that put his career and reputation at risk as well?"

"Yes, I think he would be willing to take that risk. The two are very tight." Seeing the look on Emma's face, Malick added, "No, I don't think they've ever been romantically involved. It's more a matter of being from the same money and power-worshipping tribe. They understand and relate to each other. Also, Weston, in his short-sighted view, considers Burns one of his best attorneys in terms of bringing revenue to the firm. That's because he doesn't take into account the carnage she inflicts on the rest of the office, or the number of high-quality attorneys who won't consider working at the firm because of her."

"A good case in point is our losing this bright, up-and-coming attorney." Kara added, turning to Emma with a smile.

"So," Yana broke in, "what is our next step? We're not going to let her get away with this are we?"

Emma spoke up for the first time. "As for me, I'm done. It's not that I don't think Burns deserves to be brought down. But for me personally, I need to move on and put this behind me. That doesn't preclude the rest of you from taking further steps. I'm just saying that my participation is over."

This caught the rest of the group by surprise. Yana was the first to respond. "Of course, that's understandable. Probably very wise as well." She hesitated for a few moments. "Since Emma is my only connection to this, that probably means it would make sense for me to bow out at this point as well." Yana looked over at Malick and Kara. "Although I feel bad abandoning you two, since I was the one who instigated all this. What are your thoughts on this? You two have to continue working with her."

"No, we don't!" Kara exclaimed. "I've been considering moving to a new firm for some time, and I think it's time to put that into action. The job market is pretty good at present, so this is not a bad time to see what's out there."

"Yes, come to work for Mather Anesson. It'd be great to work together again," Emma responded.

Kara looked over at Malick. "So, where does that leave you?"

Calm as ever, Malick smiled. "I just keep my nose down and manage my own clients, so I don't think Burns is going to bother me. Sounds to me like our little project is done then. Sorry we didn't get the result we were looking for."

Emma didn't seem concerned. "We gave it a try. No regrets in that."

As Yana drove home from their meeting, she pondered Emma's response versus her own. She considered that perhaps she had become too personally invested in the whole thing. Perhaps there was something for her to learn from Emma.

Sea-Tac Airport

Yana always felt flustered after making it through the harried, tense gauntlet of airport security. Now she and Ellen could relax, waiting for their flight to start the boarding process. Yana hated feeling rushed, so they had allowed plenty of time to bask in the excitement of heading to France.

Theirs was an afternoon departure on a non-stop flight, arriving in Paris mid-morning. Although Yana was not a frequent traveler, her trip to Beirut had convinced her to invest in some noise-blocking headphones. She realized that she had forgotten to pack the extra batteries she had set out on the kitchen counter at home that morning. Seeing the Hudson convenience store directly across from their gate, Yana left Ellen with their bags and headed across to pick up some batteries.

At the cashier, Yana got in line behind a tall woman picking up a magazine and some mints. As the woman turned to go, her eyes locked on Yana's. Yana almost dropped her purse in shock. The woman looked away and then suddenly looked back at Yana. A smile spread slowly across her face. "It's you," Maria

Burns spoke in her calm, menacing voice. "Have you come to take some pictures of me at the airport? Would you like me to pose next to my luggage? Just who are you anyway?"

Collecting her composure as best she could, Yana ignored Burns' questioning and proceeded past her to the register to purchase her batteries. When she finished and turned around, Burns was still there waiting for her.

Yana walked past Burns, still trying to ignore her. Not wanting Burns to follow her to her seat, Yana headed instead to the woman's restroom. When Yana reemerged, Burns was still there, waiting with an over-sized smile. Not knowing what else to do, Yana went back to sit down next to Ellen. Burns followed, picking out a seat directly across from them, and continuing to smile.

Yana didn't say anything to Ellen about the unwanted visitor, not knowing whether Burns could hear their conversation from where she was sitting. Instead, she pulled out her book and tried to behave as if nothing was amiss.

I've done nothing illegal, Yana said to herself. *There's really nothing this lady could do to me. Burns is a bully. The best thing to do with bullies is to ignore them.* Yana tried to read, but her mind wasn't registering any of it. Glancing up, she saw Burns was still there, her smile broadening for Yana. Could Burns be on the same flight? After about ten minutes of awkwardly pretending to read, Yana heard an announcement over the intercom. "Yana Pickering, please report to gate A6, Yana Pickering to gate A6."

Panicking, Yana wondered if she should respond to the page—then Burns would find out her name. That couldn't be good. But, if she ignored it, it might be important. And anyway, they would just keep repeating the page if she didn't respond. Ellen looked over at her, wondering why she hadn't gotten up. Not knowing what else to do, Yana finally headed over to the gate. Burns followed her, pretending to be in line behind her.

Yana barely registered what the gate attendant was saying. Something about switching their two seats for identical ones in the row ahead of them to accommodate a family group. Yana simply agreed to whatever he asked, and he printed out updated boarding passes. Yana returned to her seat. This time Burns didn't follow her. Perhaps she felt she had made her point.

Back at her seat, Yana double-checked to make sure Burns was not within hearing distance, then leaned over to Ellen. "Did you notice that lady sitting across from us, who got up when I did?"

"Yes, she was acting a bit strangely. Seemed like she was staring at you but in an odd way."

"Well, that was Maria Burns. Remember, the lady we staked out to get her picture."

Ellen's jaw dropped, and her hand flew to her mouth. "Oh my God! Did she recognize you from the time at the restaurant?"

"She most certainly did. I ran into her at the store just now. She followed me back here, to intimidate me, I assume—and it worked, I might add."

"Did she follow you over to the ticket counter too?"

"Yes. I'm not sure why, unless she was trying to confirm my name. She heard them page me, so maybe she was trying to catch a glimpse of the spelling."

"So much for staying anonymous. What are you going to do?"

"I don't know. I don't think there's anything I can do."

"Look. You still haven't done anything illegal. So, what can she do about it? Let her sit and stare at you all she likes. I don't think there's anything she can do to hurt you."

"From what I've heard about this lady, doing things to hurt people is one of her gifts. I just need to make sure she doesn't connect this back to Emma somehow. I think I can take care of myself, but I would feel horrible if this whole escapade ends up harming Emma. She's commented on how the attorneys in Seattle all seem to know each other."

"Well, she doesn't have any way of tying this to Emma, does she?"

Yana thought for a bit. "I can't see how she could."

By this time, the boarding had started. Burns was indeed on their flight. She was boarding early. *Of course, she would be flying business class,* Yana thought to herself.

Yana and Ellen settled themselves into their seats. They could hear the family group that their change in seats had accommodated settling into the row behind them. Yana didn't want to turn around and stare, but judging from the conversation, she guessed their child was between one and two.

Yana had been planning to sleep as much as possible on the flight. After the encounter with Burns she was far from feeling sleepy. Now, all she needed was a noisy kid behind them. She had been planning to take a Benadryl to help make her drowsy but decided this was definitely a two-Benadryl flight. She briefly considered taking three, but she wasn't the type to violate warning labels on pill bottles. Some wine should help.

Yana's mind kept coming up with things Burns might try, now that she knew Yana's identity, none of which seemed plausible when she really thought them through. Finally, she pulled her book out and forced herself to read, hoping to get her mind off the unpleasant thoughts that were threatening to interfere with this trip that she had been so much looking forward to. *This is going to be a great trip!* she told herself. *I won't let that woman spoil it.*

Paris

Yana did finally fall asleep, waking about ninety minutes ahead of their arrival in Paris. In the cramped, dark confines of their flight, it had been hard to put Maria Burns out of her mind. Now that they landed, the excitement of being in France with her best friend to share the fun made that much easier. Yana had been to Paris once before with her ex-husband, Reggie. Being here with Ellen promised less tension—the two friends were easy-going and shared similar interests.

They caught a regional train to the Luxembourg stop. Not wanting to bother with taxis or the Metro on such a fine morning—rare for October—they wheeled their suitcases to their hotel near Luxembourg Gardens. After settling themselves into their room, they were hungry for lunch. They wandered in the general direction of the Île de la Cité in search of a restaurant, choosing one of the many with outdoor dining so they could people-watch while they savored the French cuisine.

After lunch, they explored the narrow streets, passing bookshops, boulangeries, street vendors, pastry shops, and restaurants of all descriptions. Yana found the walking helped clear her mind after so much time spent on the plane. Eventually they reached the Seine and followed the promenade past couples and families enjoying some of the last good weather of the season. The afternoon sun, filtering through linden trees and under arched stone bridges, created shifting patterns of light and dark across the gently scalloped surface of the river.

As Notre Dame came into view, they paused to gawk at the beloved world icon. After a few minutes, Ellen looked over at Yana. "So, have you figured out yet where this friendship with Elias is headed? Are you interested in something more serious?"

"I wish I knew. I like Elias. He's intelligent and caring. He doesn't condescend to me because I'm female. The difficult part is that I haven't spent all that much time in his company, and we were so focused on Victor and Kamar. This trip gives me a chance to spend some time with him in more relaxed circumstances."

"So, if he passes the test on this trip, you might consider a more serious relationship?"

"No, it's not quite like that. It's more—let's see how this trip goes, and then we'll see what happens from there. Besides, I'm firmly rooted in Seattle and he in Montpellier with Kamar. Part of me wonders why I'm even here."

"Not that I'm trying to ditch my best friend, but is a move to France really unthinkable? What's keeping you rooted to Seattle?"

"Nothing, except if you count my kids, my career and all my friends!"

"Your kids and friends would love to have the excuse to visit you in France. And other people, not boring ones like us, other people do bold things such as moving to another country and starting new careers."

"That's just never been me. I like the familiar and dependable."

"And yet, here you are on this trip, which as you say, leads to nowhere."

"Yeah, it probably does lead nowhere but still, it's a great excuse to see France."

As they continued along the promenade, Yana looked over at Ellen. "What about you? Any bold moves to break out from your ordinary life?"

"Ha! No. You're the one with all the adventures—bodies in your front yard, traveling the globe to rescue refugee children, avenging tyrannical workplace bullies."

"More like being terrorized by mafia-type attorneys. You would have to bring that up, just when I had finally succeeded in putting her out of my mind. It unnerves me that she knows my name."

"No, don't worry about it. Like I said, you haven't done anything wrong. There's nothing she can pin on you."

"I sure hope you're right."

By mid-afternoon, the promenade was filling up with tourists and even a few Parisians. They decided to head back to their hotel and do some planning for their explorations the next day.

Western Syria

It was the hottest part of the afternoon, and Victor took a break, sitting on a mat and leaning against the wall of the abandoned farmhouse where his unit had set up a temporary base. Although Victor had fallen under hostile fire on several occasions as their unit moved across the countryside, he hadn't yet participated in any of their excursions. As the youngest member, he played a support role—preparing meals, digging latrines, cleaning equipment, and running errands. But he participated in all the training drills and had learned how to care for and fire rifles, machine guns, and rocket-propelled grenade launchers.

Victor was eager to be a part of the actual fighting—then he would truly be accepted as an equal among his comrades. Even so, a secret part of Victor was okay with staying behind to support the unit. He had watched the casualties returning from the unit's forays. Most were gunshot wounds. Some stood out to him, impossible to sweep from his mind—Rifat with his foot missing just above the ankle, Zahid, his once-handsome face mutilated beyond recognition by shrapnel. Victor had also watched his comrades hauling back the awkward bundles wrapped in rugs, draperies or whatever had been available. One of them had been Karam, who had taken to Victor and kindly helped him learn the many little things that improved one's chances of survival, even though in the end it hadn't worked for him.

Two from their unit had not returned. These were ones who died in open streets under heavy fire and who had to be left behind, although the men would take great risks to retrieve their comrades' bodies if at all possible.

Victor wondered about the circumstances around his brother Saif's death. He had overheard his brother's name mentioned at one point. He had not yet revealed that he was Saif's brother. When joining the unit, he used the same fake name he had given the aid group. He was no longer going to blindly trust anyone, not even his comrades in arms.

The unit was comprised mostly of Syrians like Victor, but there were several in his unit from Tunisia and one from Chechnya. Some members were gregarious, attracting groups of boisterous followers who would swap stories and carry on till late at night. Others said little and kept to themselves. Victor fell into the latter group, although he would often sit just outside a circle of his comrades to listen in on their conversations.

Nabil signaled to Victor that break was over. Nabil was one of the older men in their unit. He acted as cook, procurer of food, and medic, although, having watched Nabil work with their wounded, Victor wondered as to the extent of his medical training. Besides Nabil, there were two others from the unit who also remained at base camp. Their job was to help guard supplies. Victor slowly got to his feet and went into the kitchen to help with dinner preparations.

When the rest of the unit returned that evening, two additional casualties had thinned their ranks. After dinner, their unit leader called Victor over and told him that he was to join their expedition the next day. He explained that they were working to dislodge the militia that held control of the nearby town, which, if successful, would open the strategic highway running through this quarter of Syria. Victor was given a rifle that would now become his responsibility.

That night, Victor lay awake many hours, being equal parts exhilarated and terrified. He was determined to do his part and help his unit achieve their objective. Over the past several months, this group of men had become his family. He felt willing to die to protect his brothers, knowing they would do the same for him. He was determined not to embarrass himself. Part of his being here was to honor the memory of his brother.

There was a part of Victor that questioned their fighting. When he joined the militia, he thought they would be fighting the Assad Regime. Instead they had been fighting ISIS and were receiving tactical support from the Americans, which helped in turning the tide against the extremists.

With ISIS close to being expelled from their section of Syria, Victor thought they would strike out once more against Assad. Instead, they were now battling another rebel group, the group that had originally tried to recruit Victor when he and Kamar were living in a refugee settlement. Their unit leader talked about why it was important to defeat this group. Victor had not understood the ideologies and grievances that their leader was so passionate about. While Victor detested the rival group, he suspected the fighting was mostly a power struggle as to which group would control this section of Syria and have access to its resources. In Victor's mind, the two groups fighting against each other made them less of a threat to Assad.

Victor must have finally found sleep, because Saad was shaking his shoulder, telling him to get ready. Saad, at seventeen, was the second youngest in the unit after Victor.

Many times, Victor had witnessed this morning routine. Now,

at last, he was a participant. While evenings at base camp were often noisy and animated, mornings were subdued, quiet. Morning prayers and breakfast took place with a bare minimum of conversation. Weapons were re-checked, packs were readied. A small group of the unit's elders were gathered around the leader, finalizing plans that had been discussed and debated the previous evening.

An outside observer would be surprised at how quickly the group was packed and ready. This was a tight-knit unit where all knew their roles and could execute them in quick, silent efficiency. As they set off, Victor fell in alongside Saad, near the end of the procession. During the operation, the two of them would form the rear guard.

They timed their march to coincide with the first glimmer of dawn, hiking the mile to the edge of town and arriving just as their surroundings were becoming clearly visible in the morning light. Here they connected with another unit that had camped in town to help maintain their hold over the section already under their control.

The town was bisected by the main highway serving this region, its wide street creating a no man's land covered by machine gun posts from both rebel groups. The residents of the town had all fled the fighting.

Victor and Saad followed their unit down a side street several blocks into town. As they neared the center, the homes and stores stood closer together, sharing exterior walls. The men entered one of the homes through its front doorway, which was missing its door. They proceeded into the living room and then stepped through a hole that had been punched or blasted through the wall right into the neighboring home. From there, they crossed to another hole, which led to a store that had been emptied of almost all its wares. In this fashion, they proceeded through a maze of connected buildings that was clearly familiar to the rest of Victor's unit. This allowed the soldiers to travel through the town while avoiding open streets, where one risked being shot at. Finally, they emerged on a narrow street. Checking for snipers, they crossed the street one at a time, then disappeared into another maze of connected buildings. No one talked, and communications were via hand signals.

Eventually, they reached the edge of the main street through town. Here they joined others from their militia who were dispersed down several blocks along their side of the highway, having taken up strategic positions facing off against the opposing group. Today they had concentrated their units with the objective of breaching the highway and taking out the other militia's machine gun posts, giving them control of the highway. This would create the bridge needed for their militia to complete a sweep of the town. For the moment, they were waiting for the last unit that would be joining the operation.

Victor and Saad took up their post, which was several rooms back along the passage they had taken that morning. This room contained a damaged sofa and two matching armchairs. A framed family photo hung on the wall near where a second one had fallen and cracked. This had clearly been someone's living room. They pulled the two armchairs into strategic positions from which they could look out the front window and see the side street in both directions as well as having a clear view into the next adjacent room along the maze. They had their rifles out and ready. The street, like the town in general, was deserted.

There was time, as they sat, to chat quietly. Saad asked Victor where he was from. So, Victor told him about his mother being killed in the bombing of Aleppo and his escape with his uncle and younger sister, first to Hama, then to Lebanon where his uncle had died. He told Saad about reconnecting with his father, but not fitting in while living in Beirut.

Saad's story was not too dissimilar. He was from the city of

Homs, and his family escaped during the siege of their city. He had been living in a settlement in Turkey for several years before coming of age and joining this militia.

Saad was starting to relate the story of his journey back into Syria, when Victor waved him into silence. Someone was approaching up the street. The figure was moving with an uneven gait and looked a bit stooped. As the figure drew closer, it became apparent that this was a grandmother. Victor and Saad had heard stories of snipers or saboteurs disguising themselves as women or children, so they trained their rifles on the approaching figure. The figure walked past their window without looking up, and before either of them had time to react, walked straight in through the front door.

It was then that she looked over and saw Victor and Saad. She was definitely a grandmother. Ignoring the rifles pointed straight at her chest, she walked over to examine the hole blasted through the wall and exclaimed, "What have you done to my house!"

Saad lowered his rifle. "You need to leave immediately! This house is not safe. How did you get here?"

"I walked, obviously." She started towards the back of the house, where there was a small dining area and a kitchen. A cabinet sat against the opposite wall. It looked old but was decorated with an intricate Moorish pattern made of walnut and mother of pearl. The lady started searching through drawers, selecting certain papers, photographs, and other small items, which she placed into a bag she had brought with her. She then proceeded upstairs, where Saad and Victor could hear her rummaging. The two rebel soldiers looked at each other, both unsure what they should do about their visitor. Before they could decide on a plan of action, she returned downstairs and walked out the front door. She had taken only a few steps when shots rang out from further down the street. With surprising quickness, she darted back inside.

"We told you that it was not safe to be here," Saad told her, sounding exasperated. But Victor noticed blood coming from her hand and rushed over to her. A bullet had taken off the tip of her index finger. Victor used water from his canteen to wash the injury and then found some clean cloth in a drawer to wrap her hand and stop the bleeding.

The woman seemed unfazed by her injury and more upset that the shot to her hand had caused her to drop her bag. As soon as her hand was wrapped, she headed to the door to retrieve her bag. Victor sprang up and stopped her from going outside. "You could be killed if you go back out there!"

"If God wills it, God wills it. I didn't come all this way to return empty-handed."

"Stay here." Victor commanded, and before Saad could object or the grandmother could respond, Victor sprang out the door and, with youthful quickness, snatched the bag and dove back inside just as the bullets again started to fly.

"Here is your bag." Victor handed it to her. Her stern face broke into a smile of appreciation. "I'm sorry about the hole in your wall. That is the only way we can safely travel through the town. Here, follow me." Victor held out his hand as he helped her step through the hole into her neighbor's home.

The lady clucked her tongue at the sight. Somehow the destruction of her neighbor's home seemed to bother her more than the destruction to her own home. Victor took her through the next hole in the passageway and pointed out the next further hole. "This is as far as I can take you. If you keep following this passage, it will take you to the western outskirts of town where you will be much safer."

She turned to thank Victor, but before she could get the words out, there was a thunderous explosion, and both Victor and the grandmother found themselves on the ground. A cloud of dust and debris came billowing out from the direction where Saad was waiting. Then more explosions, and Victor pulled the grandmother through the hole into the next further room, away from the destruction, where they huddled together.

As the explosions settled, Victor heard the airplanes retreating overhead. They had been so involved with retrieving this woman's bag, that the inexperienced soldiers had missed the planes' approach.

Victor ran back through the openings across the three rooms to where Saad had been. Throwing aside debris and climbing over furniture and collapsed materials from the floor above, he found Saad lying on the floor pinned by a dresser that had come crashing through the ceiling. He checked for a pulse. Minutes ago, they were sharing life stories, and now Saad was gone.

Victor tried to release Saad's body, but the rest of the house was in danger of coming down on top of him, so he made his way over to the hole in the wall that led further on, towards his unit. The next room had been completely destroyed and was unpassable.

Victor knew the planes were Assad's. This was the perfect opportunity for a bombing raid. With one rebel group mounting an offensive against another rebel group, the two armies were concentrated into one drop zone—two birds with one stone. That meant they must have known about the offensive. Someone among their group was a mole for Assad.

This was Victor's first excursion. Now he was alone and cut off from his unit, with no one in command to tell him what to do. He was blocked from moving forward—the side street wasn't safe, and waiting here for more bombs to drop made no sense. Seeing no other viable option, he headed back along the passageway. When he reached the grandmother, she was still sitting on the floor, so he helped her to her feet.

Together, Victor and the grandmother wove their way back through the passageways. Behind them they could hear a second wave of bombing. When they reached the town's edge, it appeared that the grandmother was heading in the same general direction as Victor.

"We have a medic back at camp. He can properly dress your wound," Victor offered. The grandmother agreed to come with Victor. Her name was Rima, Victor found out. She had a large round nose, and kind crinkly eyes. Despite her stoop and slight limp, Rima was a sturdy hiker.

Once they reached the unit's base at the farmhouse, Victor would wait to see who else made it back from his unit. They would tell him what he needed to do next. Would they think he had run away from the bombing?

All was quiet as they approached the farmhouse. This morning they had left only two people behind, Nabil, the medic and cook, and just one guard, Hassan. The unit's leader wanted as much manpower as possible for their offensive.

While Rima waited outside, Victor entered the farmhouse. Other than the distant clucking of chickens, there were no sounds. The stillness didn't feel right. Searching room to room, he spotted a body lying on the kitchen floor. It was Hassan, blood trailing in a line from his head to a pool near the doorway, where flies had started to gather. He had been shot.

With the hairs standing up on the back of his neck, Victor took out his rifle and conducted a complete search of the house. There was no sign of Nabil.

Victor returned outside and explained to Rima what had happened. He checked the entire grounds and outbuildings. Nabil had disappeared. Had he been the informer? If so, he probably killed Hassan and ran. Rima looked up at Victor, a look of concern on her wrinkled face. "Would you like help in preparing his body?" she asked. Victor hadn't thought of that but nodded his head.

No words were spoken. Rima brought Victor a basin of water and then went to search the farmhouse for white cloth while Victor washed the body. Once the body was clean, Victor arranged Hassan's hands across his chest and shrouded the body with the white cloth. Next, he went outside and found a suitable place to dig a grave for Hassan, pulling out his compass to get the proper orientation.

The grave was not as deep as Victor would have liked, but it was the best he could do before sundown. With Rima's help, they managed to bring the body to the gravesite. Victor stood over Hassan's body. He had not gotten to know Hassan. Now he wondered if Hassan still had family, and if so, where they were. Victor bowed and silently prayed, while Rima also prayed, standing a short distance behind Victor. While Victor filled over the grave, Rima found a whitewashed board to serve as a grave marker. Victor took out his knife to etch out Hassan's name and the date of death.

There being nothing further they could do for Hassan, Victor found some food for himself and Rima. When they finished their meal, Rima made to leave, but Victor convinced her to stay the night, as it would soon be dark. Victor kept expecting to see some surviving comrades returning. So far, there was no one.

Victor and Rima sat outside in the cool evening air where they could see the sunset to their left and Victor could watch for returning soldiers to their right. As they sat, they exchanged stories. Victor told her about his home in Aleppo and what had happened to his family, providing more details than he had relayed to Saad, but leaving out the assault on Kamar.

Rima told him that she had grown up on a farm and had moved into town when she married. The house in town was where her husband had grown up, and that's where they raised their family. Her husband had been killed by a sniper's bullet the previous year, so she had moved back to the family farm with her older son, who now ran the operation. Her younger son had joined the rebel army and was killed earlier in the war. Her older son had an injured leg and decided not to fight. He was trying to continue farming despite the war, with limited success, amid requisitions and shortages. But they were able to grow enough food to survive.

Early the next morning, Victor again searched the house and outbuildings. No one from his unit had returned during the night. He sat for a while watching for returning rebels from the east, reluctantly reaching the conclusion that all had been killed in the bombing or captured in the aftermath. Rima took pity on the stunned young soldier and suggested that he come with her to her son's farm. Victor roused himself from his morose thoughts to consider her offer.

He had promised himself never to trust again. But he could see no future in remaining at this farmhouse. The grandmother seemed okay. He knew nothing about her son. What if he turned Victor in as a deserter?

As Victor sat, trying to decide what to do, Rima started singing. It was closer to humming, barely audible, but there was some comfort in hearing her voice. She waited patiently while Victor considered what to do, enjoying the morning coolness and sunshine. Surprising himself, he fell in with this old lady who seemed to channel distant memories of his own grandmother.

Montpellier

Elias was fidgety as they waited for the train to arrive. Kamar didn't notice because she had brought her friend Maisah along, and they were giggling as usual. They were waiting in the modern pointed-arch breezeway above the Montpellier Saint-Roch Station when the announcement came through for the arrival of the Paris train on platform D. Elias beckoned the girls and they descended the escalator just as the train breezed in. The platform quickly became engulfed in passengers, but Kamar's sharp eyes found Yana. The two girls rushed over to the two women, Elias hurrying to keep up with them. Kamar gave Yana an enthusiastic hug and Elias followed with a kiss to each cheek.

Once Ellen had been properly introduced, they made their way to Elias's car. Kamar was filling Yana in on her new school, with Maisah providing embellishments as needed. Yana struggled to catch everything due to her rusty French skills. This left Elias and Ellen, who fell into easy conversation as they walked to the car. He noticed that Ellen appeared to be slightly older than Yana, with a broader frame. Elias could see right away that

Ellen shared Yana's directness and outward awareness, and that the two were well-matched as friends.

Yana and Ellen had picked out a hotel just three blocks from Elias's apartment. Elias dropped them off to get settled, pointing out his apartment, so they could come over when ready to head out to dinner.

Elias let the girls choose the restaurant, a cozy spot in Écusson, Montpellier's historic quarter. The restaurant served a playful cuisine that did justice to Montpellier's fresh, local produce.

Seated outside at a table fit snugly along the narrow, medieval street, their dinner was a relaxed, lingering affair. There was much to catch up on—Elias's new job, reconnecting with his father's family, Kamar's new school, and their newly adopted city. Maisah had come along as well, so she shared some of her story and background. Her family had immigrated to France from Algeria several years ago. They joined relatives who had immigrated in the sixties following Algeria's War of Independence. Ellen and Yana swapped stories from their many years of working together. The only sad point in the evening was the acknowledgment that they had not received any updates from Victor.

For a time, Elias fell silent so he could survey the group and soak in their animated discussion, trying to imprint the scene in his memory. It felt like family, even though the only person he was related to was Kamar. He needed to figure out how to arrange some time with Yana alone so they would have an opportunity to discuss whether there was any possibility of a future between them. Better to do that towards the end of their visit. Allow France plenty of time to work its spell.

Towards the end of the evening, they discussed plans for the six days Yana and Ellen had allotted for Montpellier. Being new to his position, Elias was only able to arrange two days off, in addition to the weekend. The girls, however, had the week off due to the All Saints' Holiday. Yana and Ellen asked them if they would be willing to provide a tour of the shops and restaurants within Écusson, and they enthusiastically agreed. So that was set up for one of the days when Elias had to work.

Elias suggested that for one of the days he was free, they do the hike to the top of Pic Saint-Loup that he and Kamar had done when they first arrived in Montpellier. They could bring a picnic lunch and spend the afternoon visiting the town of Saint-Guilhem-le-Désert. Ellen and Yana liked that idea, so they decided to do that the next day.

The next morning Elias was up early and out buying grapes, oranges, cold cuts, cheese, and baguettes, all fresh for their picnic. Ellen and Yana, having spent the better part of the previous day dragging their suitcases about and sitting on trains, were looking forward to the hike and fresh air.

As they drove north towards Pic Saint-Loup, Ellen and Yana enjoyed seeing the vineyards and farms that stretched up the rolling hills. Elias pointed out that their region, Languedoc, bordered Provence, and that, like Provence, it enjoyed a Mediterranean climate, proximity to the coast, and a thriving viniculture, but with less sophistication and pretense.

On their hike up the peak, Yana felt a twinge of guilt, as Ellen gamely walked ahead with the chattering girls, leaving Elias and Yana to follow in their wake. But it was a chance to talk more candidly about how Kamar was doing. "Remarkably well, considering all she's been through," Elias confided. "She's resilient. Her counselor said that sometimes outward resiliency is part of the individual's survival response to an extreme crisis, especially when aspects of that crisis are too horrible to face. As I understand it, the goal in counseling is to provide Kamar with an environment where she can, at her own pace, face and process what's happened to her and to her mother and brothers. Otherwise, if it's just buried, it can resurface later and create serious problems."

"That makes total sense to me. She does seem to be doing well. You've created a safe place for her to work through all this."

"Her friendship with Maisah helps a lot. I know Maisah acts silly, but she's well-grounded and serious about school. One advantage that the immigrant kids have over those raised here is that they've seen both sides of life and are not complacent about the opportunities they have in a country like France. There's no sense of entitlement."

Talking of Kamar brought to Yana's mind thoughts of Victor—the danger he faced hung over them like a specter. Yana wanted to talk to Elias about Victor but couldn't think of anything to say. There was no news, so he remained a blank, as if a section of your retina was damaged and you had a patch in your vision where there was nothing to see. Instead she asked what Elias had heard recently from Sami and Amena.

"I think they may come to visit next year. After their trip to Lebanon last year, they weren't able to take any long trips this year."

"How nice it will be to spend time with them in more positive circumstances."

"Yes, a welcome change." They climbed a particularly steep portion of the trail, and as they stopped to catch their breaths, Elias changed subjects. "Yana is, I think, an unusual name in the U.S.? Where did your name come from?"

Yana surveyed the section of trail they'd climbed so far. "I was named after my grandmother on my mother's side. She was Jewish from Slovakia. It means 'He answers.' It's also an ancient Persian name that means doer of good toward others."

"Now that fits." Elias smiled as they continued their climb. "But I have news for you. Yana is a Syrian name as well, and there it means water lady."

"Water lady? Not sure what I think about that. Well, I have one more to add to the list. Yana is also a Native American name, from the Cherokees."

"What does it mean in Cherokee, dare I ask?"

Yana stopped again to turn squarely towards Elias in mock defiance. "Bear!"

"And, are you a bear as well?"

"Perhaps you'll need to wait and see." With a mischievous smile, Yana resumed hiking.

At this point Kamar stopped to look back at Yana and Elias, hands on her hips. "You guys are slow!" Yana and Elias picked up their pace to rejoin the others.

A short while later they reached the top and sat in the dry grass to enjoy the view. Today, a blanket of clouds covered the lowlands towards the Mediterranean coast, penetrating inland along the valleys, and isolating the higher elevations as scattered peninsulas and islands. A pair of Bonelli's eagles were circling effortlessly in the updraft off the south-facing cliff, their whitish torsos and necks offset by darker markings on their wings.

Elias started to unpack their picnic, which they spread out on a thin, blue-and-white checkered tablecloth. As she sampled some grapes, Yana thought to herself that, although she missed the lush green of the Pacific Northwest, she could perhaps get used to this place.

After hiking back down to their car, they continued on to Saint-Guilhem-le-Désert. The village is impossibly squeezed into a slender valley between steep limestone rock formations. They wandered the medieval town's stone lanes, visiting a ninth-century Benedictine abbey with its peaceful cloister and gardens.

On the drive home, Ellen and Yana chatted with Kamar and Maisah about their plans for their tour of Écusson the next day while Elias would be at work. Elias smiled to himself, vicariously enjoying Kamar's and Maisah's excitement, while sneaking glances at Yana seated next to him.

Seattle

Having just returned home from her short business trip to Paris, Maria Burns was in a crappy mood. Business travel, especially international travel, had seemed so sexy when her career was first taking off. Now it was exhausting and infuriating. Even staying at five-star hotels, she had to be on constant alert to make sure they actually delivered on all the perks they promised. And rental cars were such a hassle. She had gold-tier status with her rental company, which was supposed to mean she could skip the lines and go directly to pick out her car. She could understand that service not being available at a small-town airport, but in Paris? She had been incensed at having to wait in line with everyone else. Didn't they realize what it was like for people like her who had to travel all the time?

But those things didn't matter right now. Her first priority was to get to the bottom of what was going on with this bitch, Yana Pickering. Who was she? And why the hell was she following her around snapping photos and trying to frame her?

The obvious place to start was Facebook, and bingo! There she was. Not much of interest on her site—mostly crap. But one useful bit of data—she worked for King County. That was interesting. In their crime lab, no less.

Maria sat at her computer thinking. Now, why would someone like Pickering get involved in trying to frame her? What was the connection? The only thing that connected Maria to crime labs was the embezzlement incident with that stupid trans lady. But that was with the Seattle Police Department, not the county. Then Maria remembered. Even though the investigation was done by the Seattle Police, the evidence was handled through the King County Crime Lab. For economic reasons, Seattle contracted with King County instead of maintaining their own lab. So, would this Pickering lady have access to cases from the Seattle Police Department? If so, she might have come across the embezzlement case. But, why would she care about that? It didn't make any sense.

Maria knew who might be able to help her get to the bottom of this. As part of her work with the county, she had become friends with Marty Anderson, head administrator over the county's law enforcement division. She decided it was time to pull in some favors he owed her.

Strange things had been happening lately, and not just the photos. Margret's information about Kara snooping around her office and going through her desk drawers was mystifying. Margret thought she was being sly by pretending to let the information slip accidentally, but she was so obvious. She thought she was clever, that file clerk. She had no idea what it took to make it as a woman in the world of business, no idea what Maria had been through.

Was there a connection to this Pickering lady? Margret hinted, in what she probably thought was a discreet manner, that she might have additional information on what Kara was up to, but Maria was not biting. That lady didn't know what she was talking about most of the time. Maria was not giving any special favors.

At any rate, she couldn't have an AA that snoops, so she would need to figure out a way to get Kara fired as well. Shame, because Maria liked her and thought her to be moderately competent, unlike the usual halfwits they hired. She couldn't deal with Kara now, though. They had just fired an AA. It would look bad to have another sacked so soon. Maria would need to keep a close eye on her in the meantime.

Montpellier

Yana hated to see her week in Montpellier draw to a close, as they were having such an enjoyable visit. Everywhere they went, watching the girls' bubbly enthusiasm was like being able to enjoy each museum, restaurant, and landmark twice. The girls especially enjoyed being on the lookout for Montpellier's creative and vibrant street art, while Yana's favorite was wandering the maze of narrow, centuries-old streets and discovering small cafes hiding in the nooks of the soft sandstone buildings. This was nothing like Seattle, where a hundred-year-old building was considered ancient.

Elias had been a terrific host, devoting himself to showing them the best of Montpellier, without being domineering or trying to over-engineer things. Well, maybe he did over-engineer things just a bit, but he was quick to back off when others expressed a need to chill.

Tonight, their last night in Montpellier, Ellen was taking the girls to dinner and a play. Yana was, at last, having a serious amount of alone time with Elias. She didn't know where they were going, as Elias had made all the arrangements.

Did Yana want this to become a serious relationship? There was no doubt she was attracted to Elias, and she definitely respected him. So, yes, the impractical side of her did want things to be serious. But her practical side kept butting in with, she had to admit, very practical concerns, the top of which was the problem of geography. And there was also a part of her that wanted to keep her comfortable, less-complicated, single existence. But if that was true, why was she here? On the one hand, she didn't want to be guilty of stringing Elias along. On the other hand, they had made no commitments to each other, and she would never make a commitment out of obligation. Perhaps this was simply an extended and very expensive date?

It was a lovely evening—warm for October. Yana had packed her little black dress as her one dressier outfit for the trip. As an accent, she added the silk scarf she had picked up while in Paris. A pair of earrings completed the look.

Elias picked her up at five, and they headed into the city. Throughout their visit, they made extensive use of public transport. But tonight, Elias was driving. Their first stop was for an aperitif at one of Montpellier's top wine bars. The French are passionate about their pre-dinner ritual of sharing wine and appetizers with friends, and this seemed especially true in Montpellier. The restaurant's light tan stone walls enclosed its dining spaces with low, broad arches that set the atmosphere of long-held traditions and intimate, relaxed friendships. While enjoying a sampling of wines, along with various cheeses, tapenade, and smoked salmon, they recalled the week just spent, laughing over the reactions and antics of Kamar and Maisah.

"Elias, I've had a fantastic time here. Thanks so much for welcoming us to your city."

Elias had been looking for an opportunity to put into words what he was feeling about Yana and his foolish hope that she'd consider joining him in Montpellier. This seemed like the perfect moment.

Elias reached out for Yana's hand. A waiter behind Yana was balancing a circular tray in his right hand as he leaned over the next table to make room for the wine-sampler he was serving. A sudden movement from the lady at the next table unbalanced the waiter. Elias watched in horrified slow motion as the tray began tipping. The waiter made a desperate attempt to steady it with his free hand. Instead he knocked the tray over, sending the wine-sampler down Yana's head and left shoulder.

Yana jumped from her seat as wine glasses hit the brick floor and shattered. Waitstaff rushed in from all directions, all talking at once. They brought Yana clean dish towels to blot the wine from her hair, neck, and dress. Her scarf, stained with red wine, appeared beyond repair. While their table was changed out and the floor mopped up, Yana retreated to the lady's room to try to make her hair and dress presentable. She was able to soak up most of the wine from her dress but asked for a bag to hold her stained scarf. Yana and Elias were offered a refresh of food and wine for their table, but at this point they were ready to move on.

Back in the car, Elias asked Yana if she wanted to return to her hotel. For a moment, she considered it. What she really wanted at that point was a shower and clean set of clothes. But then she thought of the planning Elias had put into the evening. She sensed Elias's anxiety that the evening would be a loss. "Nonsense. This is our last night here, so let's not let this spoil things. But you might not want to be out with a woman who smells like a wine shop, and I'd understand if you felt that way."

"No, of course not." Elias started driving to the restaurant he had picked out for their dinner.

They arrived at the restaurant a bit ahead of their reservations but were still able to be seated quickly. Their conversation felt forced as they tried to resettle. The accident left Elias anxious that nothing else should go wrong with this evening he had been anticipating all week. Yana felt uncomfortable in a dress that was still slightly damp on one shoulder. Their waiter tried to hide it, but Yana could tell he was reacting to the strong smell of wine emanating from her head. Once they had placed their orders, Yana's thoughts turned to what waited for her back home. "I'm dreading a bit returning home."

"Oh really. Why is that?" Elias dared to hope that Yana was about to share that she wanted to stay in Montpellier.

"I don't know. This trip has been great. And it will be nice to be back home. It's just that there were some things that came up right before I left that have me a bit worried."

"What has you worried?" Elias tried to hide his disappointment that her reason for dreading her return was not because she wanted to stay in Montpellier.

"It's a long, complicated story."

"Well, we have all evening. Perfect for a long, complicated story."

Yana started to tell Elias about Emma's appearance in her front yard, about her coming to Christmas Eve dinner. How she had looked up Emma's file at the crime lab, all about their attempt to uncover Burns' conflict-of-interest violation, what took place at the restaurant when they tried to stake out Burns, how Burns had sidestepped the accusation, and finally about what happened at the airport right before flying out to France.

As Yana finished her story, she realized Elias had gone quiet. She looked over at him—his expression was unreadable. Perhaps he was still recovering from the incident with the wine. "I shouldn't have taken up all our time with this."

"No, that's fine." Elias was concentrating on his plate. "I don't understand, though, why you got involved with this attorney. She didn't really have any connection to you."

Yana started feeling defensive. "Well, she had nearly destroyed Emma's career. I felt protective of her."

"But Emma's not really connected to you either. And clearly, she has some issues she's dealing with."

"What sort of issues?"

Elias hesitated, before setting down his knife and fork, and looking directly back at Yana. "Well, this business about trying to change your gender. I confess to not understand it."

"I'm not sure I understand it either. But it sounds like this makes you uncomfortable?"

The wait staff came by to refill waters, and they paused in uncomfortable silence until they were alone again.

Elias sighed. "I can understand that people might be attracted to people of their own gender. That's part of their psychological make up, and I accept that it's something innate to each individual. But gender is a physical fact. To use an analogy, if a person believes that he or she is a dog, not a human, it doesn't make it so. They would still be a human, even if they believed themselves to be a dog."

Yana was taken aback. She tried to remain calm. "Since Emma landed in my front yard, I've done a fair amount of reading on this topic. I've come to understand that one's sense of gender goes beyond physical anatomy. What these people are saying is that one's sense of gender is also innate to the individual. Not something they can change or control."

Elias did not respond. After a few moments, Yana continued. "Elias, I don't claim to understand this whole gender thing, and from what I've read, neither does science at this point. What's clear to me is that these people are the way they are because that's who they are, not because they've been damaged, or abused, or are trying to gain attention. So, while I don't understand it, one thing I'm sure of—I will respect, support, and protect their right to be the person they feel they are and to pursue their life and personal happiness in the way that *they* choose for themselves."

After an uncomfortable pause, Yana added, "and I think I'm ready to head back to my hotel."

The drive back passed in painful silence punctuated by attempts from both parties to fill the void with safe topics. They ended up discussing French politics and what France was trying to achieve with regard to improvements in national health care, but neither of them could muster any real interest in the topic.

After dropping Yana off, Elias returned home, collapsed onto the sofa, and stared into the space in front of him, his eyes not focused on anything. How had this evening that started so promising gone so horribly wrong? It was clear that he had destroyed any chance that their relationship would become what he had dreamed it could be. He tried to tell himself that it was okay. He had good employment. He had Kamar to look after. He was settled into a wonderful corner of France. Now, all of that seemed robbed of color. He felt angry. He was always the one to help others. Why was there no opportunity for him to pursue happiness?

Kamar was not yet home. They must still be at the play. Elias's evening had ended sooner than planned. Feeling unanchored, he got up and started sorting through the mail he had picked up earlier but had dumped on the counter in his rush to get ready for the evening. He discovered a letter addressed to him from Lebanon. He ripped it open. It was from one of his contacts in the Syrian Community in Beirut, someone Elias had considered a friend during his brief stay in the city.

Elias,

I'm am sorry to bring you this news regarding Victor. I have word that the unit he was assigned to was ambushed in an air attack by Syrian government forces. The report is that everyone in his unit was killed, with no survivors.

Please accept my sincere condolences. If I hear of any additional information, I will certainly let you know. In the meantime, please let me know if there is anything I can do to help.

Elias collapsed back onto the couch. Almost everything he cared about had been taken from him. If it were not for Kamar who still needed him, he would have no reason to continue. The rift that had sprung between himself and Yana wrenched at him as he realized he had no one who could comfort him in this loss. Kamar was still a child.

This is how Ellen, Kamar, and Maisah found him when they arrived home a short while later. Hearing the others entering the apartment, Elias tried to pull himself together. As they entered the room, he beckoned Kamar to the couch and placed his arm across her shoulders. "Kamar, my dearest child, I have very sad news to tell you. Victor is dead."

Western Syria

Taking a break from his pruning work, Victor sat in the shade of a pistachio tree, removed his hat so he could wipe the sweat off his forehead, and took a drink from his canteen. As Victor rested, he stared up the line of trees, like soldiers on parade, marching up a gentle incline and ending near the dry rock outcropping that marked the beginnings of the foothills and the distant mountains beyond.

He thought about the day he first arrived at this farm with Rima. It was clear her son Mahdi had kept a worried lookout for his mother's return. Mahdi had forbidden Rima from making her dangerous trip into town, but the determined grandmother had defied her son, sneaking out of the house before the first light of morning. As Rima and Victor walked up the dusty one-lane road towards their small cluster of buildings the following morning, Mahdi hurried to meet them, walking as fast as his limp would allow. He was a tall man with a muscular, lanky build, his dark hair and beard showing the first signs of gray. He looked from Rima to Victor, his weathered face showing alarm at seeing the militia soldier accompanying his mother.

Rima waved her hand at her son, dismissing his alarm. Seeing the bandaged hand, Mahdi became even more agitated. "What has happened to your hand? Has this man harmed you?" Rima calmly relayed their story, how Victor and his comrade had been using her house as a lookout, how he had shown her kindness, in fact, risked his life to keep her from foolishly retrieving her bag from the street with its sniper, how they had spent the night at their base camp, and that none of Victor's unit had returned.

After hearing their story, Mahdi's tone changed completely. He asked Rima to take Victor back to their farmhouse so he could have something to eat and a place to rest before going on his way. But Victor had no interest in resting. "Tell me what I can do," he insisted. And that's how it ended up that Mahdi put Victor to work from the very moment he stepped onto the farm.

This farm work was nothing like the work he and Kamar had done while living in the refugee settlement. There, they did the most menial of jobs, requiring no skill and under constant criticism from their farmer-employer. Here, Victor felt part of a team, for everyone in the household—Rima, Mahdi, Mahdi's wife, Jamal, and their four children—worked together to keep the farm productive.

Today, Victor was pruning pistachio trees. It turned out Victor was a quick study when it came to plants. He surprised himself by taking to farming naturally, despite having grown up a city boy. Mahdi was his tutor. He would demonstrate to Victor what needed to be done, at each step drawing from his ancient store of insight into the world of trees. Then he calmly allowed Victor to follow, gently adjusting and teaching as they went.

Each type of tree had its own temperament—how often they needed to be watered, how tolerant they were of soggy soil, how tolerant they were of drought, the extent and type of soil amendments needed, how and when to prune, when to harvest, how to protect and store the harvest.

In addition to their primary crops of pistachios, olives, and apricots, Mahdi kept a small herd of goats and a few cows and donkeys. Their vegetable garden was for their own table, and each summer they canned and stored a sufficient amount to get them to the next harvest.

Mahdi, with his limp, needed Victor. The war had taken all the healthy, young laborers. Fuel was scarce and expensive, so sweat had replaced machine whenever possible. Seed was also becoming prohibitively expensive. Mahdi told Victor they were fortunate to be orchardists, as they only had to worry about replanting their family garden each year. But orchards needed watering through the long, dry summer. Although the Orontes River was not far from their farm, it was getting harder to run irrigation pumps due to fuel shortages. Mahdi's solution was to replace the pump engines with wind power, but his crudely constructed wind turbines required building material, also scarce.

Victor relished the physical labor and long workdays. There was much to learn, and the hard work kept his mind focused. He also looked forward to evenings at the farmhouse. To Victor's young, hard-worked appetite, Jamal's cooking seemed impossibly good. Their dinners were boisterous family affairs with their four children, the older two being girls and the younger two, boys. Unused to strangers in their home, the two boys were at first wary, peering out at the strange young man from behind their mother. In no time, they discovered Victor was quite harmless and after dinner each night would climb all over him, wrestling around him like two bear cubs on the mats that they spread out in their courtyard near their large stone fireplace. When the boys became too rambunctious, Jamal would sternly send them off to bed and Mahdi would discuss with Victor the work they would tackle the following day.

At night, Victor slept like a stone. If he dreamed, he remembered nothing upon waking.

War had claimed the Syrian educational system as one of its many victims. School attendance had been nearly universal. Now only a minority of kids were able to attend. As for Mahdi and Jamal's family, the local primary school was still intact, and the two boys would attend whenever a teacher was available. Their secondary school was in town and had been destroyed in the fighting three years ago. Marya and her younger sister, Rasha, were being homeschooled. The local primary school currently had a teacher, so the two boys attended school each day.

Despite the abundance of work to be done on the farm, Jamal was adamant that mornings be set aside for school. This was challenging because Rima had never attended school and Jamal had only completed grade eight. Nonetheless, they enforced a strict regimen of reading, math, and history, using their limited resources, including some books that had been salvaged and distributed when the town's library had been bombed.

As autumn inched towards winter, there were days when the farm workload slackened enough to allow Victor to spend some mornings helping the girls with their schoolwork. Although Victor was only a year older than Marya, his schooling had seen less disruption.

Victor could tell Marya was smart, despite the deprivations in her schooling. Yet, she seemed to need a lot of help with her schoolwork on those mornings when he stayed in. After a few days of this, Jamal started intervening to provide Marya help instead, sending Victor off to help Rasha.

Victor's life flowed easily from one day to the next, swept along in the busy current of farm and family life. He occasionally thought about the militia he had been part of. He should try to reconnect, find a new unit, but he wasn't ready to do that yet. That belonged to the future, which was conveniently out of focus. Victor had no inclination to peer out beyond his daily existence for resolution.

He thought about his sister and father. He would have called them if he still had his phone. Mahdi had a phone, and Victor was sure Mahdi would let him borrow it. But there was no coverage in the vicinity of the farm, and it wasn't safe for Victor to be seen wandering about. Perhaps it was just as well. Elias and Kamar were better off moving forward with their own lives.

Seattle

After four weeks back home, Yana's recent trip continued to darken her mood just as the gray December clouds darkened the city. Her conversation with Elias on their last night in Montpellier weighed on her. On further reflection, she realized she perhaps could have allowed him a bit of slack. She knew she couldn't consider an intimate relationship with someone who rejected an entire group of people because their belief system or who they were didn't fit one's own beliefs. But she didn't think Elias was that type of person. She'd seen the way he cared for others, even when his own life had gone horribly wrong.

Elias likely didn't have exposure to transgender people when he was growing up. She imagined his time as a resident in New York was an eye opener. Perhaps he had been shocked by some of what he saw, just as his father, during his medical studies, had been shocked by what he had seen in Paris.

She had hoped for a further discussion with Elias the next morning, after they both had a little time to reflect on what had been said. That became impossible after hearing the news of Victor's death. It had been clear Elias was feeling terrible when he dropped her off that night. And then to be hit with the devasting news regarding Victor when he was already down. She wanted to comfort the poor man. That would have been possible twenty-four hours earlier but not after their exchange that last night in Montpellier. When Elias took them to the train station the next morning, they were all formalities and discomfort.

The previous evening, when Ellen returned to the hotel from watching their play, Yana had simply told her the evening had not gone well. Yana was too tired and too upset to go into details. On the long train ride to Paris, Yana filled Ellen in on all that had taken place. She knew she was fortunate to have Ellen to commiserate with about her now-not-so-mysterious French-Middle-Eastern physician. Who did Elias have to talk to? She wasn't sure how much he had confided in Sami about his relationship with Yana, or whether Sami could be as supporting to him, so separated by geography.

Yana pondered all this as she rode her bus into work, staring out the window into the rain-soaked, early-December darkness. It had been over a year since Emma landed in her front yard. What a year it had been.

First thing on her calendar this morning was a meeting with her supervisor, Ron, head of the crime lab and forensics. She entered his office wondering why they were meeting, as he hadn't provided an agenda when he sent the meeting invite. Ron was also a long-time employee of the county, and Yana got along well with him. Yana wondered if she had been more career-driven, would she be holding his position instead of Ron? She had slightly more seniority. But Yana always made a point to end work each workday and be fully home for her family. Certainly, her gender also played a role in her lack of advancement. Law enforcement was a male-dominated field, and at the time she was rising up through the ranks, there wasn't as much attention paid to removing glass ceilings as there is now.

Still, Yana liked Ron, and they had a mutual respect and friendship based on many years of working together. As Yana sat down opposite Ron's desk, he got up to close his office door.

"Closed door? This looks serious! What's up?" Yana was teasing Ron. She knew her work for the crime lab was excellent, and she felt quite secure with her standing within the county.

Ron looked uncomfortable—his face reddened a bit. "Yana, I'll get right to the point. Did you have a professional reason for examining the file for Edward Rossi?"

Yana was stunned, caught completely off guard. Why was Ron asking her about this? Why would anyone bother to check that she had accessed that file? She didn't see any choice other than to answer truthfully. "No, it wasn't related to a work assignment. What is this about?"

"I was so hoping you could provide an explanation. Can you tell me why you accessed the file?"

"Why? Ron, what's going on?"

"Look Yana. I don't know what's going on, but Marty came to me, head of law enforcement—"

"I know who Marty is," Yana interrupted impatiently.

"Well, he had already looked up on our system that you had accessed the file, and he asked me if you had a legitimate reason for doing so. If I can't come up with one, he said you're out of here."

"What?!"

"Legally, he can do that. It's in our policy. You can be fired for unauthorized access."

"Oh, come on! Surely a warning, or something disciplinary."

"My hands are tied on this. That's why I'm hoping you can provide a reason to convince Marty not to have you fired."

Yana relayed to Ron the entire story, starting with the incident in her front yard a year ago, the subsequent visit from Emma, and then wanting to check out why there was no police action on her case. She left out the part about trying to prove Burns' conflict of interest, sensing that those details wouldn't help her case.

Ron looked disappointed. "Yana, please answer honestly. Is this the only time you've accessed a file without authorization?"

"Yes!" she replied without hesitation.

"I'll see what I can do with Marty. Normally this wouldn't come close to having someone fired, especially someone with your tenure. But, as I said, according to our policy he would be within his rights, and if he insists, I won't have a choice. He seems determined to fire you, and I have no idea why that is."

Yana knew it would be no good. If Marty was determined to have her fired, and she had nothing to offer Ron that would justify her access of Emma's file, she could see no way out. "What do you need me to do in the meantime?"

Ron looked even more uncomfortable. "Actually, there's nothing for you to do. Marty is also insisting that I place you on administrative leave until this is resolved."

"What?"

"I'm sorry, Yana. I don't have a choice. You can collect what you need from your desk, and then I need to escort you from the premises and take your access card."

"Ron, are you kidding me?"

"I would never kid you about something like this. I'm so sorry, Yana."

There being few buses serving the reverse commute out of the central business district in the early morning, Yana took an Uber home. As she rode home, she thought and thought. Burns does legal work for the county. She had to be behind this. How else would their head administrator have the time or inclination to question one specific access to their system, among the hundreds of legitimate accesses that Yana made? There was no other way in which that particular transaction would have stood out.

Once home, Yana made tea, not knowing what else to do. She had never felt more out of place in her own home. What was she doing here in the middle of a workday? Yana always kept a long list of home chores and projects that she could never get to. Now she had this empty canvas of time, but she couldn't bring herself to work on anything. She couldn't focus. Under it all was a burning, visceral hatred for Burns. That horrible lady. How many lives was she going to mess up?

At last she called Ellen. "We need to talk. Are you free?"

They agreed to meet at Volunteer Park for a walk, despite the weather. Yana needed to get outside and get her body moving to burn off some of her stress. What a friend Ellen was, to drop what she was doing and join Yana for a walk in the December wind and rain. Ellen was suitably indignant with Marty for wanting Yana fired and with Ron for not standing up more for Yana. "What are you going to do?" Ellen asked as they ducked into the steamy Volunteer Park Conservatory to check out their exotic plants and take a break from the rain.

Yana could take that question many different directions. What was she going to do about Burns? What was she going to do about her career? What was she going to do about her life?

She was reminded of the first and only time she had tried kayaking. She had ventured out into Lake Union thinking this would be a grand adventure, and had inadvertently wandered into the passage lane between the Mountlake Cut to the east, which leads to the much larger Lake Washington, and the locks to the west, which lead to Puget Sound. The lane was filled with boats bigger and faster than hers, and she was struggling to stay clear of them. Not knowing which direction to go, she sat, stalled by indecision, until the wake from a large fisheries research vessel almost splashed over the side of her kayak. She realized she just needed to move, to get out of the way. She did the only thing that made sense, which was to head back to where she had started. It was then that she realized that the most interesting stuff to explore in a kayak was close in, along the shoreline.

In her present situation, her life was being tossed about, but she saw no obvious default direction in which to head. Her life plan was built on her continuing to work for the King County Crime Lab until she retired. It had always felt like a secure foundation, and she was getting closer to the finish line. Now, in an instant, everything had changed. She had no idea of what else she might do. She certainly wasn't ready to retire.

She thought about the pain she had caused Elias. And then there was Emma. She couldn't bear the thought that she might have jeopardized Emma's career, because if Burns had traced her to the King County Crime Lab and the fact that she had accessed Emma's file, she must have already concluded that Emma played a part in the attempt to expose her conflict of interest with the county.

As Yana shared her concerns regarding Emma's career with Ellen, she realized she needed to warn Emma. She had been thinking that, should she really end up fired, she shouldn't say anything to Emma in case Emma would blame herself for the firing. Now, after thinking things through, it became clear that Emma should at least be warned so that, if Burns tried to sabotage her career in some way, she wouldn't be blindsided. She needed to set up some time to talk to Emma.

Western Syria

F arming, along with the family life that surrounded the farm, were restoring Victor, incrementally, one day at a time. Victor liked not having to think about anything other than the day at hand. What work did they need to accomplish today? What was the weather doing? What would Jamal fix for dinner tonight? Would there be an opportunity to steal a few minutes alone with Marya? Winter brought with it more free time. It also meant they were inside more and surrounded by family members. All the activity kept Victor occupied so that he didn't have time to think about either the future or the past.

He wasn't consciously aware of it, but one of the reasons why his relationship with Mahdi flowed naturally was that Mahdi reminded him of his father, the same calm, gentle authority. Sometimes, when they were working together in the orchards, Mahdi would ask Victor about his life in Aleppo, his family, his neighborhood, what he liked or disliked about living in the city, about the bombing that took away his mother.

As time went on, Mahdi gently lifted the lid on Victor's experience as a refugee, asking at first simple questions about the geographic route they had taken, the wildlife they had spotted on their journey, the weather they had encountered. Over the weeks, they eventually reached Victor's time in Beirut and how he was treated there. The part that didn't add up, in Mahdi's view, was why Victor had abandoned his chance to get out of Lebanon with his father and chose instead to return to the war. Mahdi had an accurate read of Victor by this time, and he knew Victor was not inclined towards the military.

One clear, cold winter afternoon, having finished their day's work early, they hiked up the nearest foothill and sat in a grassy section near the top to look out across the patchwork of farms, rock formations and river below. The hills on the opposite side of the valley shone in bronze as they caught the late-afternoon, winter sun. Despite the cold air, they were comfortably warm from their climb.

"Victor, why did you leave your father and sister to join the militia?"

Staring out over the valley, Victor started talking about his and Kamar's rejection from every farmer they encountered, their being turned away from the school near their second refugee settlement, the hatred directed at them by their schoolmates in Beirut, what he had heard in the news about refugees being rejected in Europe and in the U.S. Then, still staring out over the valley, he told Mahdi about the day he gave in to weakness and accepted a ride from two strangers, how he was forced to sit there, trembling, while he listened to his sister being raped, twice.

Mahdi didn't interrupt. When Victor finished his story, he placed his weathered farmer's arm across Victor's shoulders, shoulders that started to shake as tears at last came.

After a bit, Mahdi turned to look straight into Victor's face. "Victor, you are not to blame for what those men did to your sister. If I were your father, I would feel immense pride for my son."

Victor looked up, surprised. Mahdi continued, "Here is a man who has endured great loss, repeated cruelty, but he has not lost his ability to be kind. There is no higher measure of a man."

Seattle

It was several weeks before Yana and Emma were able to meet up for another walk around Green Lake. There had been a couple of weeks of colder-than-normal weather, and patches of ice were forming along the edges of the lake. Today was cold, clear, and crisp—a perfect day for a walk, provided you were dressed for the weather.

Yana hadn't talked to Emma since returning from France, so she filled her in on her vacation, leaving out the disastrous final evening in Montpellier. Then she told Emma about what had transpired at the airport, just before they boarded their plane to Paris.

Emma was shocked. "So now Burns knows your name. Do you think she will cause you trouble?"

"Yes, Emma, she is all about causing trouble. It appears that she now knows that the incident with the photos is connected to you. That's why I wanted to talk to you, in case she tries to make trouble for you."

"But how could she have made that connection?"

Yana filled Emma in on what had happened to her at work. Since Ron had not been able to provide a business reason for Yana's access of Emma's file, Marty had insisted that Yana be fired.

"Oh my god, Yana! I've cost you your job? I'm so sorry!"

"You did no such thing. This was entirely my doing. I don't blame you in the least, and I don't want you blaming yourself. I wouldn't have even told you, except I wanted you to know so that you can be prepared in case Burns tries to retaliate. I'm so worried that she'll say something to someone in leadership at your new firm."

"I don't think you need to worry about that. I've had a chance to talk with some of our senior attorneys. Burns' reputation precedes her. Seattle is still a small town when it comes to the legal profession, and apparently Burns has acted unprofessionally towards a number of the attorneys at my firm. I don't think they would take anything she told them seriously."

"That's a relief. I was so worried that my stupid meddling would cause problems for you."

"I think you can cross that off your worry list. But that's horrible that you've lost your job after so many years there."

"Well, maybe it will turn out to be a good thing. Perhaps I needed a push to break me out of my comfort zone. When I look back, I realize that I was basically marking time until retirement. Not that I disliked my job, but over the years, I had slowly lost my passion for it."

"So, what'll you do? Are you interested in something along the same lines, or are you considering something entirely different?"

"I have no idea. I guess there's some excitement in that—venturing into the unknown." She didn't sound excited.

"Yana, I feel confident there are a great number of paths you could take."

"Thanks, Emma. It still makes me so mad, though, to think that this Burns lady won. It wasn't supposed to turn out this way!"

"What makes you say she won?"

Yana was taken aback by the question. She stopped walking to face Emma. "She cost me my job, while keeping her corrupt position with the county. She caused you to move to another firm."

"To another firm where I am much happier." Emma paused, before continuing. "Yana, have you stopped to ask yourself why this has taken on so much importance to you—why you're having trouble letting go of Maria Burns? I don't want to sound ungrateful for the concern you've taken over my career, but maybe it's time to move on."

Yana felt like she had been slapped. She was trying to help Emma—trying to do something about the unjust treatment she had received. Yana felt she could easily take offense at Emma's remarks. She took a calming breath and made a conscious decision to take her comment as the advice of a friend—a friend who is willing to be honest and not just tell you what you want to hear. She looked out over the lake. "Perhaps it is time for me to move on. You've given me something to think about."

Emma realized her challenge was a bit harsh. "Look, I'm really sorry that this has caused you to lose your job. Even if it's time for a new chapter, I'm sure that's not the way you wanted to exit. But I would not want to be in Burns' shoes, even if it meant the most fantastic career possible, with truckloads of money. At the end of the day, she is who she is, and I would never want to be that person. She strikes me as someone who has struggled to find happiness."

Yana didn't know what to say to that, and Emma continued, "One of the lessons I've learned in coming to terms with being transgender is the importance of being at peace with who you are. I can't control the type of person Burns is, and I certainly can't control the choices she makes. But I can control the choices I make.

"The other big lesson I've learned is that we don't make it

through life on our own. You've been a huge support to me at a time when my parents were not there for me. I really appreciate that. But we need to concentrate on you now. What's your next step in finding a new job?"

"I don't know. This past year has changed me, particularly seeing first-hand how so many people struggle just to hold their lives together. I have a different perspective."

Montpellier

The news of Victor's death was a setback for Kamar. She lost her silliness, but thankfully, she and Maisah remained close friends. Life became more of a chore for both Kamar and Elias. The boost they had received from simply being in a new country with their newfound freedoms had worn off. There were times when Kamar complained about chores around the apartment, and Elias would lose his patience with her.

Kamar was still doing well in school, but it was no longer about her enthusiasm for learning—it was more related to her tendency towards perfection and the fact that she and Maisah remained study partners. Elias tried to keep up with his running, knowing that would improve his mood, but found his motivation dragging. To an outside observer, their lives appeared to be going well. In truth, the fire had gone out.

Elias thought about Yana. He wanted to write to her but was unsure how to begin and even more unsure whether she would welcome hearing from him.

Elias thought a lot about their conversation on their final night.

One of the things Yana had said to him was that, after finding out about Emma, she had read about transgender people to improve her understanding. Elias often took a similar approach to new issues and decided to apply that strategy here as well. He was slowly beginning, if not to understand the phenomenon, to accept it as a real and innate part of the lives of a great number of people throughout the world. As he read their stories, he was astounded at the vehement and often violent reactions against transgender people.

Being rejected by society was something Elias could relate to. He had first-hand experience of that as a refugee and had seen its effects on Victor, Kamar, and the refugee population he served. Refugees were seen as different, as not fitting in, and as a threat to an established way of life. Elias realized that many people harbored a similar view of transgender people.

Elias and Kamar continued to work and study as the weeks turned into months. For Kamar, there was a future in sight. She would complete high school, study at university, and then, who knows what? A whole world of careers and futures to choose from. As for Elias, he didn't look to the future. His future didn't look any different than his current existence.

Western Syria / Montpellier

The bond between Victor and Mahdi gradually grew stronger. They had not spoken any more about Victor's refugee experience. Still, Mahdi acted more and more like the father that Victor had left in Beirut.

As Victor became more comfortable with recalling his experiences, he thought more of Elias and Kamar. He should check in with them, just to let them know that he was still doing okay. Victor had lost his phone, but Mahdi carried one. The problem Victor faced was the lack of coverage in the area around their farm. Victor asked Mahdi if he would be willing to call his father and sister the next time he was within range.

The next week, Mahdi had to travel to a local village to pick up supplies. They usually had cell coverage there, so he took down the two phone numbers from Victor. Mahdi tried Elias's number first. No one answered. He tried Kamar's next. A young woman answered.

"Hello, is this Kamar?"

"Yes. Who is this?"

"My name is Mahdi. Victor asked me to call you."

"That's impossible. Victor is dead. What is this about?" Mahdi could hear voices in the background. Then a man's voice. "Who is calling?"

"Hello, this is Mahdi, a friend of Victor's. Is this Elias?"

"How do you know Victor? Are you from his militia?"

"No. Victor is not with the militia anymore. He has been working with my family on our farm. Kamar said something about Victor being dead. He is very much alive and doing well."

There was a long pause. Mahdi thought perhaps they had lost the connection. "Hello, are you still there?"

Elias's voice sounded thick. "Sorry, Mahdi, but I need to know for sure that you are telling the truth. What has Victor told you."

"I understand. Victor has been staying with us for some time now. He is a good kid. He has told me everything, about his flight from Aleppo, about his uncle's death, and about reconnecting with you in Lebanon. He is sorry for the pain he caused in leaving you both in Beirut."

On the other end of the phone, Elias was struggled to maintain his composure. "It's true," he told Kamar, "Victor is alive!"

Back on the phone, Elias pulled himself together. "Mahdi, thank you for this astounding news! We were told that his entire unit had been killed in a bombing raid. We understood Victor to be dead."

"Yes, there was a bombing raid, but Victor was busy trying to help my mother, who had foolishly gotten caught up in the fighting, and by a lucky result, he escaped the bombing. He really is doing fine."

"Did he tell you why he went to fight in the militia?"

"He told me about feeling rejected in Lebanon. That is what drove Victor to join the militia. But he has no desire to go back to them now. He seems to like farming. He would call you himself, but our farm does not have coverage, and it's not safe for him to venture out. Healthy young males around here are in danger of recruitment."

"Please tell Victor that we are also doing well. Kamar and I are in France now. If Victor wants to join us here, we will start the process for that to happen."

Mahdi did not want Victor to move to France, but he knew that was not his decision. "Yes, of course."

"Also, please, can we have your address so that we can write to Victor?"

The two men exchanged addresses, and after Elias thanked Mahdi many times, they hung up. After the call, Elias and Kamar stood staring at each other, until Kamar ran to give Elias a huge hug, and then proceeded to dance around the apartment, stopping suddenly when she realized she needed to call Maisah with the news.

Elias sat down at the kitchen table, listening as Kamar excitedly told her friend that her brother had returned from the dead. Still absorbing the impact of this news and vicariously enjoying Kamar's excitement, it suddenly hit him that he needed to let Sami and Amena know.

He pulled out his phone and dialed Sami's number. As the phone rang, he calculated that it was around eight a.m. in Seattle. Hopefully, Sami was not on his way to work. Sami answered, and Elias gave him the news, quickly explaining the call from Mahdi. He heard Sami calling for Amena, and then Elias was on speakerphone, providing both of them with all the details they had heard from Mahdi.

Sharing the excitement with Sami and Amena was like having dessert twice. Elias thought he might overdose on the emotional rush. When the excitement died down and they had exchanged as much news as they could, Elias casually asked Sami if he could let Yana know. "Well, of course," Sami responded. "We'll call Zaid right away. I'm sure Kayla will let her mom know."

"Yes, of course." Elias felt a bit stupid. Obviously, Yana would find out through Zaid.

"Speaking of Yana, had you heard that she lost her job?"

"What? No, I hadn't heard that."

"Yeah, I'm not sure what happened. Something about Kayla's old friend, Emma. We met her at Christmas last year. Yana had gotten involved in trying to help her and had her hand slapped as a result. She seems to be doing okay, though. She's taking it as an opportunity to rethink things, maybe try something new."

"Well, good for her," Elias responded. His mind was turning fast.

"Look, we have to take off for work. We'll call you later. If we call you at ten tonight, that would be seven a.m. your time. Would that work?"

"Yep. Talk to you then."

Elias hung up feeling he had much to think about. But Kamar, re-energized by the call with Sami and Amena, was again dancing about the room. Elias looked up at her. "I think we need to go out tonight to celebrate! You choose the restaurant."

Elias felt warmth spread back through his body, emanating from the fire that had been relit in their lives.

Western Syria

One of the chores that fell to the kids on the farm was taking the goats a short way into foothills on the border of their farm so they could feed on grass and brush. Whenever possible, Victor joined the parade of kids and goats. He and Marya would lag a short distance behind the others, allowing them some precious time to talk to each other in private. Today, they climbed partway up the hill that Victor and Mahdi had climbed several months ago. Victor was talking of his family and the life he had in Aleppo. Marya shared her dream of going to university. She wanted to become a doctor but thought that was probably not going to happen.

Victor turned to look at her. "My father and sister are in France now. If I went to France to be with them, then perhaps you could come too. In France you would be free to study at university."

"I would love to go to France, but is that even possible—?"

Victor cut off Marya in mid-sentence. In the distance he spotted a caravan of trucks and tanks raising a cloud of dust along the local thoroughfare. "Sorry," he apologized to Marya, "I need to get back to the farmhouse."

Victor took off running down the hill, through the orchard, and found Mahdi at their table working on the accounts for their farm. "Mahdi," Victor was breathing hard from his running, "a militia on the road through our village."

Mahdi ran out to their courtyard where a ladder leaned against the side of the house. He climbed up to rooftop, followed by Victor and then by Jamal. From there they watched the convoy passing up the road, following the river. After it had passed, they returned inside the house. Mahdi took Victor into his and Jamal's bedroom. Victor had never been in that room before. Mahdi moved a chest-high cabinet sideways to the left. Behind it was a half-sized door, which Mahdi pulled open and, ducking down awkwardly, managed to climb inside. He asked Victor to follow him. There was barely room for the two of them. It took a few seconds for their eyes to adjust to the scant light coming through the half-size door. The compartment was tall enough to stand in and just wide and long enough for a man to lie down, with some extra room for the small table that stood at the far end. They ducked back out, and Mahdi slid the cabinet back, covering the door.

Mahdi explained, "There have been other times in our family's history when it has been necessary for certain people to be able to disappear for a few hours. If the militia ever comes this way, this is where you are to go immediately. No questions, no delay." He saw Victor's eyebrows rise in question but cut him off. "They will not bother about the women and children. They want young men to fight for them. I am an old cripple. You are the one in danger."

Later, after dinner, Mahdi and Victor sat at the table to plan the next day, as was their routine. "I will go into the village tomorrow morning to see what I can find out about this militia. In the meantime, you are to stay in the house tomorrow." Mahdi could see Victor was about to protest but cut him off again. "Victor, this is not your war. This started as a war of patriots fighting for their country. That has changed. Now it is rival groups trying to gain control and profit. Your life is more important than that. Also, we need you here on the farm. How is Syria to have food if no one is left to farm?"

Mahdi was confirming what Victor had already come to suspect about the war, at least with respect to the fighting taking place in their region. "Okay," he finally said.

That night was the first night since coming to the farm that Victor could not sleep. He got up from his mat and crept out of the room he shared with the two sleeping boys. He sat in the communal room and looked out at the full moon, which had risen above the hills on the far side of the valley.

He had thought he was part of a normal family, living happy, productive lives on their farm. He now clearly understood what he had really always known to be true—that this was a dream. For a time, this dream had kept him safely tucked away from the rest of the world. Hearing from Kamar and Elias had begun the process of pulling him up, out of the depths of his dream. After seeing the militia today, he was now wide awake.

It was time to start thinking about his future. He liked being able to exchange letters with his family and knowing that they were doing well, although he had felt terrible when he found out they had all thought him dead. He had never meant to cause so much distress.

He knew he didn't want to go back to the militia. He had seen enough of war and wanted no more part of it. But he wasn't sure he was ready to go to France or to resume his schooling. He had felt unwanted and lost in Beirut, even though his father had tried to help him settle. Why couldn't he just stay here? Mahdi wanted him to stay. Victor was sure of that. But was it safe?

He sat for a while, staring out at the moon. Then he noticed voices coming from Mahdi and Jamal's bedroom. He sat up straight, trying to make out what was being said, but he couldn't. He silently moved to a different chair, closer to their door. From there, he could just make out their conversation.

"Mahdi, I know Victor has been an immense help working the farm, and that the farm is our livelihood. But if they make a sweep through here and find we've been sheltering him, there could be reprisals. We were surviving before Victor arrived, and we can survive without him. We will not survive if something happens to you."

"We are too remote. They won't come looking here. Besides, we have a place for Victor to hide if they do."

"You think they won't discover that hiding place? Of course, they will! Then we will not be able to claim that we didn't know he was part of the militia because they will ask why we were hiding him. And you can bet that people know he is staying with us. One of our neighbors could easily have spotted him. Or the boys might have let the information slip when at school."

"Our neighbors will not betray us."

"Mahdi, you don't know that. We don't know who we can trust. Besides, I'm sure you've noticed how he is around Marya."

"I know Victor. He would never behave inappropriately with Marya."

"Even if he is blameless, Marya is at the age where living with a young unmarried man will ruin her reputation. I know you like Victor, but you need to put your own family first."

Victor had heard enough. He crept silently back to the boys' room and laid back down on his mat, staring into the darkness for many hours while sleep eluded him, and dark thoughts crowded back into his mind.

Seattle

Having just finished dinner, Yana settled into her favorite chair with her book, a mug of tea and her classical music. For some reason, she was having trouble concentrating on her book and it wasn't the book's fault. Her mind was wandering. Ever since returning from France, her life had seemed off-kilter. Like trying to push a grocery cart with a sticky wheel, everyday things took more effort, sapping her energy. She had found employment as a lab tech in a medical laboratory. It paid the bills, but it didn't inspire her. She was searching for something more.

And the comments from Emma still troubled her. Perhaps Emma was right—perhaps she had become too invested in trying to do something about Maria Burns. She knew her motivation originated from a desire to help. Somehow it had developed into something negative—something that drained her energy instead of energizing her.

It had been one of those glorious, early-April days and tomorrow was promising the same. Yana had been planning her upcoming weekend—time to work in her garden. Spring always gave her a burst of gardening energy, with resolutions that this would be the year she'd get a head start on the weeding and expand her vegetable garden. Hoping her current funk wouldn't cross over into her gardening, she went through her mental list of what needed to be done—weeding, winter clean up, some new plants to pick up at her favorite nursery.

Lost in her thoughts, she was half aware of hearing someone at her door. It took a second knocking for her to finally respond. She opened the door, and there stood Elias. He was holding some potted daffodils, and he gave her a wavering smile beneath eyes that pleaded with her not to shut the door. He seemed misplaced, standing on her doorstep.

Kayla had mentioned that Elias was in Seattle visiting Sami and Amena, having arranged for Kamar to spend two weeks with her friend Maisah. But after the way things had ended in France, she wasn't expecting that they would see each other during his visit. Her shock must have shown because Elias immediately apologized. "Yana, I know I should have called before stopping by. Please forgive me. I thought you might not want to see me, and I didn't want to risk that. Selfish of me."

"You better come in." Yana was so surprised she didn't know what else to say.

"Thank you." He placed the daffodils on the side of her porch and stepped through the doorway. He stopped in the entryway. "If this is not a convenient time, or you don't want to talk, just say so, and I'll leave. But if you have a few minutes to talk—mostly, I want to apologize for our last night in Montpellier."

"Why don't you come sit down." The tension in Elias's face eased somewhat as he followed Yana into her living room and sat nervously across from her, Yana's small coffee table between them. "Elias, I think apologies are due both ways. I was, perhaps, a bit inflexible in my expectations."

"No, Yana. You were spot on. Which I realized once I had more time to reflect. And I've had time to do lots of reflecting. In fact, you told me you had done some reading to help you better understand Emma, and I've followed your example. It's helped me gain a better understanding as well. Of course, you were right about accepting people as they are, without trying to conform them into your own idea of what is or is not okay." He paused. He had remained seated on the edge of Yana's couch and had left his jacket on.

Yana smiled at him, but Elias couldn't shake the feeling that he'd invaded her space. He thought perhaps getting outside would offer a more neutral setting. "Would you be interested in a walk? It's such a fine evening."

"Sure, okay." Yana slipped on her walking shoes, grabbed her jacket and purse, and they started down her street, heading towards Lake Union.

"Such terrific news about Victor." Yana started things on safe territory, the void that had made this topic undiscussable in Montpellier having now been lifted.

Elias's voice was more relaxed. "Yes, he's not able to safely get within cell phone range. We've exchanged letters the old-fashioned way, via post. We're lucky that he's landed with good people. He's enthusiastic about working on their farm—he's learning how to grow apricots, olives, and pistachios."

"Does he want to stay on the farm—try to wait out the war?"

"I don't know. There's no way of knowing how long the war will last. It's gone on for so long that you'd think it must end soon. We only need to look to Afghanistan to know that's not a safe assumption."

"At least you know he's safe, for now."

As they waited to cross a street, Elias looked directly over at Yana. "It was the news that Victor was still alive that, indirectly, led to this trip."

"How's that?" Yana couldn't see a connection.

"To be honest, I'd hit a low point when I heard that Victor had been killed. When he turned up alive, it re-kindled some hope. I started thinking maybe my life wasn't destined to be all about loss."

They had reached Gas Works Park and stopped to look out across Lake Union to the Seattle skyline. It was an exceptionally calm night, and the smooth water mirrored the sparkling lights of the city. The quiet was pierced by the plaintive call of a killdeer. They settled onto a bench just above the lake shore. Elias turned from gazing at the city to look at Yana.

"Seeing Sami and Amena was not the real reason I came all the way to Seattle. But, as nothing ever escapes you, I bet you were already beginning to guess that. Yana, I've grown to really care about you. I know our situations work against us, but if we set that aside for the moment, I need to know if you feel the same way."

Yana had been anticipating this question for a long time. Had, in fact asked herself this same question many times. Even so, she was not prepared to answer it.

"Elias, I do care about you. I'm not sure where this is going, but I need to let you know that I'm not prepared to make any commitments or uproot my life to move to France at this point. Why don't we take this up where we left off before that awful final night in Montpellier? I'd like to take the time for us to get to know each other better."

"Yes, of course. That's very sensible. Forgive me for putting you on the spot." Elias felt foolish. She had voiced exactly what he had been hoping, that she would drop her life in Seattle and join him in Montpellier. How like a school child of him to think she would consider something so dramatic.

Yana sensed his discomfort. "It's okay. This whole episode has been so far outside my normal realm of experience, that I'm struggling to keep up. Our relationship has been shaped by outside forces—geographic distance, the needs of two very important kids, the difference in backgrounds. We need to allow it a chance to develop. How long do you have in Seattle?"

"I fly home a week from Saturday."

"I've just started a new job, so I don't have much in the way of vacation. I'll see if I can finagle a day or two next week."

"That would be great. What about this weekend? Do you have some free time to show me the city?"

"Nothing that can't wait until the following weekend. What about Sami and Amena? Were you planning some time with them over the weekend?"

"They've both taken this week off, so we'll have plenty of time together. Sami won't mind my spending time with you. He's already teasing me about coming to see you tonight, and this will just give him more material to work with." This brought a smile from Yana. Elias continued, "Are you free for dinner tomorrow night? Sami and Amena have invited Zaid and Kayla, and I know you would be welcome."

"Yes, that sounds great."

Elias reached for her hand. "Okay. Tell me if I'm going too fast, but how about going somewhere on Saturday? Sami and Amena keep boasting about how beautiful this part of the world is, so I'm eager to see if that's true. Where do you usually take your out-of-town, Syrian-French refugees?"

Yana thought for a minute. "Given the time of year, I might suggest the Skagit Valley tulip fields. If we can stand the crowds, they should be just starting to bloom. We could make a day of it by doing the loop around Deception Pass and Whidbey Island, and catch a ferry back."

"I didn't realize they grew tulips here."

"Second only to the Netherlands. We have a similar latitude and climate."

"Well, that sounds perfect." They were looking directly at each other. Elias inclined his head, and their lips met.

Western Syria

Victor knew he needed to leave the farm. For the first time since coming to live here, he felt cynical. Foolish to think he could spend his days hiding out here and that the world would not come find him. Also, foolish to think that he would be welcome to stay. There was no place on earth that welcomed him.

His problem was what to do. He didn't think his militia was looking for him. They didn't know he was the lone survivor, other than Nabil, from his unit. Even so, any male of military age was in danger of being recruited, killed or—worst of all—thrown in prison, tortured, and then killed. That made travel on his own extremely dangerous. He didn't want to rejoin the militia. He'd had enough of fighting. Besides, he was no longer naïve about the motivations of the various factions for pursuing this war.

His only option was to join his father and sister in France. Elias said he would make arrangements. Victor decided to write to Elias. He knew that the process would take time, and that it wouldn't even start until his letter reached his father. Unfortunately, mail was slow and unreliable in Syria during wartime. In addition to writing the letter, Victor decided to ask Mahdi to call Elias next time he would be in cell phone range.

Victor and Mahdi were taking a break from pruning olive trees, sitting side by side on the back edge of the cart that was filling up with pruned branches. "Mahdi, you've been very kind to me, allowing me to stay with your family, and teaching me about running an orchard. Now, it's time for me to move on. I've written to my father asking him to start the emigration process."

Mahdi was silent while he thought over Victor's statement. He had sensed a change in Victor. He had become guarded, reserved. While still polite and attentive, the eager desire to learn had diminished. Also diminished was the unacknowledged closeness that had created in Mahdi a bond to Victor as a father to his son.

"I don't want you to go. You've been a tremendous help to us, and I like working with you. But you must do what's right for you."

"I know I can't stay here indefinitely. I'm not sure how long it will take my letter to reach my father. Could you call him to let him know, next time you are in range?"

"Of course. I should have an opportunity to do that tomorrow. How will you get out of Syria?"

"I don't know. I made it over the border through Lebanon once before. Perhaps I can do it again."

"No, I don't think that will work. Many of the borders are closing. Syria's neighbors are starting to say 'no' to more refugees. Also, travel to the border is very dangerous."

"But my father will get me papers to emigrate to France. Surely that will get me across the border."

"Yes, you may be right. But it would still be too dangerous to try to get to the Lebanese border from here."

"What about getting to the coast and catching a boat?"

"Those are being intercepted by militia forces. You're not likely to get out that way either. I think your best bet may be to head to Damascus and fly to France. Elias can get you tickets."

"But how would I get to Damascus?"

"Some of the bus lines are resuming between here and Damascus. It would still be risky, because the buses are often stopped by the militias, but it's safer than trying to travel on your own."

It was time to get back to pruning. Both Victor and Mahdi were deep in thought about logistics, risks, and what they could do to reduce the danger of travel.

Seattle

Yana thoroughly enjoyed dinner at Sami and Amena's. It was a reunion of the six of them, the first time since Beirut, and under completely different circumstances. Sami and Amena's home sat several blocks north of the Ballard Ship Canal Locks, with a partial view to Puget Sound and a glimpse of the Olympic Mountains, which were smothered in snow this time of year. In honor of their time in Beirut, they had lamb expertly roasted on their outdoor grill, skewered alongside marinated vegetables—the result being a truly memorable meal.

Kayla kept smiling knowingly at her mom and Elias, until Yana had the urge to slap her. Actually, she didn't mind. For some reason, now that Elias and Yana were "an item," Kayla no longer acted as if Yana had horned in on the trip to Lebanon, and Yana no longer felt like the outsider peering in. Instead, she felt part of an extended family that now included all six of them.

Kayla and Zaid left a short while after dinner, as Kayla was about to start another three-day stretch of twelve-hour shifts, and she wanted to get to bed at a good time. This gave Elias a chance to talk shop with Sami about a range of current topics in pediatric medicine. Yana filled Amena in on her new job with the medical laboratory and caught up on Amena's work at the local library.

Yana glanced up at the clock. "Ten o'clock already. I better head home. Tomorrow's a workday for me." She was gathering her coat from the front hall when Elias's phone rang.

"Hello. Yes, this is Elias. Oh. Hi, Mahdi. Is everything okay?"

Amena, Yana, and Sami all froze and turned to watch Elias as he stood conversing with Mahdi. Only Sami and Amena could understand what Elias was saying, because he had switched to Arabic.

"Yes, of course. What timing does Victor have in mind? How is he intending to get out of Syria? I see. I'll get started right away. Thanks for letting us know. Please send our love to Victor."

Elias pocketed his phone and turned to the group. "Victor wants to come to France."

"Tremendous news!" Sami looked ready to hug Elias but put his arm around Amena instead. "What else did Mahdi have to say?"

"Victor wants to move as soon as possible. Getting him out of Syria is the challenge. The border through Lebanon is no longer a good option. Mahdi thinks it's best for Victor to fly out from Damascus. The important thing is to get started right away on the paperwork for his visa."

A single phone call can change everything. In that instant, the group switched from a relaxed gathering of friends to a team on a mission. It reminded Yana of their time back in Beirut. Since it was Thursday night, Sami, Amena, and Elias immediately cancelled their plans for Friday so they could devote the day to launching Victor's visa application. Elias started by describing to Sami and Amena the work he had already accomplished so that the application would be as far along as possible. Yana debated returning her coat to the front hall closet but decided there wasn't anything she could do to help this evening. She bid them all good night, and immediately they came over to say goodbye, as if just now remembering that she was still there. Elias walked with Yana out to her car.

"Elias, I would love to spend the day with you on Saturday, but this takes precedence."

They had reached Yana's car, and Elias took her hands into his own. "We have all day tomorrow to work on this, so let's just see how things go. I think getting away on Saturday will still work. I'm very much looking forward to it. What this may mean though is that I cut my trip short, assuming I can get my flight changed. There are some things that can only be done on the ground in France."

"I understand."

They continued to gaze at each other. "I think you may have guessed by now that I love you, Yana."

Yana stared into Elias's deep brown eyes. "I love you too, Elias." They shared a lingering kiss.

Western Syria

The children were heading out once more to graze the goats. Jamal typically found chores for Victor when this happened. She had become more vigilant about preventing opportunities for Marya and Victor to be on their own. Today, some burning flatbread distracted Jamal. Victor slipped outside and ran to catch up with the group. Once more, he and Marya fell behind the others. "I need to leave the farm," Victor announced as soon as they had fallen out of earshot.

Marya stopped to look at Victor, her forehead wrinkled in dismay. "Why? Where are you going?"

Victor hesitated and then decided to confide in Marya. "Your mother doesn't want me here. I overheard your parents talking in their bedroom. She worries about the militia raiding your farm and the reprisals that might come if they find me here. Also, she worries about your reputation if I stay, and rightly so."

"I don't care about my reputation. I want to go with you."

"No, you should care. Your mother is right. Besides, you won't be able to come with me. My father can get visa papers for me because I have French citizenship and because he and my sister are already living in France. It would be near impossible for you, and definitely not without your parents' permission." Marya started to protest, but Victor gently placed his finger across her lips. It was the first time he had touched her, as he had always been careful to show respect for her. In fact, this was the first time in Marya's memory that she had been touched by a male that was not a member of her family. Startled, Marya fell silent.

"You will need to wait here until this war is over. Then I will come for you. That is, if you still want to come to France."

"Of course, I will come. But I've spent so much of my life with this war. How old will I be when it is finally over?"

"I don't know, but what else can we do? It's too dangerous now to get you out of here. Besides, your parents will never agree to your leaving with me."

"I don't care if they agree. I can sneak out with you, then it will be too late for them to stop us."

A vision flashed across Victor's mind of the attack on Kamar while they were in Lebanon. "No!" he said, but it came out too harshly. Seeing Marya's face crumple, he quickly added, "I will do everything I can for us to be together. And I will write to you. Please try to understand." Victor wanted to placate her. "You need to work on your schooling as much as possible. Maybe when you are ready to start college you can get a study visa."

Marya's voice caught. "When are you leaving?"

"I don't know. I can't leave until the paperwork comes through from my father. Your mom wants me gone, but I think your dad has overruled her for now."

They paused for a moment, then Victor reached out and touched Marya's cheek, just inside the edge of her hijab. This time she didn't flinch. She looked boldly into Victor's eyes, feeling that they had now made an unspoken agreement.

Coupeville, Whidbey Island

Yana and Elias were in the small town of Coupeville, waiting for their food at a cozy restaurant that looked out over Penn Cove. Coupeville was like a number of small towns scattered across the islands and peninsulas of the Salish Sea. In the early 1900s, shipping, salmon, and timber spawned big-city dreams that were destined to come true only for those towns situated along the eastern shore of Puget Sound. Now their time-capsule Victorian homes and shops, and their picturesque waterfront settings combined to make these quaint towns perfect get-away destinations.

There had been an off-and-on, light drizzle all morning. The low clouds and scattered rain patterns stretched out across the water to the distant, forested shoreline, composing an impressionist study in shades of gray. Elias was starting to understand the cozy, coffee-shop warmth that Puget Sound residents relish during their long rainy-season.

They had made an early start to the day in an effort to avoid the weekend crowds for the annual Skagit Valley Tulip Festival.

The grayness of the day accentuated, rather than dampened, the expanses of bright yellows, intense reds, and lurid pinks and violets.

From the Skagit Valley, they had crossed onto Whidbey Island via Deception Pass, where they stopped on the bridge to enjoy the fresh air and gaze down 180 feet to the turbulent water driven by changing tides through the narrow passage. A bald eagle circled out over the water at eye level, while below them a colorful pair of harlequin ducks bobbed and resurfaced, in search of breakfast.

By the time they arrived in Coupeville, they were hungry for lunch, and since their view was of Penn Cove, decided to try the Penn Cove oysters. Elias pulled his gaze away from the water and looked over at Yana. "Okay, you've convinced me. This is unarguably a beautiful corner of the world. But do you really get used to the rain? I'm not sure I could."

"There have been cases of non-natives making the adjustment, but that's rare. You don't stand a chance. You've spent too much time in the desert."

Elias chuckled at that, and then turned more serious. "So, I gather you're not inspired with your current work in the medical lab. Do you have any thoughts about what you'd like to be doing?"

"Yes, many thoughts, but no 'voice of god' telling me what to do with my life. Lebanon was a unique experience. Watching reports on the news doesn't prepare you for what it's like being there in person, being among people simply trying to survive. It's changed me. Things that used to worry me seem trivial now. After Lebanon, the thought of simply collecting a paycheck feels flat. I guess I'm looking for something in my career that will have some of that engagement. But I'm approaching sixty. I don't know how practical I'm being."

Elias simply smiled. "Very impractical, I'm sure. How great is that? I had similar feelings leaving the refugee clinic. I still think about them, wondering how they're managing."

Yana reached over and took his hand. "You did the right thing, getting Kamar out of that situation. And now, hopefully Victor."

"I think so too. Also, I needed the break."

"As they say, 'put on your own oxygen mask first before trying to help others.' Speaking of helping others, how is the work on Victor's visa application going?"

"We've done as much as possible from out of the country. The fact that Kamar and I are already living in France should help."

Elias looked back out at the view of Penn Cove before continuing. "I'm sorry to cut my trip short. It seems we're destined to always be short-changed on time together."

"If this will help get Victor to safety, it's the right thing to do. I would be horrified if he were put at risk just so we could have a few more days together. So, you're flying out Tuesday morning?"

Elias waited for the waiter to clear the table before continuing. "That's right. Monday night we're going out to dinner with Sami, Amena, Zaid, and Kayla. I'm hoping you can join us again."

"Yes, that sounds great."

"So that leaves only Sunday. Can you join me for dinner tomorrow? I'd like to take you out, but you should choose the restaurant. You know Seattle better than I do, obviously, and it needs to be somewhere where they don't dump wine over their patrons."

Yana laughed. "That sounds lovely as well. I think I know just the place."

Later that day, catching the ferry back to the mainland, they ventured out on the forward deck, braving the cold April air driven against them by the speed of the ferry. Yana leaned out over the railing, and Elias stood beside her, his arm wrapped around her shoulder as they watched the town of Mukilteo approach and, to their right, the sun setting over Whidbey Island. Feeling Elias's warm embrace sheltering her from the blustery wind, Yana thought to herself that perhaps she did like the idea of a man back in her life.

Seattle

Elias had returned to Montpellier, and in his wake, Yana was as unsettled as ever. She busied herself with the minestrone soup she was preparing for a light supper with Kayla. Zaid was in Spokane for a work project. The timer went off, and Yana pulled some rye bread out of the oven to go with their soup.

Before Elias's visit, Yana had come to terms with the relationship being over. Now she could no longer deny that she wanted it to continue. But how was that to happen? Yana's family was here, in Seattle. Yes, her kids were grown, but she still played an important part in their lives and they in hers. If she moved to France, she would be abandoning them and would miss them terribly. Plus, what would she do in France? She kept coming back to the question of what to do with her life. Most people sorted that out in their twenties and thirties. What was wrong with her?

The Sunday night before Elias flew back to Montpellier, Yana and Elias had an opportunity to discuss their future over dinner. Yana had chosen one of her favorites, Place Pigalle. Tucked away in the Pike Place Market so the tourists don't find it, the small restaurant had an airy, light-filled dining area looking out on Puget Sound. Elias confided to Yana how much he missed her presence in his new life in Montpellier, which was saying something, given that they had not spent a great amount of time together. Yana assured Elias that his feelings were reciprocated, but that their being together meant a complete upheaval of her life. "I need time, Elias. I hope you can understand that."

He had been gracious in his response. "So unfair for you to be in this position. I wish I could do something to make it otherwise. And you're right. This would be a major change for you. You should take the time you need to make sure you're doing what's right for you. I'm not going anywhere. I'm just delighted that you would even consider such a thing."

Kayla arrived, pulling Yana away from her reminisces. Although Kayla and Zaid lived close by, their busy schedules meant there were, at times, long stretches between visits. And while Yana enjoyed visiting with the two of them together, it was great to have time with Kayla alone.

After supper, mother and daughter lingered around the kitchen table. This was the first Yana had talked with Kayla since Elias's visit. Kayla was the one to bring up the topic. "What have you heard from Elias?"

Yana got up to start heating water for more tea. "He texted recently to say that he thinks they're making progress on Victor's visa. He's done everything he could to expedite the process, but bureaucracies across the globe seem united in their aversion to speed."

"That's great. But what about the two of you? What's happening with your relationship?"

Yana was reminded of the adage about the acorn not falling far from the tree. Kayla was as direct as her mother. It felt odd, though, discussing her personal life with her daughter. It was always the other way around—Kayla's high school romances, the much-debated choice of colleges, her career plans, her new relationship with Zaid. Usually kids weren't terribly interested in their parents' lives. They just wanted help with sorting out their own, and then only at those precise times when they were ready for a bit of parental input and never at any other time.

Yana sat back down at the table. "Good question! I don't know. And, it's pretty much a moot question."

"Why is that?"

"Elias can't relocate to the U.S. That would involve too much upheaval for Kamar and Victor. And I'm firmly rooted in Seattle."

"Why are you firmly rooted in Seattle? You hate your job. I know you do, even if you're not admitting it to yourself."

Yana chose not to challenge Kayla's assertion. She got up again and started clearing away dishes, wondering why she was being so fidgety. "It's more than that. For one thing, my family is here."

"What law says you have to remain your entire life where your family lives? I'm not saying we won't miss you, but I'll be damned if I'll be the reason you don't live your life."

"But I have no idea what I'd do in France. My French language skills aren't that good."

"You don't have any idea of what you should be doing here, so I don't see there'd be much difference with you in France. Maybe some new horizons are what you need to figure this out. Maybe that's why you're stuck."

Yana sat down once more. She was losing the argument. Who was this young lady that used to be her little girl? She was sounding so adult, and wise even. Yana decided in that moment that she was exceptionally proud of her daughter, who had grown up self-assured and independent, even as she also felt the pain of losing that young girl who once relied so heavily on her mother.

But Kayla wasn't finished. "If you always play life safe, you'll never know what else it has in store for you. You can always move back to Seattle if it doesn't work out."

"I can't afford to keep this house and move to France, and I'm not going to rent it out and become a long-distance landlord. Once the house is sold, I can't move back here. This is where you and Kyle grew up. We have so many memories here."

"Yes, we have great memories from this house and perhaps a few that aren't so great. The point is, Kyle and I have moved on with our lives. Maybe it's time for you to do the same."

Yana was running out of objections, so she opted for a strategic retreat. "Perhaps you're right. This is a really big decision, and I have a lot to think about. Maybe you're okay living on the other side of the globe from your mother, but I'm not sure I'm ready to live so far from my family and friends."

It was time for Kayla to head home. With her twelve-hour work-days, she was careful about getting to bed early so that her sleep did not get short-changed. Yana gave her daughter a hug. "Thanks for your help in thinking this through."

"You'll get it figured out. Thanks for the soup!"

Once Kayla had left, Yana texted Ellen to see when they could meet up for lunch. She needed a sounding board, someone who wouldn't have quite as strong opinions as her daughter.

Western Syria

The arrival of travel papers with permission to emigrate to France triggered conflicting emotions for Victor. He was both excited about going to France and dreading what he would find there. He was distraught about leaving Marya behind, not knowing if he would see her again, yet eager to escape from under Jamal's watchful gaze. Over the last two months she had kept an ever-closer eye on Victor, assigning him more tasks around the house—ones that would usually be assigned to the children—and generally making it clear that he was no longer welcome. Fortunately, with the coming of summer, Victor could escape to work in the orchards. Mahdi continued to treat him well and to teach him the ways of farming, but there was a distance between them that had not been there at the start.

Victor was sitting at the family table with Mahdi and Jamal, discussing the bus trip to Damascus. "You will need to disguise yourself as a young woman," Mahdi announced.

Victor looked over at Mahdi in shock. He was outraged. "What are you talking about? I couldn't wear woman's clothing."

"You must," Mahdi insisted. "You don't have a choice. Traveling as a young man through this section of the country is too risky. Once you get to Damascus, you should be okay."

"That's crazy! As soon as I talk, they will know what I am."

"I will go with you, so you won't need to say anything. It's a good thing you're not very tall and your beard is not yet thick. You will need to shave closely right before you go."

Jamal, alarmed to hear her husband's plans to join the expedition, cut in. "You can't go with him! It would be too dangerous. What will happen to your family if you are taken? This is Victor's journey, and he must take it alone. You have done enough for him."

"Nothing will happen to me. I am a cripple, remember? They will know that I am not part of any rebel group, and they need farmers to continue farming the land."

Jamal started to argue, but she was cut short by Rima, sitting in her rocking chair in the shadowy corner of the room patching up holes in the children's clothing. "I will take Victor to Damascus. No one will bother a grandmother traveling with her granddaughter. I brought Victor here, and I will take him on to Damascus."

The three at the table looked up at her, as if just remembering that she was in the room. Mahdi began to protest, but Rima's mind was made up. "Jamal is right. The family needs their father. I've been to Damascus before the war. It will be fine. Mahdi, you will need to take us to Hama to catch the bus."

Marya looked over at her grandmother sitting next to her, then over to Victor. Turning back to her grandmother she said "I will go with you. That way you will not be alone on the return trip."

"You will do no such thing!" Jamal glared at Marya. "Kids, to bed. Now!"

Marya looked as if she were about to protest, but seeing the look on her mother's face, she turned instead and stormed off to bed with the other children.

With just the adults and Victor left, Mahdi tried to reassert his place as head of their household. "It's decided then. I will take Rima and Victor to Hama, and Rima will accompany Victor to Damascus."

Elias had wired money to an account Mahdi kept for purchasing farm supplies. The funds would cover both Victor's and Rima's bus tickets, with cash for Victor to use during the trip, and additional money that Elias insisted Mahdi keep to cover any other expenses that might arise. The plane ticket had been purchased online by Elias in Victor's name. The plan was for Victor to arrive in Damascus two days ahead of his flight's departure, allowing time for unexpected delays.

That night Victor's mind raced. He was going to France. He had studied French in Aleppo and also while in Beirut, but his French skills were not great. What would he do in France? Would he be so far behind in school that he would be with kids much younger than himself? Would the other students shun him the way they had in Beirut? Maybe he would be done with school and find work at an orchard. And was he really going to dress as a woman? What would Marya think of him? Would Marya's brothers and sister laugh at him? What if the bus is stopped and the soldiers discover he is a man dressed as a woman? What would they do to him then?

Finally, Victor grew tired of tossing about on his sleeping mat and slipped out into the moonlit courtyard. Sensing movement, he turned and jumped. Someone was sitting in the shadows at the far end of the courtyard. Then he realized it was Marya.

Victor crossed the courtyard. "What are you doing up at this time of night?" He kept his voice low so as not to wake anyone.

"I couldn't sleep. I keep thinking about you leaving. Something dreadful could happen to you."

Victor sat down beside her. "Mahdi and Rima have thought this through. They've come up with a good plan to get me to Damascus. Even if it involves me making a fool of myself."

"If you do make it to France, you will probably never come back here. Either way, it's the last I'll ever see you."

Victor placed his hand on her shoulder. "Didn't I tell you that I would not forget you. We will write to each other, and the time will come when you will be free to travel as well."

Marya looked down at her feet. "I don't see that happening. I will be stuck on this farm until my parents arrange my marriage with another farmer. Then I will forever be a farmer's wife." Sobbing, she fled back to the girls' room.

Victor sat in the darkness. His conversation with Marya only added to his turmoil. He had not shared with her his thoughts of becoming a farmer. He had assumed that Marya loved him. Now he wondered if she wanted to go with him because it would mean going to college and perhaps fulfilling her dream to become a doctor?

She's still a child, Victor said to himself. *How can she know what she wants?*

The next couple of days passed quickly for Victor. He tried to put as much work as possible into the farm. It would be difficult for Mahdi to go back to managing on his own, and Victor wanted to give him as much of a boost as he could before he left.

The morning of his departure, they arose before dawn for the long trek into Hama. Mahdi had used some of the cash he received from Elias to buy precious gasoline for his old farming truck, which would get them into town much faster than the cart. Victor had packed the night before, carrying his few possessions in a single bag, with a set of men's clothing hidden at the bottom. He would change once he reached Damascus. He felt ridiculous putting on women's clothing. He was glad they left the house before any of the children were up.

Since their midnight conversation, there had been no further opportunities for Victor to talk with Marya alone. When they were together with the family, she would not meet Victor's eyes. Victor could tell that Jamal's sharp eyes had caught the awkward distance between Victor and Marya, but since she had never openly acknowledged their relationship, she was not in a position to comment on this change.

It was a relief to be on the road, away from the tension with Marya, out from under Jamal's scrutiny. Rima coached Victor on how to behave so as to avoid suspicion. "You must always walk behind Mahdi and keep your gaze down. Don't look anyone in the face, especially not any men."

The trip into Hama passed without incident. Victor remembered the city from when his family had visited it long ago. Hama had experienced a prelude to war, having been bombed decades ago by the current Assad's father to quell a Sunni uprising. Victor had seen from the remnants that the ancient city had once been a thing of beauty. He was shocked to see the additional destruction wrought by the more recent bombing, street after street of apartment buildings, stores, and office buildings, all half standing and surrounded by rubble.

They found a place to park near the bus station, and the three of them got out of the truck. It was mid-morning and already hot. Victor's head started to sweat under his hijab. He wished he could rip it off to let in some air.

Sentries were posted at the entrance to the bus station, their automatic weapons in their hands at the ready. Mahdi proceeded straight past them to the ticket desk. Victor followed, keeping his eyes down and attempting to shorten his stride, as instructed by Rima. With their tickets purchased, there was nothing for them to do other than wait. The bus was supposed to leave Hama at ten-thirty, but finally pulled into the station at eleven-ten. They stood, and Mahdi pulled Victor into a hug, before thanking him for his work and wishing him Allah's blessing. Then Victor and Rima joined the group of boarding passengers. The bus was newer, with curtains between the rows of seats, and, Victor noticed right away, air conditioning. As they made their way down the aisle, Victor observed that the bus was about half full. Rima and Victor found seats near the back.

Since Victor did not have the liberty to talk, they passed the time in silence. Victor studied landscapes that he might never see again. The bus was passing through the countryside between Hama and Homs when it suddenly braked and pulled to a stop on the side of the highway. The bus driver announced that they were passing a military checkpoint, and that all passengers must disembark while the bus was searched.

The soldiers lined up the passengers alongside the bus in the hot sun. Victor remembered to keep his face down but tried to surreptitiously take in as much as he could of the scene. Four soldiers went into the bus to conduct their search, several others supervised while all the luggage was unloaded from the baggage compartment on the opposite side of the bus. A contingent of soldiers stood guard. Others loitered around. Two of the soldiers started down the row of passengers, searching some of them and looking into handbags. Victor gathered from the things they said to each other that these men were from the militia group that had tried to recruit him when he and Kamar were refugees. Sweat started filling up his armpits and dripping down his forehead. He knew this militia by reputation.

When they reached Victor, one of the soldiers stopped. "You're an ugly one! What happened to you, sister?" The others laughed.

He stepped in for a closer inspection, but Rima stepped out of line in front of Victor, looking up defiantly at the much taller soldier. "May Allah forget to have mercy on you! Treating my granddaughter in this fashion and at her time of the month, no less. Shame on you! She has lived her life a servant of Allah."

The other soldiers laughed even harder, but the one backed off in the face of Rima's wrath. "It's okay grandma. We're just doing our job here, which is to make sure none of you are spies for Assad."

They finished their inspection of the bus and the baggage compartment, and the passengers were allowed back onto the bus. Back in his seat, Victor's pulse slowly returned to normal. He leaned over and whispered, "That was impressive, Rima."

Rima continued looking straight ahead, but a small smile appeared on her face.

They soon arrived at Homs where a few passengers got off and more boarded the bus. Their next stop was Damascus.

Damascus

As they neared Damascus, the bus pulled over for another checkpoint, this time by Syrian government forces. With great effort, Victor hid the hatred he felt at seeing the government soldiers strut down the line of passengers. These were the supporters of the demon who killed his mother and his brother and destroyed his city. Victor clenched his fists under his long sleeves and felt his legs shake. But he kept his gaze down, and the inspection passed without incident.

At last they reached the bus station. They had made it to Damascus. Rima would not be able to catch a bus home until the following morning, so they set off on foot to find a place with a room for the night. Once they secured their lodging, and Victor could at last change into his own clothes, they set out in search of dinner. All they had eaten since their early breakfast was a few dried apricots and some bread they had brought with them, and they were both hungry.

Walking around Damascus, they found the amount of war damage similar to that in Hama, except here there was more progress towards clearing streets and even some rebuilding. The restaurant did not appear to be short on food, but their prices were shocking. It was a good thing Victor's father had been generous with the money he sent.

Exhausted from the tension of their trip, they returned to their lodging, where Rima settled down on the bed while Victor spread some blankets in the corner on the floor. Despite the sleeping arrangement, he slept well that night, the first time in many days.

The next morning, Victor accompanied Rima back to the bus station where they waited for her bus. Rima, that tough old grandmother, teared up as she gave Victor a farewell hug, and whispered something in Victor's ear that he couldn't quite hear over the noise of the station. Victor watched until her bus had pulled out of the station and then out of sight. He turned to start back towards the center of the city.

His flight wasn't until the following morning, which gave him an entire day to wait. His father had instructed him to use some of the money he had sent to purchase a cell phone and some minutes so they would be able to coordinate on his arrival.

Victor found a place to buy a phone and headed back to his room. After crossing the Barada River, he found himself in front of an impressive building, the National Museum. Unlike the National Museum in Aleppo, this building had not been shelled. Victor remembered coming to this museum on a family trip to Damascus before the war, when he was six years old. Although the war had closed the Damascus museum and its treasures had been hidden away, the sign in front indicated that the museum had now reopened some of its wings.

Victor would have nothing to do back in his room, and he had money from his father to cover admission to the museum, so he decided to take the opportunity to look around. After all, he didn't know if he would ever return to this city.

When he was six, the museum had been just rooms full of old

stuff. At sixteen, Victor could appreciate what these ancient artifacts represented. He was fascinated to learn that his heritage included the world's oldest cities and the birthplace of agriculture, that throughout many centuries his homeland had led in medicine, astronomy, math, and art. He walked past tablets displaying the world's first alphabet.

Victor enjoyed being on his own. In no hurry, he took his time, reading about everything that caught his interest. After a leisurely break for lunch, he returned to the museum, spending most of the afternoon there. Finally, leaving the museum, he set out following the Barada River, winding through Damascus' historic Ancient City, and arriving at the Citadel. Victor recalled that, even as a six-year-old, he had been impressed with this ancient fortress, whose site dated back to the time of the Greeks.

Remembering that he had an early start the next day, Victor decided it was time to find a place for supper before heading back to his room.

That night Victor dreamt he was in a boat. It was a small but ancient boat, with only one paddle. Across the noise of the river and the slapping of water against his boat, he heard his name called out. He looked to the shore. There stood his sister and his father. They were calling for him to come ashore. He picked up the paddle and paddled as hard as he could, sweat breaking out from his arms and head. The current was too strong, and his hajib kept getting in the way. Why was he wearing a hajib? He ripped it off. Still he could not overcome the current. As Victor's boat drifted away, Kamar sat down and started sobbing. Victor tried to yell out to them, but the wind took away his voice. Continuing to drift downstream, Victor heard his name again, this time coming from the opposite bank. There was Marya, Rima, and Mahdi. They called to him, waving their arms frantically. He tried to steer the boat over to them. Again, the current was too strong, and the paddle wasn't capable of providing much power. Finally, he gave up, set the paddle in the bottom of the boat, and sat, watching the shoreline flow past. He came upon an ancient city with bridges, docks, and giant water wheels churning with the flow of the river. As he drifted past the city, Victor became aware of sound ahead of him. It grew suddenly louder, and, too late, Victor realized he was heading towards a thunderous waterfall. He paddled furiously. Even so, the current was too strong.

Victor woke to the sound of the alarm he had set on his new phone. He had a feeling of panic, but the dream he had been dreaming dissipated quickly, as steam will do in the hot desert air.

Victor dressed quickly and went out into the early morning to flag down a taxi. He planned to get breakfast at the airport. His EgyptAir itinerary would take him to Kuwait, then Cairo, and finally Charles de Gaulle airport in Paris.

It took all of Victor's nerve to walk up to airport security for screening, his voice almost shaking as he responded to their questions. Having overcome that obstacle, Victor quickly located his gate and confirmed his departure. Next, he stopped at a small gift shop to pick out a book to read during his trip. Then he picked up some breakfast and found a table at which to wait for his flight.

Using his bag to prop up his book, Victor started to read between bites of breakfast. Glancing up for an instant, he saw something that made his heart freeze. There was Nabil, the cook and mediocre medic from his rebel unit, the only person besides Victor to survive the bombing. Seeing him striding confidently through the airport confirmed in Victor's mind that he was indeed the spy who tipped off the government forces, leading to the ambush bombing that killed all of Victor's comrades.

Nabil was heading past Victor's table. Victor quickly buried his head in his book, praying he had not been recognized. He looked up again to watch Nabil continue off to the far end of the airport. He was wearing the same uniform as the other guards stationed around the airport. Not wanting to take any chances, Victor picked up his belongings and moved to a different sitting area, picking out a seat in a corner that gave him a view of people passing in either direction.

Seeing Nabil alive, well, and confident, walking openly through the airport arcade, made Victor's blood boil. It would be suicide to attack Nabil in the airport with people and sentries everywhere, but it would be worth that to avenge his comrades. What could he use as a weapon? He would need a weapon, even with the advantage of surprise—Nabil was a much larger man than Victor.

Victor was so absorbed in plotting his avenging deed, that he didn't register the initial boarding call for his flight, nor the second call, nor even the third and final call. It was only when they announced his name over the intercom asking him to report to his gate, that he suddenly became aware again of his surroundings.

Why were they calling his name? Had Nabil recognized him after all? Victor hadn't seen any signs of recognition on his face. Maybe the ability to mask his response was part of his training as a spy. Were they waiting at the gate to seize him? Then Victor remembered that Nabil had never learned his real name—Victor had used an alias when he joined the militia. Noticing the time on his phone, he realized his flight was supposed to be departing now. Maybe they were simply calling his name because he was about to miss his flight. Victor hesitated, frozen between fear of being taken prisoner and fear of being left behind in a country where he was no longer safe.

They called his name again. How could he choose? Finally, he took off running for his gate. He was done with hiding. If they took him prisoner, then it was Allah's will.

The people at the gate, a man and a woman, looked at him with disdain. His clothes were dirty and worn, and now sweaty as well. He showed them his boarding pass and papers. They were examining them against their information on their computer screen.

He expected that at any moment they would summon the sentries standing less than ten meters away. They didn't do that. They motioned for him to pass through the gate and down the ramp to his plane. He was the last passenger to board on his first-ever flight. Victor's heart continued to thump until, at last, he felt the plane lift into the air, leaving behind the ground of Syria, his homeland. He was on his way to France.

Seattle

Yana was surprised to see an e-mail from Elias. Since his visit to Seattle, they had been FaceTiming each other every week or so and texting from time to time, but it had been a long time since they had communicated via e-mail.

My Dear Yana,

Please forgive the e-mail, but I thought this might be easier to communicate in writing, and then we can talk live when you are free. Two things to communicate. First the good news:

Victor arrived in Paris two days ago. We met him at the airport and accompanied him straight back to Montpellier via train. He was understandably tired (and to be honest, quite smelly), so the last two days have been getting him rested and set up with basics.

When you have given up hope on someone you love, and then they are miraculously returned to you, I can't describe how that feels. And to see Kamar and Victor reunited, after all they've been through. I have joy that I thought would never be mine to experience again. Yet, the hard work lies ahead, as we help him feel that France is his home and allow him an opportunity to heal and resolve the trauma and rejection he has faced. But we celebrate this amazing step forward.

Now, on to some news we are not celebrating. I was diagnosed last week with stage II melanoma. Fortunately, it has been caught relatively early and that means a positive prognosis. They have removed the offending tissue, and in the next few weeks will perform a test to confirm that it has not spread to the local lymph nodes. They expect that it has not. Once they confirm that, it will simply be a matter of keeping a close eye on things. So, please be assured that this is not a big worry, but I didn't want you to find out indirectly through Sami and Amena, with whom I am also sharing this news.

Are you free tomorrow to FaceTime? I can update you further on Victor's situation. I won't know any more about the melanoma until next week.

My love to you,

Elias

Yana read the e-mail through twice and then sat staring out her living room window. What if this had been terminal cancer? She continued to stare. She'd been clinging to things—the family home, her kids still being her kids, the parts of her life that were comfortable and familiar. She'd wasted time worrying about the wrong things.

She thought about what was important to her. She knew from her reaction to the e-mail—she had known for a while—that Elias was important to her. Yes, her kids and friends were also important, but they were ready for her to move forward with her life.

It was also important to be making a contribution with her life—that damn trip to Lebanon had changed her. But as she looked back over the past year, she realized this need to contribute had been there all along. Was that why she became over-involved with Emma? Maybe her life had been in need of change for some time.

She wasn't finding what she needed in Seattle. Her heart was elsewhere. She thought of the challenge that lay ahead for Victor, about the healing that Kamar still needed, of Elias struggling to hold them together. She couldn't let go of this family in France that needed her now.

She thought of Emma and her courage. She had accepted risk in order to do what she felt was right for her own life. She thought of the disruption that had come to Victor, Kamar, and Elias. They had all found the resilience to make new lives for themselves. Elias had not lost focus on what was important to him. Yana felt she had much to learn from these people. How fortunate that they had entered her life.

Yana knew it was the right thing for her. She had known for some time, if she was being honest with herself. She was moving to France! She felt settled. She hadn't felt this settled in many months. She also felt excited. In fact, she hadn't felt this much excitement in a very long time.

And she felt nervous. She was really going to do this. She needed to enroll in intensive French classes as soon as possible. She would need to get her house sold, start the visa application. So much for her to do. She couldn't wait to tell Ellen.

First, she needed to respond to Elias.

Montpellier

The burst of joy over Yana's plans to relocate to Montpellier had not worn off in the intervening months. Elias hadn't dared to hope that she would decide to leave everything in Seattle and do this. They hadn't yet talked about whether she would move in with him, or into her own apartment. Oh, well. That didn't matter at this point. It would work itself out.

Still, Elias couldn't afford much time to celebrate. He had his hands full with Victor. Between Yana's visit and his trip to Seattle, he had already exhausted all of the time-off opportunities available to him as a new employee, so he was stuck having to head to work each day, leaving Victor alone in their apartment.

Victor seemed empty to Elias. He wasn't in a hurry to enroll in school, and Elias had decided to let him do that in his own time. There was so much that needed to be done for Victor those first few months—establishing a wardrobe, updating his medical and dental care, and adjusting to their new household rhythm. Just as with Kamar, Elias made learning French a priority for Victor. Fortunately, Victor liked the intensive language classes. As much as possible, they spoke French at home.

Elias had taken an opportunity when Kamar was not around to bring up the attack on Victor's sister. Elias was emphatic that Victor should in no way consider the attack his fault or failure. Surprisingly, Victor was okay with talking about it, and told Elias that Mahdi had told him the same thing. From that, Elias concluded that Victor must have confided in Mahdi at some point. He wondered what else had transpired during Victor's time with Mahdi and his family.

When Elias and Kamar first arrived in Montpellier, they had time to explore the city and make it their home. Now with Victor, despite the lack of time, Elias tried to work in some of those same activities. The problem was, whereas Kamar had been enthusiastic about everything, Victor seemed not to care.

Elias tried to put all those worries aside. He was getting ready to FaceTime with Yana. One of the challenges of their long-distance relationship was coordinating times, given the nine-hour difference between Seattle and France, and the busy work and home schedules. Elias had set his alarm a half-hour early this morning so he could talk with Yana before the kids were up.

"Hi, Yana. How has your week been?"

"Hectic! Between work, French classes, and getting ready to move, it's been crazy. My house is looking empty now. They're getting ready to stage it. Given the location and Seattle's current real estate market, we don't think it will take long to sell. In fact, they expect to see a bidding war."

"What have you done with all your furniture?"

"What the kids didn't want, I've gotten rid of in an estate sale. There were a couple of items I didn't want to part with, and Kayla and Zaid are storing those for me."

"So much change."

"Yes, indeed. Also, I keep forgetting to ask you about apartments in Montpellier. Do you think there are any units available in your building?"

"I don't know, but I'll check. You, of course, are welcome to stay with us."

"Thank you. But I think your household is crowded and hectic enough as is. The last thing you need at this point is the disruption of moving to a larger apartment. Having my own place close by would work great. Provides maximum flexibility and the ability for us each to have our own space as needed."

"That makes sense. If they have a unit available, do you want me to go ahead and try to secure it, or would you like to do a virtual tour first?"

"A virtual tour would be great, but if you need to snatch it before someone else gets it, go ahead, unless of course, it looks dreadful."

"Will do."

"It's still seems surreal that I'm doing this."

"I'm very excited, as are the kids."

"By the way, how was your six-month follow-up visit on the melanoma?"

"No sign of any reoccurrence. So, they don't need to see me again for a year."

"Great news!" Elias noticed Yana's face relax as she sat back in her armchair. "What's the latest with Victor?"

"He still likes the French language classes. He's not showing much interest in his regular classes. He has his heart set on farming, so I've been gathering information on vocational programs that would fit that interest."

"Mahdi must have been a good influence on him."

"Yes, we're so fortunate he landed with them. Hey, Kamar is up. She says 'hi!' I'd better get ready for work. Love you! We'll talk soon."

"Love you too and send my love to Kamar and Victor."

Seattle

Yana put down her phone and gazed around her empty house. She still believed she was doing the right thing, but there were times she felt less sure. It was excruciatingly difficult to go through the accumulations of decades of family life. There were many boxes of pictures and memorabilia that she passed on to Reggie, since he had part ownership of those memories. Not being in the same stage in his life as Yana, he seemed more inclined to hang on to such things. That was fine with Yana. He could keep them.

Difficult though it was, Yana experienced an incredible feeling of freedom once she made it through the process of sorting through all her belongings. Her outlook was no longer focused on the past. She liked the idea of giving her full energy to what lay ahead of her.

In exploring job opportunities in Montpellier, Yana focused on organizations doing research geared towards addressing world health issues. Fortunately, being a strong university town, Montpellier had a lot of interesting work taking place. Yana also explored volunteer opportunities, deciding she wanted to involve herself in the community as a way to build connections in her new home city.

Contemplating the move, however, was bittersweet. Her kids, Ellen, Sami, Amena, and her other friends in the city she loved, she would miss them all. But she made a promise to return to Seattle at least annually, and hopefully during the summer when Seattle's temperate climate would be a welcome escape from the hot weather in Montpellier. After five and a half decades in one city, she was moving on.

Western Syria

E ver since Marya had heard the news from her father that Victor was safe in France, she had felt relieved, but also tormented by their parting. She was not proud of her final conversation with Victor. She knew he had to leave, and it was impractical to think she could go with him. She couldn't stand the thought that Victor's final impression of her would be that of a child, not capable of dealing with difficulties.

It had been many months, but she still thought of Victor. She decided there was something she could do about it. The easy part was sneaking some paper from the household school supplies. She planned to ask her father to mail the letter, as she was sure her mother would throw it away if she found out about it. The difficult part was finding an opportunity to write her letter where she would not be noticed by anyone in the household. One afternoon, when her mother and the kids were taking their afternoon break, she snuck up on the roof. It was hot up there in the afternoon sun No one would think of coming up there at that time of the day.

Victor,

I'm happy for you that you are now safe in France. I hope that you are enjoying being reunited with your father and sister.

I'm sorry for not understanding that you needed to leave and that I could not go with you. I realize now that you were right, even though that doesn't make it easier to have you gone.

I hope that you will write to me and tell me everything about your new life. Trust me, nothing you have to tell me will be boring. I am excited for you and what your life will become.

Not much has changed here except that Rima is not doing well. She has developed a cough and spends more time lying down than she used to. My mother and father have not said anything in front of me, but I can see that they are worried about her.

Also, once again, we have no teacher at the primary school, so the boys are back to being homeschooled. I hope they find a new teacher soon, because I miss the times when I can study in peace and quiet.

I hope you are doing well. I think about you always.

Marya

Also, if you write to me, put your envelope into a larger envelope and address it to my father. I don't know what my mother would do if she found out we were writing to each other.

Montpellier

V ictor was stretched out on his bed, his laptop propped in front of him. He should have been working on his school homework. Instead he was looking at the vocational program websites that his father had found for him. There were some that looked like great programs, but he couldn't get excited about them. His thoughts kept wandering back to Syria.

He had abandoned hope that he and Marya would ever be allowed to be together. But then, Yana had moved all the way from Seattle to be with his father and that was much further away than Syria. Yana would be joining them for dinner again tonight, as she did most nights. Sometimes she'd invite the family to her apartment. And then there were times when his father had long dinners alone with Yana at her apartment while Victor and Kamar ate dinner here, usually with Maisah also present. The point being, if Yana could do that, move across the globe, maybe Marya could end up here as well.

But the situations weren't the same. First, Victor and Marya had parted badly. He didn't know if she still wanted to be with him. Those last days at the farm, she wouldn't even look at him. Secondly, she expected Victor to go to university and get some advanced degree here in France, when all he wanted to do was farm. Then there was the problem of Marya's parents, particularly her mother. Victor didn't think she would ever agree to Victor and Marya being together. He wasn't sure why she distrusted him so much.

And as if that were not enough, there was the war. By the time the war ends, Marya's parents would probably have already arranged a marriage for her. There were just too many hurdles. It would never come to be.

Victor heard his father arriving home from work and talking to Kamar out in the living room. Then there was a knock on the door. His father poked his head in. "Mail for you! It's from Syria."

Victor usually tried to mask from his father any excitement over anything at all. He didn't like it when adults over-reacted and read all kinds of things into stuff Victor said or did, and his father tended to do that. But it was difficult to act nonchalant about this. Victor never received mail, let alone a letter from Syria.

His father left the room, closing the door to allow Victor his privacy. Victor ripped open the envelope. It was from Marya. He read the letter, picking through each word, as he lay stretched out on his bed. She does still want to see me, he realized. But does she want that because she thinks I'm her ticket to France, or does she really want to be with me? I need to know. How can I find out?

Victor thought of Rima, that small but fierce grandmother, wondering what it was she whispered in his ear just before boarding her bus back home. Rima was someone he could talk to, just as he had been able to talk to his own grandmother. He missed them both.

Victor put the letter aside, put on his ear buds, and started listening to his music while pondering the things Marya had written to him. He had just dozed off when Kamar knocked on his door to tell him dinner was ready.

Maisah was having dinner with her family tonight, so it was just Victor, Kamar, Elias, and Yana. They fit together well as a family, and, although Victor still missed his mother, he liked being a part of this group.

They were well into their dinner conversation before his father asked the question Victor knew was coming. "So, who was your letter from, Victor?"

"Marya." Victor's attention was focused downward on his dinner.

"She's Mahdi's daughter—right?"

"Yes."

"What does she have to say?"

"Not much. Her grandmother is sick, so they're worried about her." Victor looked up at his father, having reached a safer discussion topic.

Elias had finished his meal and pushed back his chair. "That's unfortunate. Wasn't she the one who brought you to their farm in the first place?"

"Yes, and went with me to Damascus."

Yana joined the conversation. "How old is Marya?"

"She just turned sixteen."

"Did she have anything else to say?"

"She wants me to tell her all about what life is like in France. If she could, she would move to France so that she can study to be a doctor."

Elias perked up at that. "Really? Good for her. That sounds ambitious."

Victor got up from the table and took his dishes over to the sink. "Yeah, but I don't think she's told her parents about that, so don't say anything to Mahdi. That's why she's writing—she thinks I can get her into France somehow." Yana studied Victor as he reported this.

After dinner, Kamar retreated to her room to study, and Elias left to run some errands. It was Victor's turn to clean up after dinner, and Yana came into the kitchen to help him. "Sounds like you got to know Marya during your time there."

"Yeah"

"What did you think of her?"

"She's nice, and she's smart, but she still has some growing up to do." Victor found it easier to talk standing side-by-side rinsing dishes and loading them into the dishwasher.

"Would you like it if she was able to come to France?"

By now, Victor was used to Yana's directness and tried to answer honestly. "I'm not sure."

"Why is that?"

"I'm not sure what her real reason is for wanting to come here."

Yana started wiping down the counters. "Are you wondering whether her reason for wanting to come to France is because of the opportunities here or because you are here in France?"

Victor realized that Yana had seen to the heart of the matter. "Yeah, that's pretty much it."

"That's a tough position to be in. What makes you think she might not want to come to be with you?"

Victor hesitated. "She told me she doesn't want to become a farmer's wife. She wants to go to university to study. She doesn't know that I want to be a farmer. I think she has higher ambitions than I do. Either way, it's not going to work for her to come here, so I think I just need to forget the whole thing."

Yana saw the puzzle pieces falling into place. "Yes, that's certainly an option. You could forget the whole thing, and you wouldn't risk anything that way. Except, you would risk not ever knowing what she thinks and wondering whether she might really be interested in you."

Victor considered this as they finished cleaning up the kitchen. Yana sat down at the kitchen table, and Victor came over to join her. Yana smiled over at him. "I found that I'm sometimes a slow learner." Victor was surprised to hear her say this. Yana didn't strike him as being slow at anything. Yana continued, "It took me a while to learn how to identify what in life is important to me. Once I did that, it made it easier to decide which risks were worth taking and to focus on the things that are important."

"Yeah, I'd like to find out what she thinks, but how can I do that when we can't even see each other."

"You could write to her and ask her."

"What?" Victor looked up at Yana.

"You could ask her. Tell her what you're thinking, what you want your life to be. Ask her if that fits with what she wants. You would be taking a risk, because she might not want what you want, but at least then you would know."

That seemed too straightforward. Adults were always either overcomplicating things or pretending that something was easy when it wasn't. "How would I know if she's telling me the truth? I know she really wants to go to university. What if she lies to me because I'm her best hope of making that happen?"

"Yes, that's a risk as well. It might come down to how well you feel you know Marya and whether you feel you can trust her." They sat for a few moments while Victor thought about that. "By the way, if she wants to go to university and become a doctor, and you want to be a farmer, does that mean you can't be together?"

Victor had assumed that a university-educated doctor would not be happy being with a plain old farmer. Besides, Marya had said she didn't want to be a farmer's wife. But maybe what she really meant was that she didn't want to be confined to just being a wife and not being able to pursue her own dreams. When Marya made that statement, she didn't know what Victor's plans were.

As he mulled this over, Victor felt a kernel of excitement growing. That lasted only a few moments. "It doesn't matter anyway. There's no way she can go anywhere without her parent's permission and not while there's a war going on."

"This war has gone on a long time. So, that's another risk. The war could go on another ten years. But I don't think that will happen. What do you think about that?"

"She's not old enough to leave her family or apply for an educational visa anyway, and I need to finish my schooling, so who knows?"

"It might make school a bit more interesting if you have something at the end of it to hope for."

At that point Elias returned from his errands. Victor looked up at his father, and then got up from the table. "Hi, dad. Thanks for the chat, Yana." He disappeared into his room.

Elias looked questioningly at Yana. She simply smiled and reached out for his hand. "Come sit down," she said. "Let me fill you in on what's going on with our son."

Acknowledgements

I am indebted to a number of individuals who helped make this book possible. My editor, Laura Wally Johnston, was key to bringing the story to the level needed for publishing. Beyond editing, she graciously filled the role of teacher, making up for the college writing class that I never had. Professor Heaven Crawley of Coventry University provided much appreciated guidance with the plot, keeping it from straying too far from the hard realities faced by refugees in today's world. She also offered helpful comments and suggestions on the manuscript. Mary Kooistra and Susan Evans provided valued insights and encouragement as beta readers. Margaret Daisley provided the final edit and proofreading, with many helpful tweaks that accumulated to a substantial improvement in the final product. Dawn Daisley did marvelous work with the layout, design, and cover. Many thanks also to Michael Tompsett for his permission to incorporate his inspired city-skyline artwork within the cover design. My greatest debt is to my wife, Carol McClain, who reviewed several drafts, but more importantly, willingly gave her support, advice, encouragement, and patience throughout my little obsession.

Information and resources related to transgender issues

According to the 2015 U.S. Transgender Survey, 46% of respondents reported being verbally harassed, 9% reported being physically attacked, and 10% reported being sexually attacked during the previous year, due to being transgender. Data is sparse on the number of transgender individuals, but a University of Michigan study, using 2014 data, estimated that 1 in 189 U.S. adults identify as transgender, which translates into well over a million people in the U.S. alone. The Employment Non-Discrimination Act, a federal bill to protect workers from discrimination based on sexual orientation or gender identity, was first introduced in 1994, and has stalled or failed numerous times over two decades. Focus has now turned to the broader Equality Act, which was first introduced in 2015.

National Center for Transgender Equality:
www.transequality.org
GLAAD (Gay and Lesbian Alliance Against Defamation):
www.glaad.org

"2015 U.S. Transgender Survey." National Center for Transgender Equality, January 2016.
"Transgender Demographics: A Household Probability Sample of U.S. Adults, 2014." *American Journal of Public Health*, December 2016.

Information and resources related to the Syrian refugee crisis

As of April 2020, the United Nations had registered 5.6 million Syrian refugees since the war's inception in 2011. The UN estimated an additional 6.6 million Syrians were internally displaced and 2.98 million were in besieged or hard-to-reach areas, for a total of 13.1 million Syrians in need of help. Starting in May of 2015, Lebanon discontinued allowing the UN to register Syrian refugees, so the true number of refugees is not known.

Approximately 50% of UN-registered Syrian refugees are under the age of 18. By late 2017, KidsRights reported that 43% of Syrian school-age children in Lebanon, Jordan, Egypt, Turkey, and Iraq have no access to education. Generational gaps in education will add yet another obstacle to the rebuilding of Syria, once the war ends.

UNHCR (United Nations High Commissioner for Refugees):
www.unhcr.org/en-us/syria-emergency.html
Mercy Corps:
www.mercycorps.org/blog/quick-facts-syria-crisis
International Rescue Committee:
www.rescue.org
ANERA (American Near East Refugee Aid):
www.anera.org/priorities/syrian-refugees

"Operational Portal – Refugee Situations." United Nations High Commissioner for Refugees, April 2020.
"The Widening Educational Gap for Syrian Refugee Children." KidsRights Foundation, March 2018.

CPSIA information can be obtained
at www.ICGtesting.com
Printed in the USA
LVHW011405300720
661946LV00002B/61